Sand Queen and The L̲_____ _____

On *Sand Queen*

"Every war eventually yields works of art which transcend politics and history and illuminate our shared humanity. Helen Benedict's brilliant new novel has done just that with this century's American war in Iraq. *Sand Queen* is an important book by one of our finest literary artists." —**Robert Olen Butler**, author of *A Good Scent from a Strange Mountain* and *Perfume River*

"Every American who claims to value the lives of our soldiers should read this powerful, harrowing, and revelatory novel."
—**Valerie Martin**, author of *The Ghost of Mary Celeste* and *Sea Lovers*

"Helen Benedict's compelling story provides an intimate picture of what it means to be a soldier, what it's like to live on the battlefield, and what the ethical choices are that our troops have had to make in Iraq.... At times funny, at times grimly painful, *Sand Queen* offers a new chapter in contemporary American history."
—**Roxana Robinson**, author of *Cost* and *Sparta*

"This is *The Things They Carried* for women in Iraq." —*Boston Globe*

"If you missed out on serving in the Iraq War, you can, if you're willing, be catapulted right into the midst of some of its more challenging moments courtesy of Ms. Benedict's gutsy prose.... *Sand Queen* [is] a novel that will leave you deeply unsettled if not shaken to the root of your being." —*Herald-Dispatch*

"Told in compellingly vivid detail with the clear ring of truth every step of the way." —*Free Lance-Star*

"[A] completely heartbreaking, vivid story of the particular difficulties of being not just a soldier, but a female soldier." —*Bustle*

"In writing what might be the first major woman's war story and alternating points of view between opposing sides, [Benedict] has created something enormously fresh and immediate." —*Chronogram*

"[Benedict] is an exceptional writer and storyteller. Her gritty depiction of a soldier's life in the Iraq desert is particularly well done."
—*New York Journal of Books*

"Benedict's writing is impressive, passionate, and visceral.... Reading this book is the best literary path to understanding the particular challenges of being female in the military during warfare."
—*Publishers Weekly* "Best Contemporary War Novel" citation

"Funny, shocking, painful, and, at times, deeply disturbing, *Sand Queen* takes readers beyond the news and onto the battlefield."
—*Booklist*

"An eye-opening glimpse into a life that many Americans have never seen." —*Library Journal*

"A convincing and affecting portrait of two resilient young women caught up in war." —*Shelf Awareness*

On *The Lonely Soldier*

"It's outrageously immoral that our female soldiers have to fear many of the male soldiers they serve with, as well as being let down by the very Veterans Affairs system that's supposed to help them out. Thanks to Helen Benedict, the world is watching!"
—**Roseanne Barr**, Emmy Award–winning actor

"*The Lonely Soldier* is an important book, a crucial accounting of the shameful war on women who gave their bodies, lives, and souls for their country." —**Eve Ensler**, author of *The Vagina Monologues* and *In the Body of the World*

"No matter your politics, this book is vital. Helen Benedict's brilliant and compassionate reporting is neither left nor right—it's human."
—**Dale Maharidge**, author of *And Their Children After Them* and *Bringing Mulligan Home*

"*The Lonely Soldier* tells an important and often ignored story about our military women. Benedict writes with skill and compassion, helping us understand what it feels like to be a woman soldier in Iraq. I recommend this book to everyone who cares about our soldiers."
—**Mary Pipher**, author of *Reviving Ophelia* and *Seeking Peace*

"*The Lonely Soldier* will shock you and enrage you and bring you to tears. It's must reading for everyone who cares about women, justice, fairness, the military, and the United States."
—**Katha Pollitt**, award-winning columnist, *The Nation*

WOLF SEASON

WOLF SEASON

Helen Benedict

BELLEVUE LITERARY PRESS
New York

First published in the United States in 2017 by Bellevue Literary Press, New York

For information, contact:
Bellevue Literary Press
NYU School of Medicine
550 First Avenue
OBV A612
New York, NY 10016

© 2017 by Helen Benedict

Library of Congress Cataloging-in-Publication Data
Names: Benedict, Helen, author.
Title: Wolf season / Helen Benedict.
Description: First edition. | New York : Bellevue Literary Press, 2017.
Identifiers: LCCN 2017015974 (print) | LCCN 2017022200 (ebook) |
ISBN 9781942658313 (E-Book) | ISBN 9781942658306 (softcover)
Subjects: LCSH: War and families—Fiction. | Domestic fiction. |
BISAC: FICTION / Literary. | FICTION / War & Military. |
FICTION / Family Life. | GSAFD: War stories.
Classification: LCC PS3552.E5397 (ebook) | LCC PS3552.E5397 W65 2017(print) |
DDC 813/.54—dc23
LC record available at https://lccn.loc.gov/2017015974

Bellevue Literary Press would like to thank all its generous donors—
individuals and foundations—for their support.

 This publication is made possible by the New York State Council on the Arts with the support of Governor Andrew Cuomo and the New York State Legislature.

 This project is supported in part by an award from the National Endowment for the Arts.

Book design and composition by Mulberry Tree Press, Inc.
Manufactured in the United States of America
First Edition

1   3   5   7   9   8   6   4   2

paperback ISBN: 978-1-942658-30-6
ebook ISBN: 978-1-942658-31-3

To the widows and orphans of war
To my mother, and Iggy

Behind each sociable home-loving eye
The private massacres are taking place . . .

—W. H. Auden, "In Time of War," 1939

Mothers have been stolen from their own tears.

—Kareem Shugaidil, "Flour Below Zero," 2005

WOLF SEASON

Part One

AUGUST

1

STORM

The wolves are restless this morning. Pacing the woods, huffing and murmuring. It's not that they're hungry; Rin fed them each four squirrels. No, it's a clenching in the sky like a gathering fist. The wet heat pushing in on her temples.

Juney feels it, too, her head swaying, fingers splayed. She is sitting on the wooden floor of their kitchen, face raised, rocking and rocking in that way she has. Hair pale as a midday moon, eyes wide and white-blue.

"It smells sticky outside, Mommy. It smells wrong," she says in her clear, direct voice, no hint of a whine. Soldiers don't whine. And Juney is the daughter of soldiers.

"Nothing's wrong, little bean. Maybe we'll get a summer storm, that's all. Come, eat."

Juney is nine years old, the age of curiosity and delight before self-doubt clouds the soul. Fine hair in a braid to her waist. Bright face, wide at the temples, tapering to a nip of a chin. Delicate limbs, skinny but strong.

She lifts herself off the floor and wafts over to the kitchen table, a polished wooden plank the size of a door, where she feels for her usual chair and settles into it with the grace of a drifting leaf. Starting up one of her hums, she dips her spoon into the granola Rin made for her—sesame seeds, raisins, oats, and nuts, every grain chemical-free.

"More milk, please."

Sometimes, when Rin is not hauling feed, chopping wood, weeding, or fixing some corner of their raggedy old farmhouse, she stands and watches Juney with wonder, her miracle daughter, and this is what she does after pouring the milk; she leans against the kitchen counter, still for a moment, just to absorb her. Juney moves like a sea anemone, fingers undulating. She can feel light and sun, shadow and night, and all the myriad shades between.

"I want to go weed," she says when her bowl is empty, sitting back to stretch, her spindly arms straight above her, twiggy fingers waving. The scrim of clouds parts for a moment, just enough to allow a slice of sun to filter through the windows, sending dust motes spinning and sparking into the corners of the kitchen. She rocks on her chair inside a sunbeam, hair aglow, fingers caressing the air. She can hear their cats, Purr, Patch, and Hiccup, stretching out on the floor. Smell their fur heating up, their fishy breath slowing into sleep.

"Me, too," Rin says. "Let's go."

Juney was born in the upstairs bedroom, amid Rin's outraged yells and the grunts of a stoic midwife; she knows her way around their ramshackle house and land as well as she knows her own body. Rin only helps by keeping unexpected objects out of the way, as even the dogs and cats have learned to do. No tables with sharp corners; no stray chairs, bones, mouse corpses, or drinking bowls. The house itself might be a mishmash of added rooms and patchwork repairs, windows that won't open and trapdoors that will, but everything inside has its place.

Out in the backyard, Juney stops to sniff the thickening heat—the clouds have closed over again, gunmetal gray and weightier than ever. "Itchy air," she declares, and makes her way to the vegetable garden. Ducking under the mesh Rin erected to keep out plundering deer and rabbits, she squats at the first row of tomatoes. Weeding is Juney's specialty. Her fingers climb nimbly up the vines, plucking off the brittle spheres of snails, the squishy specks of aphids. Her palms caress the earth, seeking the prick of dandelion leaves and thistles, the stubs of grapevine and pokeweed, and out they come, no mercy for them.

Her father loved planting. Jordan Drummond was his name, Jay to all who loved him. Jay, flaxen-haired like Juney, face white as a Swede's, eyes set wide and seaglass blue. Tall and rangy, with enormous feet, and so agile he might have been made of rubber. He, too, was born and bred on this property, back in the time when it was a real farm. Helped his parents raise cows and corn all his life, until the farm failed and drove him into the army. When his platoon razed the date groves around Basra, acres of waving palm trees, their fronds a deep and ancient green, their fruit glistening with syrups—when they ploughed those mag-nificent trees into the desert just because they could, he wept as if for the death of a friend.

Now Rin arranges her days around forgetting, pushes through a list of tasks tough enough to occupy her mind as well as her muscles. Juney comes first, of course, but her wolves take con-centration, as do her chickens and goats and vegetables. She has staked out her ground here with all her companions. If anyone wants to find her, they have to negotiate half a mile of potholed unpaved driveway, barbed wire, electric wire, a gate, and her four dogs, who are not kind to strangers. Not to mention her army-trained marksmanship.

Juney feels her way around the spinach and carrots, pulling and plucking. "Mommy, what are we doing today?"

"Going to town. The clinic. Not till we finish the chores, though. Come on, let's feed the critters."

"Which clinic?"

"Yours."

She hesitates. "Have I got time to do the birds first?"

Juney's favorite job is tending the bird feeder. Rin wanted to throw it out after that mama bear knocked it off its squirrelproof stand, plunked herself on the ground and dumped the seeds down her throat like a drunk—Rin watched the whole thing from the kitchen window, describing the bear's every move to Juney. But the feeder means too much to Juney to relinquish. She judges how empty it is by feeling its weight in her palms, plants it between her feet to hold it firm, fills it to the brim from the seed sack, and deftly hangs it back up. Then she sits beneath it, head lifted while she listens and listens. "Shh," she says this morning. "There's a nest of baby catbirds over there." A faint rustle, the quietest of hingelike squeaks. "Three of them. They want their breakfast."

Leaving her to sit and listen, Rin kicks the sleepy cats outside to make their way through the day and eases her car out of the barn. The barn sits to the side of her house, on the edge of a flat field that used to hold corn. Beyond that, a hardscrabble patch of rocks and thistles meanders up a hill to scrubby hay fields and a view of the Catskill Mountains to the south. Otherwise, aside from her yard, the ancient apple orchard in the back, and the vegetable patch, she is surrounded by woods as far as the eye can roam.

Ten acres of those woods she penned off for her three wolves, leaving them plenty of room to lurk. Wolves need to lurk. They are normally napping at this time of morning, but the seething heat has them agitated and grumbling. Rin can sense their long-legged bodies moving in and out of the shadows, scarcely more solid than shadows themselves. Even her absurdly hyper-active mutts are feeling the unwholesome weight of the day, but instead of expressing it with restiveness like their cousins, they drop where they stand, panting heavily into sleep.

The entire compound is preternaturally still. The yard, the woods, the porch cluttered with gnarled geraniums and fraying furniture; the rickety red barn with its animal pens clinging to its side for dear life; the piles of lumber and rusting machinery—all are as somnolent as the snore of a summer bee.

Rin looks at her watch. "Time!"

Juney straightens up from under the bird feeder, wipes her earthy hands on her jeans, and walks toward her mother along the little path planted with lilac bushes, a path she memorized as an infant. She puts her head on Rin's chest, reaching the exact level of her heart.

She smells her mother's fear even before she hears it in her voice. The sweat breaking out slimy and oyster-cold.

Juney was conceived in the back of a two-ton, Camp Scania, Iraq, under a moon as bright and hard as a cop's flashlight. A grapple of gasp and desire, uniforms half off, bra up around Rin's neck, boots and camo pants flung over the spare tire. Jay's mouth on her nipples, running down her slick, sandflea-bitten belly, down to the wet openness of her, the salt and the sand of her, the wanting of her, his tongue making her moan, his fingers opening her, his voice and hers breathing now and now and now.

Wartime love in a covered truck, that desert moon spotlighting down. His chest gleaming silver in its glare, eyes glittering, the scent of him sharp and needing her, the voice of him a low growl of yes like her wolves.

But even through the slickness, even through the wanting and wanting, she felt the desert grinding deep into her blood. Toxic moondust and the soot of corpses.

As Rin drives her rackety maroon station wagon along the rural roads that take her to town and the clinic, Juney hums again beside her, rocking in her seat, her warbly tune following some private daydream. The windows are open because the AC refuses to work and the sweat is rolling down Rin's arms, soaking the back of her old gray T-shirt, the waistband of her bagged-out work pants. She glances down at herself. She is covered with dirt from the yard. Probably has burrs in her hair. Once she was slim with just enough curve and wiggle to make Jay smile. Long hair thick as a paintbrush till she cut it for war. These days, squared-out by childbirth and comfort food, she looks and moves more like a lumberjack. Still, she should have had the decency to shower.

Juney is mouthing words now, rocking harder than ever to her inner rhythm. Rin should teach her not to do that—it makes people think she's retarded—but she doesn't have the heart. Juney rocks when she's happy.

"Tweetle tweetle sang the bird," she croons in some sort of a hillbilly tune.

"Twootle twootle sang the cat.

You can't get me, sang the bird.

I don't want to, sang the cat.

Tweetle and twootle, tweetle and—"

"Juney?" Rin is not exactly irritated but needs her to quit. "You're going to be okay at the clinic, right? No screaming like last time?"

Juney stops singing long enough to snort. "I was a baby then. And they stuck me with that long needle." She takes up her song once more, then stops again. "Are they going to stick me this time?"

"Soldiers don't mind needles. It's just a little prick, like you get every day in the yard from thistles."

"Yeah. Who cares about needles?"

"It's just an annual checkup to see how much you've grown. Nothing to worry about. They'll probably tell you to eat more, skin-and-bones you."

"That's 'cause you won't let me have candy. I'm going to tell the doctor to order you to give me candy."

This is an old battle, Rin's strictness about food. She is strict about a lot of matters. No TV, no cell phones. No radio, either, not even in the car. Yet there are limits to how much even she can cushion her daughter. Thanks to the law, she is obliged to send her to school, and there, as if by osmosis, Juney has absorbed the need for the detritus that fills American lives. Despite all Rin's efforts, Juney has caught the disease of Want.

Rin wonders if Juney's daddy would approve of how she's raising her: Jay, the only man she's ever wanted, ever will want. Jay, gone for as long as Juney has been alive. And look what he left behind. A broken soldier. A fatherless daughter. The wolves who patrol the woods like souls freed from the dead, their thick-furred bodies bold and wild—the ones who won't be tamed, won't be polluted, won't be used.

It was Jay's idea to raise wolves. His plan was to do it together once they were done soldiering—he had always wanted to save them from extinction, the cruelty of zoos and those who wish to crush them into submission. "They need us, Rin," he said to her once, his big hand resting tenderly on her cheek. "And we need them." So when she found herself alone and pregnant, she decided to carry out the plan anyway. She tracked down a shady breeder over by Oneonta and rescued two newborn pups, blue-eyed and snub-nosed, blind, deaf and helpless, their fur as soft as goose down, before he could sell them to some tattooed sadist who would chain them up in his yard. One was female, the other male, so she hoped they would breed one day. As they did. "Never try to break wolves," Jay told her. "They've got loyalty. They might even love you, who knows? But we must never tame them. They're wild animals and that's how it should stay."

Her guardian angels. Or devils. She hasn't decided which.

"We're here!" Juney sings out. She knows the town of Huntsville even when it's midmorning quiet and raining: the asphalt steaming, the wet-dust funk of newly soaked concrete.

Rin drives down the main drag, a wide, lonely street with half its windows boarded up and not a soul to be seen. A Subway on the left, a Dunkin' Donuts on the right, its sign missing so many letters it reads, DUK DO. The CVS and three banks that knocked out all the local diners and dime stores. A Styrofoam cup skitters along the gutter, chipped and muddied by rain.

Pulling up the hill into an asphalt parking lot, Rin chooses a spot as far away from the other cars as she can get, her stomach balling into a leathery knot. She hates this town. She hates this clinic. She hates doctors and nurses. She hates people.

Pause, swallow, command the knot to release. It won't. She sweeps her eyes over the macadam, down the hill to the clinic, over to the creek bubbling along behind it. Back and forth, back and forth.

"Mommy, we're in America."

"Yeah. Sorry." One breath, two. "Okay. I'm ready."

If Rin could walk with her wolves flanking her, she would. Instead, she imagines them here. Ebony takes the front guard, his coat the black of boot polish, eyes green as a summer pond, the ivory curve of his fangs bared. Silver brings up the rear, her fur as white as morning frost, her wasp-yellow eyes scanning for the enemy, a warning growl in her throat. And the big stately one—the alpha male, the one Rin named Gray, his body a streak of muscle, his coat marked in sweeps of black and charcoal— walks beside her with Juney's fingers nestled into the thick fur of his back, his jaw open and slavering, ready to tear off the head of anyone who so much as looks at her.

With her invisible wolves around her and her daughter gripping her hand, Rin plows through the now-strafing rain to the clapboard box of a clinic and up to its plate-glass front, on which, painted in jaunty gold lettering, are the words *Captain Thomas C. Brittall Federal Health Care Center's Pediatrics/U.S. Department of Veterans Affairs.*

"Department of Vaporized Adolescents," she mutters, pushing open the cold glass door and its cold metal handle. They step inside.

❖

Naema Jassim is standing in the white starkness of that same clinic, suspended in one of the few moments of tranquillity she will be granted all day. Her hands, long-fingered and painfully dry from constant washing, press down on the windowsill as she gazes into the hot wetness beyond. The sky has turned an uneasy green, tight with electricity and tension. Even from inside her clinic office, the air smells of singed hair and rust.

"Doctor?" Wendy Fitch, the nurse, pokes her head into the room. "Your nine A.M.'s here. We have four more before we close. TV says the hurricane's due around two."

"Yes, the rain, it has already come." Naema turns from the window, so slight she is almost lost inside her voluminous white coat, her black hair gathered in a loose knot at her neck. Face long and narrow, eyes the gold of a cat's. A star-shaped scar splashes across her otherwise smooth right cheek.

Behind her, a sudden wind catches the weeping willow outside, sending its branches into a paroxysm of lashing and groaning. But the tightly closed windows and turbine roar of the clinic's air-conditioning, set chillingly low to counteract the bacteria of the sick, render the premature storm as silent as dust.

Naema slides her clipboard under her arm and moves to the door.

Outside, the trees bend double and spring back up like whips. The clouds convulse. A new deluge drives into the ground, sharp as javelins.

A mile uphill, the wind seizes a tall white pine, shaking it until its ninety-year-old trunk, riddled with blister rust, splits diagonally across with a shriek. It drops onto the Huntsville Dam, already thin, already old, knocking out chunks of concrete along its crest until it resembles a row of chipped teeth.

❖

Rin grips Juney's hand while they sit in the waiting room, her palms sweating as she scans every inch of the place: walls too white, lights too bright, posters too cheerful, a television screen as big as a door blasting a cooking show. But she refuses to look at the other women. Their calculating eyes. Their judgments. Their treachery.

The monologue starts up in her head, as it always insists on doing at the VA, even though she is only in an affiliated pediatrics clinic, not a full-fledged hospital full of mangled soldiers and melted faces. She fights it as best she can, trying to focus on Juney, on her wolves growling in their hot fur by her feet, but it marches on anyhow, oblivious to her resistance: *Where were you ladies when I needed you, huh? I saw you fresh from your showers; I saw you listening. Scattered, every one of you, like bedbugs under a lamp. Where were you when, where were you. . . .*

"Stop." Juney pulls Rin's hand to her chest. "Mommy, stop."

Rin looks for her wolves. They are crouched around her still, tongues lolling, their musky fur and meat-breath reassuring. She should have brought Betty, her service dog. She keeps telling herself she doesn't need Betty. But she does.

Juney lifts her nose and Rin can tell she is smelling the medicinal stinks of the clinic. All scents are colors to Juney, an imagined rainbow Rin will never see. The disinfectant in the wall dispensers, sickly sweet and alcohol sharp—this is her yellow. The detergent of the nurses' uniforms, soapy and stringent, she calls bright orange. The chemical-lemon odor of the floor polish: purple. The pink of freshly mown grass, magenta of oatmeal, green-bright breath of their cats, black of their dogs panting. The glaring white of her mother's alarm.

Rin sends her mind to her hand, still clasped against Juney's narrow chest. Juney's heartbeat reminds Rin of the chipmunk she once held in her palm, soft and weightless, alive and warm—a tiny bundle of pulsating fluff.

Another soldier mother is squeezed into the far corner, holding a feverish infant to her breast. A second sits by the wall with her child, its back in a brace. A third walks in with her toddler daughter, whose right hand is wrapped in a bandage. The beams of the women's eyes burn across the room, avoiding one another yet crossing like headlights, smoldering with their collective sense of betrayal.

Time inchworms by.

Finally, a hefty nurse with frizzled blond hair steps through the inner door, the name FITCH pinned loudly to her bosom.

She runs her eyes over Rin and Juney and all the other mothers and children suspended in this stark, white room. "Rin Drummond," she calls.

Rin cannot speak.

"Mommy?" Juney lifts Rin's hand off her chipmunk heart and jumps down from her chair. "We're ready," she tells the nurse and pulls her mother's arm. She and Rin follow the nurse's broad back down the corridor and into an examining room.

"Just strip to your undies, honeypie, and hop up here," the nurse tells Juney. "Doctor Jassim will be here in a jiffy."

"Thank you. I know what to do. I'm nine years old and my name is June Drummond."

"Of course it is," the nurse says, unruffled.

"Did you say 'Jassim'?" Rin asks, finding her voice at last. "Who's he?"

"Doctor Jassim is a woman. She's been a resident with us for half a year now. She's very good, don't worry."

"Where the fuck is she from?" Rin's hands curl up tight and white.

"Mrs. Drummond, relax, okay? She's the best physician we have here. You're lucky to get her." The nurse leaves, closing the door with a snap that sounds more as though she is locking them in than giving them privacy.

Juney peels off her T-shirt and shorts and kicks away her flip-flops. Both she and Rin are dressed for the heat of the August day, not for the clinic's hypothermic AC, so her skin is covered in goose bumps. Rin finds a baby blue hospital robe hanging on the back of the door and wraps Juney's shivery body in it before lifting her onto the plank of the examining table, its paper crackling beneath her. She is so fragile, her Juney, a wisp of rib cage and shoulder blade, legs pin-thin as a robin's. Rin holds her tight, not sure who is comforting whom.

❊

The wind rampages through woods and parking lots, streets and gardens, seizing sumacs, maples, and willows and shaking them until their boughs drop like shot geese. Up the hill, the rain-bloated creek presses its new weight against the crumbling dam, pushing and pounding until, with a great roar, it bursts through, leaps its banks and rushes headlong down the slope toward the clinic; a foaming wall of red mud, branches, and rocks flattening every shrub and tree in its path.

Inside, the air-conditioning hums. Voices murmur. Babies whimper.

Wendy Fitch hovers by the door of the examining room, checking her watch. Dr. Jassim might be great with her patients but the woman has zero sense of time. Whether this has something to do with her culture or is only an individual quirk, Wendy doesn't know, but the doctor needs to finish up here and fetch her son from his friend's house, the boys' summer baseball camp having sensibly closed against the impending storm. The rain is beating on the windows now and Wendy can feel the patients' parents growing more restless by the minute, as eager as she is to get back to their canned food and bottled water, their batteries and candles. Her pulse quickens. As a lowly nurse, she has to bear the brunt of the parents' ire, and these are no ordinary parents, either. They are all military veterans, half of them ramped up or angry. Like that pit bull of a woman, Rin Drummond.

"We better hurry, storm's coming on quick," Wendy says when Naema emerges at last from the first examining room. "Watch out for this one," she adds in a whisper, touching her temple. "Room three."

Naema nods with a resigned smile and walks toward the door.

❖

Rin can't believe they gave Juney an Arab for a doctor. Typical of the VA to hire the second-rate. The woman probably bought her certificate online, did her training on YouTube. Probably blew up some sucker of a soldier or two on her way here, as well.

"Mommy, what's wrong?"

Rin takes a breath. And another. "It's okay. It's just this place." She strokes her daughter's hair and pulls her close once more, feeling her frail body shiver.

A knock on the door. Gentle, yet it sends a spasm through Rin's every nerve.

The door opens and in walks a woman in a white coat, as if she's a real doctor. No head scarf, at least, but there's that familiar olive-brown skin and blue-black hair. She's carrying a clipboard file, which she reads before even saying hello, which Rin considers damned rude. Then she looks up.

A splattered white scar on her right cheekbone. Most likely a shrapnel wound. Rin would know, having some fifteen herself.

"Good morning," the doctor says to Juney, voice snake-oil smooth, accent not much more than a lilt but oh so recognizable. "You are June, right?"

But Juney isn't listening. Her head's up, cocked at the angle that means her mind is elsewhere. "Mommy?"

Rin is shaking. The face. The scar. Her breath is coming short and airless.

"Mommy?" Juney's voice is more urgent now. "I hear something."

"There is no need to be frightened, dear," the doctor says, and Rin can't tell whether she's talking to Juney or her.

"Mommy!" Juney jumps down from the examining table, her

robe falling off, leaving her in nothing but white cotton under-pants, skin and bone. "Something bad's happening!"

"Get out of here!" Rin yells at the doctor.

"What is the matter?" The doctor looks confused.

"No, not her!" Juney cries. "Run!" And she hurls herself into the dangerous air, unable to see the metal table covered with glass bottles and needles, the jutting chair legs on the floor.

Rin reaches out and catches her, but she wriggles free in true terror. "Let us out!" she screams, and the doctor turns around, bewildered, saying something Rin can't hear because at that moment the window bursts open and a torrent of red water crashes through, smashing them against the wall, knocking them over, pounding them with a whorl of mud and branches and shattered glass. . . .

Rin's soldier training, her war-wolf heart, these are not in her blood for nothing. She struggles to her feet, seizes Juney around the waist and forces the door open, kicking away the flailing doctor tangled in her white coat, her long hair, her scar, and her legacy.

Rin slams her face down in the water and steps on her, using her body to lever her daughter through the door and out of the water to safety.

2

WOLVES

On the morning after the hurricane, two ten-year-old boys climb onto the wall of a stone-knobbled bridge and peer down at the remains of the creek beneath. For years they have waded its waters, built forts by its banks, explored its icicled caves in winter, lain in wait for its beavers in spring, but the storm ruined all that. Now the creek is so plugged with logs and mud it's nothing but a mess of trickles wandering lost and directionless, like the spill from a kicked-over bucket.

"We can't even fish in this," says Flanner, freckled, orange-haired, and bony as a goat. "Bet the fishes are all drowned."

Tariq, equally bony but brown and loose-limbed, pushes away the curls irritating his brow. "Fish can't drown, dummy."

"They could if mud gets gunged up in their gills."

This is what happened to Tariq's mother in the clinic, but he's not about to say so in case he cries. He raises his head to survey the wet and ragged woods around them. The ground is smothered with so many leaf-covered branches the trees seem to be standing on their heads.

"Now what're we gonna do?" Flanner says. "Everything's gone to hell."

"We could hunt for the wolves." Tariq slides off the wall, his prosthetic leg making a light, fleshy thump as he lands.

"How do you know there are any wolves? They might just be dogs or coyotes." Flanner jumps down, too.

"I don't. But it'd be chill to find out."

Flanner hesitates. "How many are there, you think?"

"Seven, maybe? Twelve?"

"A whole pack?"

"Yeah. Let's go."

The boys struggle through the trees for some time, clambering over trunks as slick and fat as manatees, dropping to crawl under bristling logs, their knees pressing into the cobbled mud. Tariq sniffs the air, sour-sweet and steamy, with a tinge of rot—not the way his woods normally smell at all.

"If we do find the wolves, what do we do then?" Flanner asks.

"Feed them."

"Feed 'em what? Your fatso butt?"

"Shut it, Flanner."

They hike on, sweating their prepubescent sweat, slapping at mosquitoes, batting away deerflies. The mugginess left over from the storm seems to have drawn every mean biting bug for miles.

"S'pose the wolves want to eat *us*?" Flanner adds after they have walked farther into the woods than they have ever walked before—so far, it is as still and quiet as a vast room. He is panting now, the words coming out in staccato gasps. *S'pose. Wolves. Eat. Us.* "I think we need weapons. Sticks. Big heavy sticks. And we need to sharpen one end to make spears."

They kick through the mucky underbrush for several minutes, branches snatching at their hair, brambles raking their shins, until they find a sturdy stick each. "You got a knife?" Tariq says.

"Yeah, the one Dad gave me." The fact that Flanner is the only boy of the two with a father, and a father who happens to be a marine sergeant fighting in Afghanistan, adds considerably to his authority. "It's blunt as a thumb but I think it'll work."

He and Tariq whittle the ends of their sticks with a series of deft scrapes until they are honed to pleasingly sharp points. Armed with a spear each, they move deeper into the woods.

Then they hear it: a long, low, pulse-freezing growl.

They stop, a sensation like ice-cold ants running over their skins. They listen without moving. Listen a long time.

Nothing.

"That-was-like-a-dog-right?" Flanner says.

"I don't think so." Tariq's voice is charged with excitement. "I don't think so at all."

They press forward. Or Tariq does. Flanner lags behind.

They hear it again. Even closer, or so it seems. It is hard to tell about sounds in the woods. Sounds bounce against trees, detour through clearings, slap against bluffs. Still, it's the same low growl they heard before: long, deep, and scalp-shriveling.

"Fuck," Flanner gasps, even though his mother shouts at him every time he says it. "Fuck, that's close."

And then, a howl. An actual howl. And each boy knows with an instinct carved deep into his genes by his cave-painting ancestors that this howl is nothing like the howl of either a dog or a coyote.

Flanner can neither move nor, for the moment, speak. But Tariq speeds up, crashing through the underbrush with his peculiar loping gait, as if he can't wait to meet a wolf or even shake its paw. In no time at all, his curly hair is indistinguishable from the patchwork of leaves, and the back of his T-shirt has dwindled to a tiny red stamp.

"Damn," Flanner mutters. Slowly and a safe distance behind, he follows, his surroundings electric with danger now. Twigs snap like jaws. The air pants. Something slavers behind him. An invisible squirrel rattles the leaves nearby and he jumps.

"Flan?" he hears Tariq call, his voice sounding small and oddly far away. "Come."

Flanner creeps through the trees, his heart somersaulting.

"Look." Tariq points at a towering chain-link fence a few feet away. "What do you think that's doing here?"

❧

Juney is squatting beside Rin in the remains of their vegetable patch, running her fingers over boggy lettuces and gashed tomatoes to feel for any plants that might have survived the storm. She is singing one of her off-tune songs again, something about rain and mud and drowning birds, when her hand falls still and she stops.

"Hiccup?" She pulls a small and matted clump from under a cabbage. "What happened to you?" And she starts to cry.

Hiccup was the littlest of their cats, a tiny gray thing only a year old, slight as a comma, and the only one who would consent to sit on their laps. Had Rin switched on her car radio for once and put aside her clusterbomb of paranoias, she would have known the hurricane was coming. Then she could have locked the cats inside to keep them safe. Along with a whole lot else.

"Soldiers don't cry over the dead," she almost says. Then shuts herself up. This is not a lesson she wants her daughter to learn; not the way she and Jay had to learn it.

"Poor Hiccup," she says instead. "We'll give her a special burial, okay, little bean?" But she wishes she had been the one to find the kitten. Juney has gone through enough. After Rin hauled her out of the mud and screams and water the color of bloodied milk, she ran with her up the hill to the car, bundled her inside, and wrapped her in a dog-haired blanket, holding her close until she stopped shaking. "We're safe now," she called over the racket, rain battering the roof, wind rocking the car. "You all right?"

"Yes, you saved me, Mommy. 'Course I'm all right."

But the entire drive home, while Rin maneuvered through sheets of water, roads morphing into mud, branches hurtling at her like missiles, she wondered how much Juney knew of what had just happened and how much she understood.

Juney rubs away her tears with her forearm. "We'll bury her under the bird feeder," she says, her voice still a wobble. "That was her favorite place."

It's true. Hiccup used to crouch there for hours, tail twitching, eyes fixed, watching the birds with the unwavering devotion of a creature addicted to murder. But when the stream behind the barn breached its banks, it washed the bird feeder to kingdom come, along with half of Rin's chickens and the newest-born of her pretty white goats. She found him drowned in the runoff ditch by the driveway, skinny legs snapped. Juney was feeding him from a bottle only two days ago—she had just named him Twigs. Rin hasn't the heart to tell her about that yet.

The animals are not all that's suffered, though; Rin's entire property looks as though it's been mortared, which has shaken her more than she cares to admit—this is, after all, the only true home she has known. As a girl, she was always moving, her parents—father a furniture salesman till booze got the better of him, mother a kindergarten teacher sunk-stuck in depression—hauling her and her brother from one hidey-hole to another. All those nights of being poked awake. "Get up, we're leaving." Tiptoeing out under the silence of the moon. Slipping away from towns and landlords. Crossing state borders. Minnesota, Wisconsin, Iowa, Pennsylvania . . . Driving for hours and days and more hours, her nose in a book to shut it all out. Changing their names, changing their schools. Three suitcases on a bare floor.

At least the storm left the house unscathed, thanks to Jay's ancestors, who built it more than two hundred years ago to withstand this northeastern weather, floods, hurricanes, snow, and all. Once grand and proud, the old farmhouse does look a wreck now, lopsided and paint-peeled, more gray than white, a string of rooms pinned to its side as if in afterthought, the porch dangling like a dropped jaw. Half its green shutters are missing, too, leaving the double row of windows on the front looking asymmetrical and confused. But at heart the house is so solid Rin would bet it could last through a dozen more hurricanes, along with whatever else this haywire climate might have up its sleeve.

Juney lifts her head in her listening way, the fingers of one hand caressing the air, the other resting on Hiccup's corpse. Juney doesn't mind handling dead animals. She is so at home with the earth and its creatures, Rin sometimes thinks she gave birth to a sapling, not a girl at all: a blond wisp of a willow who only pulls up her roots to walk.

"Mommy? There's somebody in the woods."

Rin raises her head, too, trying to hear what Juney hears through the steamy thickness of this new poststorm heat. "Go inside. We'll bury Hiccup later."

Juney knows not to argue. You don't, not with a soldier alerted to danger. Nestling the kitten into a tattered head of a lettuce, she picks up her cane and, with her feet testing every step, makes her way past the lilac bushes to the house. Closes the door behind her and locks it.

Rin runs to the barn, grabs her shotgun off its rack over the corncrib, and heads out to the woods. Nobody, but nobody, is allowed near her wolves.

She sees the boys before they see her, the first tall and acorn-colored, the second white and orange-mopped. She is relieved they are only kids, but she can't be liable for them leaning their ignorant selves up against her fence or sticking their equally ignorant fingers through it. Especially not now when Gray, Silver, and Ebony are so amped from the storm. So she steps out of the shadows, raises her weapon, and trains it right at the boy in front.

❈

Tariq's words stop in his throat, his heart tangling in his ribs, but the rest of him remains peculiarly aloof, as if it has sidled away a moment to busy itself with something else. Flanner, on the other hand, stands locked to the spot behind him, mouth open and stuck there. For a long time, nobody moves.

The woman holding the gun studies them over the stretch of it. Tariq studies her back. A body solid and square. A cap of short, bristled black hair. A round, sunburned face. Eyes the steel gray of a knife, mouth thin as one. And most intriguing of all, barb-shaped scars pockmarking her arms all the way up to the sleeves of her dark green T-shirt.

"Can't you peanuts read?" Her voice is deep and scratchy; the voice of someone who used to smoke but now only coughs.

Neither boy answers.

"You." She jabs the shotgun at Tariq, nearly bumping him in the chest. "You hear me?"

"Yes, ma'am."

"Yes, ma'am what?"

"Yes, ma'am I can read."

"And what do you read on that bigass sign right in front of your nosy little nose?"

"Uh . . ."Tariq peers around her bulk. "No trespassing?"

"And what does 'trespassing' mean? You."This time she swivels her gun to Flanner.

He flinches. "Um. It means can't go in there?"

"It means, chowderhead, no walking on other people's property without their permission. Which is exactly what you are doing. It also means, in this case, not messing with my wolves."

"You mean they're real?"Tariq blurts.

The woman ignores this. But she does lower the gun at last, letting it hang by her knees. Her jeans are mud-spattered and baggy, her feet in tan workman's boots, despite the summer heat. "Lucky you aren't any bigger or I'd shoot you up good and feed you to Gray and Silver and Ebony over there."

The boys strain to see through the fence behind her, which is at least eight feet high and appears to stretch the entire width of the woods. The chance to see actual, live wolves so appeals to their adventure-hungry minds it overpowers any sense of danger. But all they can see is the shadowed darkness between the trees, shot with sunbeams and clouded by gnats.

"Now scat," the woman says. "Before I pepper your balls with buckshot."

They obey, doing their best to walk, not run, each clinging to his spear, feeling her shotgun boring into their backs. They walk for some time without speaking or looking at each other, kicking aside sodden clumps of leaves and slapping at deerflies, fiercer than ever now the afternoon has reached its height. But eventually, Flanner, who considers himself leader, feels duty-bound to speak.

"That lady's crazy. Not just crazy, she's mean. A mean-ass bitch with a mean-ass mouth." No one has ever threatened his balls before and he doesn't know whether to find it horrifying or thrilling.

"Yeah. But I didn't believe that stuff about feeding us to her wolves. She was just trying to scare us."

Flanner is quiet a moment. "Nah, me neither. Who is she anyhow?"

"I think she's the mom of that blind girl."

"What blind girl?"

"You don't remember that girl in third grade?" The boys have just finished fourth, a world away from the babies in third.

"Don't know any blind girl. Don't want to, either."

That closes the conversation, so they walk on in silence. Then Tariq stops. "Where are we?"

They look around. They have often bragged that they know these woods well enough to find their way out even in the dark. But that was before the storm rerouted every path, downed every landmark tree.

"Where's the birch?" Tariq says.

They look around again. No birch.

Tariq has known that birch since he and his mother moved to Huntsville their second year in America. He has carved on it, hidden things in it. Peeled off its papery bark and written secret messages on it. He has always felt—and this is private—that the birch is a guardian spirit, a silvery beacon standing at the edge of the woods to point the way home.

"R.I.P. birch," Flanner intones.

"No, I think we're just lost. We need to go back and ask that mean lady the way."

"Are you nuts? She'll shoot us!"

"No she won't. That's just bluff." Tariq wants to go back. Not because he really believes he and Flanner are lost—his sense of direction tells him pretty clearly where he is. No, something else is drawing him there, something powerful and strange. "I'm going. You can do what you want."

Flanner looks at him. "But we can't split up! We made a sacred pact never to do that!"

"It wasn't sacred. I'm going."

"No you're not! I won't let you."

Tariq turns and starts back along the way they came.

Flanner watches in disbelief. "Fuck you, cripple leg!" he screams, "Towelhead! Traitor!"

3

MOSAIC

Naema lies in her hospital bed without moving, her face trapped under an oxygen mask, her arms wired to tubes, her mind weaving in and out of memory and dream. Her every breath catches like a sob, the tissues of her lungs as shredded as the plastic bags left clinging to telephone wires by the storm.

At the moment, she is sewing Tariq's leg back on, doctor that she is. Needle plunging . . . thread pulling . . . wounds closing . . .

A mosaic lamp spins petals of color over the whitewashed walls of her home. She keeps sewing.

Baby Tariq crawls, perfect and whole, across a carpet woven with flowers. She keeps sewing.

Out in the courtyard, lemons hang as heavy as breasts, while olives hide among their silver leaves, nuggets of powdered green. She threads a new needle.

The call of the muezzins rise, summoning the faithful to prayer, their voices cracked and splintered by aging loudspeakers. . . . She keeps sewing.

Khalil moves up to kiss her, calling the prayer with them. His arms embrace her even as the explosion shatters him into a rain of flesh and jelly, blood and bone. . . . She keeps sewing.

Tariq shocked stiff in her arms, his leg an incomprehensible rag. . . . She chooses a sharper needle.

Black Hawks throb through the sky, pounding chisel and hammer into her temples. . . .

The eyes of Syrians black and blank because they are the eyes of strangers. . . .

The blinding green of the American countryside . . . Tariq digging in a flower bed, the soldier looming over him like a shadow . . .

She keeps sewing.

4

VISITOR

"I don't give a damn about your act of God," Beth Wycombe yells into her phone. "My insurance contract states it right here: Branch falls on it, I get damages."

Using her free hand to pull up her hair, dangling heavy as a horse tail in this new wave of heat, she gazes across the lawn at the crushed remains of her husband's Camaro, which only two days ago was lipstick red and sleek as a fish. "I'm trusting you to look after this baby," Todd told her before he left. "I don't want to see a single scratch on her, understand?"

"Yes, of course that's what I mean," she says. "I can't even move the thing. It looks like a smashed Coke can." She listens a second, frowning, then slides the phone into her jeans pocket and returns to raking the leaves and branches heaped all over her lawn. Yesterday afternoon, right in the thick of the hurricane, she, Flanner, and Tariq crept up from the basement to peer out of a back window. Trees were whipping from side to side, branches harpooning the air, rain pounding the windows like fists. The valley behind her house, normally a bucolic cup of a meadow, had transformed into a roiling rust-red sea, waves cresting into angry white spumes. "Holy crap," she whispered, and hustled the boys back down to safety.

All that has receded now, but what's left looks like a demolition site; the meadow clotted with mud, yard ankle-deep in tree debris. It'll take her days and days to clean all this up without Todd here to help. Not that he ever is here to help.

Flanner comes tramping around the corner, his face set in a sulk, ginger hair studded with burrs. Beth leans the rake against the porch, crosses her arms and watches him, her freckled, button-nosed gangle of a son. "Flanner McAllister, you're a mess. Where on earth have you been?"

"No place." He glances at the remains of his father's Camaro and trails over to sit on the bottom step of their porch. The porch is painted white, but the rest of the house, inside and out, is the blaring yellow of a daffodil.

"You went into the woods, didn't you?"

"Maybe."

"I told you not to, honey. The storm's weakened the trees and a branch could drop on your head at any moment. It won't be safe for a while yet."

He looks again at the car; the chassis flattened under a log, branches wrapping it like tentacles. The windows littering the ground like shattered ice. "Dad's gonna be mad as hell."

"I know. So let's not tell him, okay?"

Flanner nods, bending to scratch his legs, poking white and knobbly out of his desert camouflage shorts. "The bugs are bad today. I'm, like, bitten all over."

"Go shower and wash those burrs out of your hair. You're probably stuck with ticks, too. You should've worn long pants. Where's Tariq?"

"Gone to see the wolves."

"What?"

"You know those wolves over the hill near Potterstown? He went to see them and that wacko lady over there."

"There aren't any wolves, honey. That's just stories."

Flanner looks at his shoes.

Beth bends to peer into his face. "Are you talking about Mrs. Drummond? Tariq walked all the way to her house?"

"Uh-huh."

"And you let him go by himself?"

Flanner shrugs.

"I thought you knew the rule about not leaving each other alone in the woods." She straightens up. "Remember what Dad always tells you? 'Never leave a fallen comrade behind. *Semper Fi.*'"

"Tariq wasn't fallen."

"I'm ashamed of you, Flan. You should be sticking by poor Tariq after what happened to his mom. Think how upset he must be."

Flanner's mouth presses closed.

Beth decides to call Louis Martin, her neighbor down the road and one of Todd's military buddies. Louis knows Naema Jassim better than anybody—he can be the one to rescue her kid.

He answers on the fifth ring. "You all right after yesterday?" His voice, flat and low, always sounds to her as if it doesn't want to be talking at all.

"More or less. A tree fell on Todd's new car, though. He's going to kill me. Listen, you got a moment?" She hates asking Louis for favors, even though he promised Todd to help her out when needed—be the man while Todd is running around shooting Afghans. She hates it not only because it makes her look like the very type of helpless woman she least wants to be but because Louis is so difficult to be around, weighted as he is by his history and the town's suspicions. He's been like this for six years now, ever since his accomplished young wife astounded everybody by killing herself.

"Of course. Is there a problem?"

"Might be. Tariq just walked through the woods to Rin

Drummond's place. By himself." She frowns again at her son, who examines a scar on his left knee.

"You sure? That's not like him."

"I know, and I'm worried. Remember what she did last year when she caught that prowler snooping around her property? Shot him right in the butt—"

"I'll get him. Last thing Naema needs now is anything happening to Tariq."

Beth studies her nails, which she painted a glossy gold only two days ago but are already chipped, thanks to her hours of hauling wood. "Yes. Of course. How's she doing?"

"Not good."

"I'm sorry to hear that." Beth searches for what to say next. "I wish we could warn Rin that Tariq's coming. I don't want her taking potshots at him. You have her number?"

"No, but don't worry. I'm sure not even Rin Drummond would shoot a kid."

❊

"Are they gone, Mommy?" Juney says when Rin returns from chasing off the boys. Juney is standing in the kitchen with a tiny red trowel in her hand, the toy one Rin gave her when she was three. It touches Rin that Juney would choose her babyhood spade to dig a grave.

"Yeah. It was just a couple of kids. You okay?"

"'Course I'm okay. Can we bury Hiccup now?"

"Sure, if you're ready."

"I'm ready."

"That's my girl."

Juney picks up her cane and follows Rin to the empty bird feeder pole, where they settle onto the damp ground and dig in silence, scooping out a tidy, if muddy, grave the shape and size of a shoe box. Rin is just wondering whether to raise the subject of the storm again, see if Juney needs to talk any more about it, when Juney breaks into another of her songs, giving it a lullaby tune while she rocks the rhythm over the mouse-gray corpse in her lap.

"Rest, little kitty, rest your sorry eyes.

Sleep, little kitty, sleep under the skies.

You'll be gone soon, kitty, so here are lots of hugs.

You'll be gone soon, kitty, eaten up by bugs."

Shush, Rin wants to say, *please shush, Juney.* The song is making her think of when she and Jay buried his family dog behind the barn. An old sheepdog, comforting as a slipper. And of Jay himself, reaching for her in his grief.

Juney falls silent then and lifts her head, her entire body alert and still. Rin is about to ask what's wrong when a voice pipes up directly behind her, "Excuse me?"

She leaps up and spins around. That boy is standing here, the one she just chased away with his carroty friend, right in her own private, protected, sodden sanctuary of a garden. How did he get back here without her hearing—without even the wolves hearing? Or the dogs, for that matter? They aren't even chained up. But they stayed quiet—they're still quiet.

"What do you want?" she snaps.

He steps back, rocking a little. Dropping her eyes over him, she sees why. Something is wrong with his legs.

"Sorry to bother you again, ma'am," he says, his voice a child's but with a man's rasp around the edges. "It's just that I'm lost."

He doesn't look lost. He doesn't look as scared as he should be, either, given she just poked her shotgun into his chest.

"I know you," he says, turning to Juney. "You're in Ms. Peterson's class, right?"

Juney lifts her petal-pale face in his direction. "Yup. I'm Juney. Who are you?"

Rin looks from one child to the other. Juney cross-legged and calm on the ground, her toothpick arms bare in a red T-shirt, trowel in her hand, dead kitten in her lap. The boy, mud-spattered and burr-stuck; black curls, earnest eyes. Rin a speechless lump between them.

"I'm Tariq. What happened to your cat?"

"She drowned in the storm."

"That's sad. You burying her here in this hole?"

"Uh-huh. Want to help?"

"Sure." And as if it's the most natural thing in the world, the boy pulls up the left side of his jeans, presses something Rin can't see on his thigh and drops half his leg off. Settling himself down, he crosses his good leg beneath him and rests his stump along the grass, the empty pant leg below it crumpling like a discarded sock. Kids usually gape when they first meet Juney, pull faces to test if she truly can't see. It slices into Rin every time. But this kid only picks up Rin's trowel and starts digging. "Are you going to put your kitten in a box?" he asks.

"No. I want her to melt into the earth quick, you know? So it doesn't hurt? A box would make it take longer."

"Good idea. A box might make her feel lonely, too."

She and the boy dig for a few minutes in companionable silence.

"Mommy," Juney says eventually, "stop hovering. I can hear you hovering."

She's right. Rin has been glued to the spot, staring at them like a fool. She and Juney have never had a kid visit before, let alone a kid like this. Juney has learned not to ask for one, knowing that even if Rin could handle a child, she couldn't handle the parents.

"Mommy, maybe you could make us some lemonade?" Juney's tone has a bossiness to it that is entirely new. "It's hot out here. You want some, Tariq?"

"Yes, please, if it's not too much trouble. Thank you, Mrs. . . ." He looks up, waiting for Rin to tear her eyes off the molded leg lying beside him, its lifelike skin the exact color of his real one, complete with its own blue cotton sock and mucky sneaker. "I'm sorry, ma'am, but I don't know your name."

What is this kid, thirty? "Drummond," she just manages to say.

"Thank you, Mrs. Drummond," he says calmly.

"Okay, Mommy?" Juney urges, and in her voice Rin can hear her saying, *Don't worry, I'm safe and so are you. Now leave me alone.*

So she does.

❖

"Why's your mom keep pointing guns at people?" Tariq asks once she is out of earshot. "And why does she keep wolves? I mean, it's chill to keep wolves. *I* want wolves. But I just wondered."

Juney pats the little grave to make it smooth and even around the insides. "It's to protect us."

"Protect you from what, robbers?"

"I don't know." She stops what she is doing to sway back and forth a moment. "My mom was in a war." She leans forward to feel the bottom of the grave. "You think it's deep enough yet?"

"No. We should keep going if you don't want animals digging it up." He scoops out another handful of earth and adds it to the tidy pile beside him. "I was in a war, too."

They dig a while longer, deepening the grave and patting it smooth again. "I think it's ready now," he says. "It looks nice."

"Are there lots of earthworms in there?"

He peers in. At least five liver-colored worms are writhing greasily from the shock of being uncovered. "Yup."

"Good. They can keep her company." Juney brushes the earth off her hands, lifts the kitten from her lap and places her carefully inside the grave, feeling around to make sure she is centered. "Was it scary being in a war?"

Tariq scoops up a handful of damp earth and molds it into a patty. "Yes. A lot of bad stuff happened. You ready to put the dirt on top of the kitty now?"

"Her name's Hiccup. Does she look comfy?"

"She looks like she's sleeping. Why's she called Hiccup?"

"'Cause she does. Did. I think we should put a flower in there with her, don't you?"

Tariq hunts around in the rubble until he finds a half-drowned marigold. He shakes off the mud and puts it in Juney's earth-stained hands. "Here. It's orange."

She sniffs it. "No, blue." Bending forward, she runs her fingers over Hiccup until she finds her ears, then nestles the flower between them. "What kind of bad stuff?"

"Well, my leg and . . . other things. You want to shovel the dirt back in now?"

"In a minute." She strokes the dead kitten one more time. "Bye, little Hiccup. I loved you a lot. I hope the maggots come quick." Picking up her trowel, she reluctantly trickles some earth back into the grave. "What do you mean about your leg?"

"Half my left leg got blown off by a bomb. Can I put some dirt in, too?"

"Yup, but it isn't dirt; it's earth." She trickles in a little more. "Can I feel where your leg was?"

Tariq hesitates. He can't stand anyone touching his ampu-
tated limb, even doctors or his mother. It has had seven years
to heal, to harden into a shiny round knob just above his knee,
knotted and folded like the end of a sausage. But when it's
touched, the sensation is both unbearably intense and sicken-
ingly numb, as if someone is tickling an inner organ.

"You can touch the fake one if you want." He lifts his prosthesis off the ground and puts it in Juney's lap in place of the
kitten.

"Wow, it's heavy." She runs her hands over its vinyl surface.
"It's got skin. I thought it'd be hard, like a plastic bucket."

"No. But I have a metal one for when I do sports. That one's
hard."

Leaving the prosthesis on her lap, she shovels the earth back
into the grave in earnest now, Tariq following suit. "Are kids
mean about your leg?" She raises her pale oval of a face, her long
whiteblond hair curving around it. The way she moves is peculiar, swaying her head around on her neck like a sunflower in a
breeze, but this is more intriguing to him than strange.

"They used to be. Not so much anymore." He takes her hand
and brings it to his own face, wanting her to see him as he can
see her. "What about you? Do kids tease you?"

She runs her palm up his cheek to his forehead, down over
his bump of a nose to his lips, his pointed chin, and over to the
other side, sensing a narrow face with deep eye sockets. When
she tucks her fingers into his thick hair, the curls wrap around
them like little hugs. She withdraws her hand. "Sometimes kids
are mean, yeah. But soldiers don't care about that kind of thing."
She returns to filling the grave.

"You're a soldier?"

"Yup. Me and my mom both."

"My dad was a soldier, too. And my mom's a doctor for soldiers' kids." A claw twists in his chest. "Or she was."

❖

Rin leans against her kitchen sink, watching Juney and the visitor through the window while she stirs lemon juice and honey into a jug of cold water. She knows she shouldn't spy like this—she should leave her daughter some privacy. Jay would certainly tell her so. But this boy's brazen invasion has rattled her badly.

She hears the dogs burst into a frenzy of barking, so stops stirring to listen. These aren't the excited barks triggered by a bitch in heat or a rival dog in the distance; nor are they the cousinly barks they send out to the wolves and local coyotes, barks as full of longing as they are territorial warnings. No, these are the vicious, hysterical barks they reserve for human strangers, which means that somebody else has invaded her property now, somebody who has ignored the PRIVATE KEEP OUT I MEAN IT sign at the head of her driveway and driven on in anyhow.

Seizing the M16 she keeps racked over the kitchen window (she stores a loaded weapon in every room, although well out of reach of Juney), she runs out to the porch. A car is insinuating itself up the driveway; a slinky, silver, untrustworthy car that makes her think of military recruiters and Bible salesmen. She sees a man inside, tall and dark and wearing sunglasses. Cropped black hair, shoulders bulked. And she sees on the faded remains of his bumper sticker the words HOOAH. IT'S AN ARMY THING.

Hooah, my ass.

She raises her rifle, aims it at him and makes no move to call back the dogs, who are clumped behind the gate now in a moil of snarling and leaping, urging one another on in brotherly delirium. She is no more interested in some war-crazed hooah veteran coming to bother her than she is in some slob of an overweight civilian doing the same thing.

"Get off my property!" she yells. But he can't seem to hear her because he keeps on coming. Up her purposely ill-kept driveway. Past all the NO ENTRY, GO AWAY signs she has planted along its edges. And all the way to her gate, which she has secured along the top with a coil of army-strength razor wire and a string of electric wire, too, in case anyone fails to get the point.

Locking and loading, she steps forward.

For a long moment, Rin and Louis are at an impasse: she on the porch, rifle aimed with sniper precision at the center of his forehead, dogs yowling; he in his car, heels dug into the floor, back pressed against the seat, hands wrapped tight and sweating around the steering wheel.

He stares at her weapon, adrenaline burning along his veins. Nobody has aimed a rifle at him for years, let alone from this close. A familiar screaming starts up in his head, a screaming he had hoped never to hear again.

Wishing he had his own M16 so he could shoot the damn dogs quiet, he breathes long and slowly, in and out, his eyes fixed on the rifle. He forces a count of twenty.

One . . . Two . . . Her aim pushes between his eyebrows; a hot, bullet-shaped circle.

Three . . . Four . . . He will not hit the ground. Will not crack.

Five . . . Six . . . The barks slam into his eardrums.

Seven . . . Eight . . .

He reaches twenty. Adds another ten for good measure.

Checks himself, eyes still riveted to Rin's rifle as if they alone could stop a bullet. Only when he has successfully wrestled the screaming back into its lockbox and slid the iron bolt home does he allow himself to roll down his window.

Torso clammy, fingers clammier, he leans out, the M16 aimed like a blowtorch at his head. "Ma'am, lower your weapon, please!"

"Not till you haul your ass out of here!"

"I don't mean any harm. Just came looking for a boy."

"Don't know any boy," she yells back, not sure why she's lying. "Leave or I shoot!"

Tariq steps through the front door just then, holding the hand of a wispy towheaded little girl. Louis's spine springs loose with relief. He cannot imagine how he would follow one breath with another if anything happened to Tariq. He eases his arm out of the car window and waves, taking a gamble Rin won't blow his hand off.

She watches this audacity with no idea the children are on the porch behind her.

"Mrs. Drummond?" Tariq ventures. "That's my uncle Louis. You don't need to shoot him."

"Mommy, please?" Juney sidles over and slips an arm around her mother's thick waist.

Rin is shaking now. She does, however, manage to ease her finger off the trigger and lower her rifle. "Betty, Ricky, Pop, Rufus!" she calls. "Get over here!"

She shouts it three times before the dogs stop barking, but finally, with a long growl each they slink back, hackles up, and gather around her, panting. The invisible wolves are there, too, Gray pressed up against her, his sizzling eyes fixed on the stranger.

"I like dogs," Tariq says, stretching out a hand to stroke Betty.

"They don't like you," Rin snaps.

"They're guard dogs and Betty's a service dog," Juney explains. "They're not pets."

Tariq has no idea what a service dog is, but he understands to let them alone. "Hi, Louis!" He looks up at Rin. "Can he get out of the car now, Mrs. Drummond?"

"No. But you can go over there and get into it."

"Mommy!"

"Enough, Juney. That's enough for one day."

"Ma'am." Louis has opened the car door and climbed out anyway. His nerves are still shooting sparks, but he lifts off his sunglasses so as to seem less of a threat. The dogs bristle and growl. He stays behind the gate, an eye on both them and Rin, who may be no more than five foot five but looks every bit the former soldier she is: boxy and muscular, dark hair short and scrubby as a nailbrush, rifle dangling by her knee. He wills Tariq to come to him and come quickly. "Ma'am, if you need any help clearing this up, I'd be glad to oblige." He gestures at the storm wreckage, half to make peace, half to call her bluff.

"Like hell you will," she mutters. "Bye, Tariq. Now scat."

Tariq descends the porch steps, looking little and spindle-shouldered compared to Rin's menacing bulk. "Bye, Mrs. Drummond. Bye, Juney." He turns back to them. "See you soon."

Rin glares at him as he unlatches the gate, carefully shuts it behind him, and climbs into the soldier's car. She watches it back up to turn around and keeps watching while it bumps slowly down her driveway, rounds the corner, and lurches out of sight.

"Good riddance." She looks down at her daughter, whose arm is still around her waist. "Right, Juney?"

But Juney isn't listening. She is only smiling to herself. And then she lets go of her mother, raises her pale arm and waves into the empty air. Waves and waves, as if Tariq can still see her.

❀

"You okay?" Louis asks Tariq while he maneuvers around the potholes and ruts of Rin's driveway, not entirely certain he is okay himself. "That woman didn't scare you, did she?"

"Of course not."

"You sure? Waving her rifle around like that?"

Tariq looks out of the side window, gazing at the row of neon orange KEEP OUT signs posted along both sides of the road. "She doesn't mean anything by it."

"Oh no? Well, she shouldn't threaten people like that. Somebody could get hurt." Louis inhales, still needing to breathe in short, sharp intakes.

Tariq says nothing. He doesn't feel like talking. He only wants to absorb all he has just seen. The wolves undulating through the woods, their throats rumbling like earthquakes. The girl with her antennae fingers and mirror eyes. The dead kitten, a marigold between its ears. The soldier mom and her dilapidated farmhouse listing like a boat in the wind.

"You want to come home with me or go back to Flanner's?" Louis asks after a spell of quiet. The car is out on the road now, no longer lurching.

"You. Flanner's a jerk."

"Oh? Since when was your best friend a jerk?"

"Since always." Tariq considers telling Louis about Flanner's insults, but the words are too ugly to repeat.

"You look like you've been dunked in a mud bath. Flanner's mom said you were in the woods. Were you?"

"Yeah."

"That wasn't so smart, bud. The trees are too unstable. What were you doing?"

"Exploring." And then, because Tariq has known Louis since he was six, and because he knows Louis would never make fun of him, he adds, "I saw Mrs. Drummond's wolves. I crept up to her fence and I saw them!"

"You did? I thought they were just a story."

"Oh no." Tariq smiles to himself, a secret warming his insides like a swallow of hot chocolate. One of the wolves, the biggest one, the one Juney said was named Gray, walked right up to the fence and stared at him. Stared so hard his eyes shimmered like melting gold. He didn't seem fierce or frightening. He seemed like a big, friendly dog. No, Tariq corrects himself, he seemed like what he was—a wild, majestic, beautiful beast. But best of all—and this Tariq will never tell anyone, not even Louis—he seemed about to speak.

Louis has never seen a wolf in his life and is pretty sure Tariq hasn't, either. All he saw, no doubt, was a dog and a wish. But Louis has seen war-warped vets before. "Well, you better stay away from that place, wolves or no wolves. That woman is not cool."

"She's fine."

"Oh yeah? What about her little girl, is she 'fine,' too? Imagine having a mom like that."

Tariq returns his gaze to the window. He refuses to talk about Juney. Talking about Juney would be like spilling oil into a perfectly clear, crystalline pond.

When they reach Louis's house, a two-story beige clapboard just down the hill from Beth's, Louis switches off his engine and turns to Tariq. "Listen, bud, I asked at the hospital if you can visit your mom today, but I'm afraid they said it's still too early. You will be able to soon, though, I promise." He can't bring himself to add more, the details Wendy Fitch told him too raw in his mind. How she was hurrying the patients out of the collapsing clinic when she saw a white coat floating by like a great lily, a tangle of black hair straggled across it. How she had taken a moment to realize Naema was inside that coat, face down. How she had waded back into the flood, the water snatching at her knees, to seize Naema under the arms, haul her up to dry ground and give her CPR. How it had taken the ambulance forever to get to them through the floodwaters, Naema lying there with a stillness you rarely see in the living.

Tariq and Louis climb out and stand in silence a moment, gazing at the shambles the hurricane made of Louis's home. The right corner of the roof is dangling like a dislodged eyebrow. The roof itself is covered in bald patches, the wind having ripped off a number of shingles. An upstairs window is punched in and gaping. The whole place looks as if it's been in a fight.

"Where's the linden?" Tariq spins about as if to catch it sneaking off somewhere. The huge, fan-shaped tree has always towered over the house like a benevolent giant. Tariq has daydreamed and read under it for years, climbed its branches, collected its seeds and sent them twirling all over the garden like tiny helicopters. Now all that's left of it is a ragged hole in the earth, like a wound. "What happened to it?"

Louis rests a hand on his head. "I'm afraid it got knocked over by the wind. I had to have it hauled away." He glances at Tariq. "Shame, I know, but it was too close to the house to be safe anyhow. Come see what I found on my deck."

He leads him around the back, where a branch as wide as three boys holding hands in a circle has dropped across the deck floor, splintering the planks beneath. Resting on top of it is a bright green garage door.

"Whoa, whose door is that?"

"No idea. My deck furniture blew away, too. Probably sitting on somebody's roof."

"But how are you going to fix all this?" Tariq lifts his face to Louis. "I mean, it's so . . ." His lips pinch tight, his brow drawing into a cluster of little lumps. He looks exhausted, dark patches under his eyes. Louis, too, cannot sleep out of fear for Naema.

He slips his arm around Tariq's narrow ledge of a shoulder. "You want to stay with me while your mom's away? You don't have to go back to Flanner's or camp if you don't feel like it. You can come to work with me, help keep the store in order."

"I can?"

"Of course. Your mom'll be all right, you'll see. Just hang in there, okay?"

Tariq keeps his gaze on Louis. But he doesn't say a word.

5

MAGHRIB

Naema is gathering laundry on the roof of her house in Baghdad, a basket at her feet, a black sheet slapping her face. She reaches up to pluck the pieces from the line: strips of flesh, a burqa, her mother-in-law's shroud. Folding them one by one, she places them in the basket, where they squirm and settle like sleeping goslings. They hold the warmth of the sun still, even as the air is cooling, and they smell of dust and death.

"The stench of death permeates every crevice of a city at war," she remarks to a vulture flying by, its talons gripping Tariq's severed leg. "I can smell it even on my own tongue."

An explosion in the distance strikes through her chest, startling the pigeons on the roof next door into flight. Rising with them, she and the birds wheel and dip in circles, as if trying to escape an invisible tether, the flap of their wings sounding like applause. Around and around they fly, over the jumble of flat, sand-colored rooftops and spindly minarets of her doomed city; under the sun caught in a snarl of telephone wires. Her hair streams behind her like a net, trapping the pigeons, binding their wings. Shrieking, they drive their beaks into her eyes. She plummets into the basket with a thud.

"Mama?" Tariq runs over, his curls dancing behind him like a cloud of midges. "Play with me?" He tugs at her skirt, the black of it coming off on his hands.

59

The sun dips behind the roofs, turning the sky a blood-streaked gold as the muezzins once again take up their call to Maghrib, their voices curling into her like hooks. Soon the curfew will begin, when nobody but a soldier is allowed on the streets and Baghdad sinks into dark and sinister emptiness. She peers over the roof's edge. Her husband, Khalil, is out there somewhere, perhaps alone, perhaps with soldiers. Perhaps already a ghost.

"Here," she says to Tariq. "Help me pair up Baba's socks."

"But they're all the same, Mama. They're all black. And they don't have Baba's feet in them." He takes off his leg and puts a sock on it.

"No, no, you still have your leg. Put it back on."

He does, but he puts it on backward, the foot pointing behind him. She squats beside him and tries to fix it, twisting and pulling until it begins to bleed.

"Stop, Mama, stop!" he cries. "It hurts!"

A nurse adjusts the mask over Naema's nose and mouth. "Shh," she whispers. "It's all right now. Go back to sleep." She checks the IV drip and turns off the lights.

6

HOPE

Beth and Louis lean on their rakes in the shadows of her front yard, catching their breath as the dusk purples around them. All afternoon, they've been hauling branches off her roof and sawing up the maple crushing the Camaro. Now, Louis's green T-shirt is patched with sweat and Beth's long ponytail is sticking to her back, her bare legs damp and scratched.

"Want to come in for a drink?" she says. "You've earned it."

He glances at his watch. The hospital's evening visiting hours begin in fifty minutes. "Just a quick one. But sure, thanks."

She rubs the back of a knee with her foot. "Shit. Mosquitoes. Let's go."

Inside, she directs him to the ground-floor bathroom and climbs the stairs to another. His is narrow and tubular and just as yellow as the rest of the house: curtains bright as lemons, matching towels, gold faucets. Soap the shape and color of a bee. He wonders if Todd had anything to do with all this.

He washes his hands and face and joins her in her large and equally yellow kitchen. "Sit," she says, pointing to a chair at the table, which is at least white. "Bourbon good?" She hefts a liter of Old Crow down from a cabinet, along with two heavy-bottomed highball glasses. "Ice?"

"That'd be great."

She pours them each a large slug and hands his over,

emptying hers in a series of quick gulps. Refilling it, she takes a seat across from him, kicks off her sneakers, and props her feet up on the table. Her toenails are painted the same glossy gold as her faucets, and her cutoff shorts are very short indeed. Louis is not quite sure what to make of Beth, but he has to admit she's attractive. Small, and still lithe from her years as a dancer. Eyes the blue of jay feathers, face as tidy as a doll's. Hair a thick and wavy auburn. She's just a little frayed around the edges, that's all. Only thirty-four, his own age, yet lines are already scratched around those eyes and across her forehead. But then, as his wife used to say, waiting day and night for that death knock on the door could age even an angel.

"To never having to spend another Saturday like this again." Beth raises her drink with a weary smile. "Thanks for all your help, though. Really."

He shrugs.

"Mind if I ask you something?" She lowers her husky voice to a near whisper. Flanner is upstairs, getting ready for bed, but she doesn't want to risk him overhearing. "Has Tariq said anything to you about why he hasn't shown up here all week?"

Louis knocks back the rest of his bourbon. He can't very well tell her that Tariq refused to come even today, insisting on staying with a neighbor instead. So all he offers is another shrug.

This annoys Beth. She finds Louis annoying in quite a few ways—his tendency to drift off when she's talking to him, the reticence he wraps around himself like a coat. Ever since he and his wife moved here some eight years ago, he has been the object of gossip in town, yet he talks so little about himself nobody is even sure where he's from. They do know he served in Iraq at least three times. They also know he was deeply in love with his wife, Melody Long, a young woman from Albany rumored to have been half black, or maybe Hispanic, as Beth guesses he might be—a woman who seemed fine until she wasn't. But what nobody knows is why she killed herself or what, if anything, he had to do with it.

"I mean," Beth says, "one minute Tariq was staying with us; then he suddenly moves to your house, and now he hasn't come over since. Is he mad at Flanner or something?"

Louis checks his watch again. "I think he's too upset about his mom to see anyone. It's nothing to do with Flanner, I'm sure."

Beth puts down her glass, unconvinced, but decides not to push it. "I can't believe that happened to Naema. Poor Tariq, he must be so scared. Some people get nothing but trouble, you know?" Gathering up her ponytail in both hands, she pulls it apart like wings to tighten it. "Damn this heat. My hair feels like a rug."

Rising, she walks over and cranks open the window above the sink, admitting a waft of viscous air, along with the pulse of crickets and fricative snores of cicadas. She gazes through the insect screen, its mesh blurring her view of the twilit lawn beyond, thinking of her own troubles. Raising a child by herself. Working a dead-end job selling clothes and teaching dance at a boutique with the humiliating name of DanceHi. Todd's Camaro crushed in the driveway.

Returning to her chair, she picks up her glass and drains it, while Louis sits across from her, off in one of his dazes again. She takes the opportunity to study him, tall, lean, and muscled as he is. High-boned face. Black hair short and tight with curls. That coppery-bronze skin she can't quite place on the racial scale. His eyes are so intensely green that every time he raises them to her, she feels a little shock.

"Did you actually meet that Drummond woman the other day?" she asks to break the silence.

No answer.

"Louis?"

He glances at her. "What? Oh. Yeah, kind of." His skin pricks at the memory.

"She as loony as everyone says?"

"She's got a bad case of nerves, that's all." Realizing this sounds like a reprimand, he tries to lighten his tone. "Tariq told me she keeps wolves." He raises his eyebrows.

"Yeah, Flanner said something about that. You think it could be true?"

"'Course not. The kids are just playing."

She stands again, picking up the bourbon bottle and pointing its bottom at him. "Another?"

"No thanks, I need to go."

Ignoring this, she presses fresh ice cubes into both their glasses with a series of loud thunks. "Well, if those wolves are real, I sure hope she's got them caged up."

She pours them each half a glass more and slides his over. Sitting back down, she takes another long swallow, trying to avoid the sight of Louis's right hand cupped around his drink, the middle and ring fingers having been torn off during his last tour in '08. The stubs are purple and scarred and he is usually more careful to keep them out of sight, stuffed into a pocket or tucked under a folded arm, his thumb curling around them in a self-conscious twist. She glances at his face, his eyes fixed once more on the table, and wonders again about Melody.

❖

Upstairs, Flanner is sitting against his pillows, playing a video game on his laptop. In the game, the bad guys are green skeletons and the good guy a soldier in desert camouflage. If Flanner can get his hero to beat the skeletons, he'll let himself go to sleep, and, so far, he's winning. But then his eyes drift to the window, attracted by the moon peering through the blinds, and when he looks back, three skeletons have piled on top of the soldier and are busy whacking him in the head.

Flanner groans and hunches over, his fingers hammering the keyboard. He tries to make the soldier get back to his feet, whirl and kick and fire the humungous machine gun right there in his arms. But the skeletons are creaming him now, along with a swarm of flying screws who have appeared out of nowhere and won't stop pecking holes in his face. The soldier is rapidly weakening, points sliding. Flanner makes him stand up but he only crashes back down again, his weapon disintegrating into pixilated fragments. "No!" Flanner shouts. "No, get up!"

"What's the matter, honey?"

The door swings open, revealing his mother silhouetted against the hallway light. "Are you playing with that thing again?" Her words sound runny. She marches over and snatches up the laptop, glancing at the frozen image on the screen: a pile of green skeletons flailing at the corpse of a soldier.

"What *is* this?"

"Nothing." Flanner's voice quavers.

"Oh, Flan." She sits down on the bed and closes the lid. "You shouldn't play games like this. I told you. Come here."

For a moment, he allows himself to sink into her soft comfort, a luxury he usually rejects these days. But just as he is snuggling into her chest, her breath reaches him. He jerks up and pushes her away. "Leave me alone!"

She stands, clasping the laptop to her stomach. "Get into your pj's, honey." And she creeps out of the room.

❁

Down in the kitchen, Louis is pacing the floor, waiting for Beth to return so he can say good-bye. He only hopes he is sober enough to drive. He poured the remains of his second bourbon down the sink the minute she went upstairs, but even so he feels unsteady. Normally, he never touches anything stronger than beer, not anymore; not since his first year out of the army, the memories rushing at him like a train.

Beth appears at last, clutching a laptop and looking stricken. "Shit." She drops into a chair. "It wasn't one of his nightmares. Look." She puts the laptop on the table and pushes it over.

Louis lifts the lid. One glance at the image—the soldier in DCUs, the skeletons—and his guts clamp. He closes it quickly.

"Take it," she says, the words slipping into one another. "I don't want that damn thing in this house."

He picks up the computer, which dangles like a toy in his big hand, and nestles it into the dust on top of the refrigerator. "I'll leave it here." He backs toward the door. "You'll be all right?"

She looks at him with a crumpled smile, her hair straggling across her face. "Oh yes. Strong little military wifey, that's me."

When he reaches the hospital some forty minutes later, Louis squeezes onto an elevator with a crowd of other visibly anxious visitors and hurries to Naema's room, only to find the door firmly closed. He knocks, worried he has come too late, and waits for some time. Finally, a tall, broad-shouldered nurse opens it and nods in weary recognition, her eyes as darkened with fatigue as Tariq's.

"Any change?" Louis whispers.

"I think she's breathing a little easier. Come see." She takes him inside, past an empty bed and over to a set of blackish-green drapes. "I'm afraid you can't stay long. Visiting hours end in ten minutes." Swishing open the curtains, she hurries away.

Louis steps over and gazes down at Naema's sleeping face, half obscured by her mask. Her eyelids are the color of bruised petals, her wrists punctured with tubes. Her skin has turned waxen. Only her hair, thick, black and full, looks itself, spread in disarray over the pillow.

He leans over her. "Breathe," he whispers. "Please, breathe."

Drawing a chair up to the bed, he clasps her cold hands in his and kisses them—something he would never dare do were she awake—his eyes on the rise and fall of her chest. Every day since the hurricane, he has come before and after work to watch over her like this, the dread heavy within him. He cannot imagine what he would do if he lost her, how he would make it from one day to the next.

He first came across her four years ago at the government's Refugee Center in Albany, where he had been volunteering in the hope of palliating the rot inside him planted by war and Melody's suicide two years earlier. The center had made him a chauffeur, explaining that several hundred Iraqi refugees had been settled in the area, most in need of jobs and all lacking a car. One morning, he was assigned an interpreter's widow who had come to the United States with her mother-in-law and child. They had been staying with their sponsor, he was told, a soldier for whom her husband had translated in Iraq, but something had gone wrong, and now Louis was to help them find a home of their own.

"I was expecting a woman," Naema said in accented but near perfect English when they were introduced, and turned her eyes away. Taking in the tightness of her lips, the white star on her cheek, he hoped she would never learn he had been a soldier, too.

He drove her to three places that first day, each in a neighborhood defiled by poverty and crime. A windowless basement, a tenement that hadn't had working plumbing in years, the back room of a house littered with needles and excrement. She bore all this with equanimity, saying little, pulling at her fingers, sitting with her narrow back straight. She wasn't wearing a hijab or abaya, only blue slacks and a jacket, her hair in a long black rope of a braid. But he felt her holding herself away from him and knew she was humiliated by having to sit alone in a car like this with an American man she didn't know.

"I do not mind somewhere small or even in bad repair," she told him at the end of the day. "But I did not take my son out of war only to bring him to yet more danger. Cannot the center find us a safer place to live?"

The second time they met, she brought Tariq, explaining that her mother-in-law, Umm Khalil, whose given name was Hibah, had been hospitalized with pneumonia and so could not look after him. Tariq was only six then and so proud of his newly fitted prosthesis, the first he had ever had, that he lifted his pant leg to show it off within minutes of their meeting, and then dashed about, a red scarf pinned to his shoulders, insisting in surprisingly good English that Louis call him Nabil Fawzi.

"Who's Nabil Fawzi?" Louis asked Naema.

"Oh, he is some sort of superhero he found in a Syrian comic book." She gazed at Tariq a moment. "It used to break my heart to see my little one on his crutches pretending to fly with the grace of a bird."

That evening, as Louis was driving them back to their lodgings in Slingerlands, the day having proved as fruitless as the first, she looked at him and said, "My sponsor, Sergeant Donnell, he and his wife, Kate Brady, they were soldiers like you, Mr. Martin. Or is it Sergeant?"

"Sergeant. How could you tell?"

She turned her head away.

The third time he picked her up, she was friendlier. "After we see today's apartment, could we take my son somewhere more suitable? These dangerous streets and run-down buildings, they are not good for his spirits."

"They're no good for mine, either."

She pushed her braid behind her shoulder. "Perhaps we could go to a museum? Or, as it is a pleasant day, to a park? If you have time, that is."

"Oh, I've got plenty of time." He stole a glance at her. "Tariq can walk on dirt trails, right?"

"He can walk on anything."

Louis drove them to his favorite refuge, a nature preserve called Myosotis, just south of Huntsville. During those nights in Iraq when the sleep was driven from him by doubts or heat, aches or illness, the deeds of the day burning into him like a branding iron, he would try to escape by walking through this park in his memory, forcing himself to recall every twist of its trails, landmark oak or hemlock; every hawk or bald eagle he had seen sailing over its lake. Myosotis, he knew, was Greek for forget me not.

Parking on the edge of a tree-shaded road, he led them down a pebbled path, a stream on one side, a mossy bank on the other, a wash of golden-green light trickling through the dense woods around them. It was a torpid August day, but here the air was leaf-cool and fresh, and as he gestured for Naema and Tariq to move ahead of him, he saw her lift her face and inhale.

"See that bridge?" He pointed to a small wooden footbridge arcing over the stream. "When we get to it, you'll find a surprise."

"It is safe? For Tariq, I mean?" Naema turned to face him on the narrow path, and he was struck by the grace with which she moved, dressed that day in loose jeans, her back slender under a royal blue tunic, the braid swaying over her hips.

"Sure, as long as he sticks to the trail. He can walk for a while?"

"Oh, yes. Now that he no longer needs crutches, he can walk for hours." She fell in beside him, Tariq trotting ahead of them. "He was only three when he lost his leg, you know, and for years, he had to hobble and limp on crutches. Now, he can go anywhere. Now he is free." She smiled then, for the first time, and Louis felt his heart, which had been so crimped for so long, shake itself like a small, cold animal, and stretch.

The surprise was a waterfall, hidden by a fern-covered bluff and visible only from the bridge. Tariq was already there, jumping with excitement at the sight of the water tumbling in great sheets of white and silver, weaving itself into ribbons, scattering at the touch of a rock into a rush of foam. He reached out as if to hug it, and each time a splash caught him, he laughed.

Naema joined him, bending to kiss the top of his head. And then she, too, stretched out her arms as if to grasp the waterfall. Louis stayed back, watching. He knew from the Refugee Center that her husband had been killed by the same car bomb that had mutilated her son and scarred her face. That she had also lost her father and brother to the war. Yet there she was, laughing.

For the next four weeks, Louis drove Naema and Tariq from one calamity of an apartment to another, interspersed with restorative trips to lakes, movies, playgrounds, and museums. Once Khalil's mother was released from the hospital, she would sometimes come, too, a bent and silent old woman in a black hijab and abaya, with an unsmiling face as withered as a prune and dim, suspicious eyes. But usually it was only the three of them.

"Try to understand if Umm Khalil, she does not warm to

you," Naema told Louis in the car one of the mornings Hibah was absent. "After Khalil and his father, they were killed by the bomb, she managed to cope as long as it was necessary to help us survive in Damascus. But now we are here and relatively safe, she has fallen into a depression I am afraid might kill her." Naema paused. "It was very hard for her when Khalil, he chose to work for your American army. He had to change his name and live away from us so we would be in no danger. Often, we did not see him for months. He did this because he wanted Saddam brought down and he wanted true democracy in Iraq. Did you work with interpreters like that when you were a soldier?"

"I did."

"In return, Sergeant Donnell, he promised to protect Khalil. But he did not protect him. And now we find ourselves staying in the back room of this same Donnell's house."

"You're all in one room?"

"Yes, but that is not my point. My point is, I am living with the man who hired my husband for the job that killed him and I cannot bear being the object of his attempts at restitution, his guilty charity. It is suffocating. And it is even worse with his wife." She paused again, as if to gather herself. "Do you understand this, Louis?" she asked, using his given name for the first time.

"I do. It's not your job to help us soldiers forgive ourselves."

She regarded him gravely, the gold of her irises and the white of her scar vivid in the morning's silvery light. "Exactly. This is why I must leave."

"We'll get you out of there as soon as we can."

They kept looking until, at the end of the month, Louis took her to a new place on the center's list in a slightly better neighborhood than those they had seen so far. She gazed up at the brown brick building, four stories high, its windows cracked and filthy, its front door slashed with graffiti. "Ah, this looks like home," she said, her voice dry. But then she turned to him and he saw she was joking. "Come, my friend, let us go inside. There is always hope, no?"

7

MOON

Rin is worried about Juney. She moves her wafty little self through her chores willingly enough, helping to resurrect the shell-shocked vegetable garden, put up a new bear-luring bird feeder, and repair what other storm damage she can, but she is doing it without any of her usual chatterbox joy. And when she hums in that secret-private way of hers, fingers fluttering, head swaying, she sounds so sad it winches up Rin's heart tight as a high wire.

So, at lunchtime, while Rin is making egg salad sandwiches and Juney is sipping lemonade at the kitchen table, both dirt-grimed and due for showers, Rin asks if something is wrong.

"Nope."

"You sure?"

"Leave me alone, Mommy." Rin is about to object to her tone when Juney takes up a new song, its tune meandering and frail, giving it lyrics that catch Rin's words in her throat.

"Hiccup is a kitty, Hiccup is a cat.
She lives in a box under the ground.
Her box is dark and lonely;
Her box is quiet as earth.
Her only friend is a flower,
A blue and sad little flower.
And maybe one worm."

She sings it again and again, rocking in her chair until Rin can't bear it. "Are you lonely like Hiccup?"

Juney stops singing. "Mommy, I'm not a baby. I know Hiccup's dead. It's just a song."

It isn't until later, after lunch and showers, when Rin finds her sitting still as a shrub in the vegetable patch, head tilted in her listening pose, that she gets it. Juney is waiting for that boy. The one who appeared out of nowhere and dropped his leg off, bringing back memories Rin had hoped were erased for good. Juney is lonely. Naturally, she is. She is nine years old, so of course Rin isn't enough anymore. Even the dogs and remaining cats and goats—even the wolves aren't enough.

Rin sits next to her on the warm ground and strokes her cheek, so soft to her calloused hand she can scarcely feel it. Juney is only wearing a faded blue T-shirt and shorts today, but she looks like a fairy-tale princess nonetheless, her hair braided into the coronet Rin pinned around her head to relieve her from the heat. This muggy pressure hasn't let up for all ten days since the storm and it's cooking the drowned plants in their garden to mush. They reek of mildewed washcloths and sneaker feet.

"What's your friend's name again?" Rin asks, although she remembers it only too well.

"What friend?"

Rin feels a splat of annoyance, along with no considerable wonder. Her little Juney, who only a moment ago was as free of guile as a newborn, is being coy. "I mean that kid who popped up in our yard like a gopher."

That makes Juney smile, which allows Rin's inner winching to relax a fraction. "His name's Tariq." And then: "Mommy, what's he look like?"

"Who, the gopher?"

"Mommy, come on."

"He looks like any kid."

"Mommy!"

"I'm sorry, little bean, I wasn't thinking. Let's see. He's tall for his age, taller than you. Skinny. He's got a narrow little face, curly black hair—"

"I know *that*. But what are his eyes like?"

"Oh. Well, they're big and round and the color of—they're brown. Reddish brown." Rin realizes that won't tell Juney anything. Rin has tried to teach Juney to name the true colors of things, but Juney isn't interested, and given that blue is green to some folks and vice versa, while others can't even recognize red, Rin doesn't see that it matters. Who is she to railroad her daughter into the vocabulary of the seeing? "You know when I roast chestnuts in winter?" she says in her earthbound way. "That color."

"Hmm. And how's he walk on his fake leg? Does he hop?"

"No, he walks normally. Maybe just the tiniest limp, like when you get a thorn in your shoe."

Juney pulls up her pale, pointy knees and rests her chin on top of them, making herself into an egg. "He told me his leg got blown off in a war."

Rin closes her eyes.

"Tariq," Juney says, drawing out the word. "What kind of a name is that?"

Rin stands up, the few pebbles of tolerance she has for this topic rolling clean away. "Ask him. I need to work on the barn. You going to be all right?"

"Yep. I'll do the veggies." So Rin leaves her to feel for leaf-munching beetles and flood rot while she tries to purge Tariq from her mind for long enough to figure out how to remove the two enormous trees the hurricane sent crashing into the back of her barn.

The trees are ancient, one a willow, the other an oak, and she is deeply sorry to see them die. The willow was a beauty, forty feet tall and some seventy-five years old, with vine-thin branches bursting from its trunk like a fountain and a mass of slender, feather-shaped leaves. But the oak was her favorite. Its little acorns with their crocheted berets. Its rough, wise old bark. Its thousands of intricate leaves, like tiny elongated hands with too many fingers, jammed against the barn roof now, unaware of their impending doom. Rin reckons this oak must be a century old, if not more. It has watched Jay's farm prosper, fade and fail. Seen the woods spring up thick and wild, only to be razed for fields and then left to spring up again. Witnessed his parents come into this life, age, and die. Housed generations of birds inside its branches—woodpeckers, nuthatches, cardinals, hawks, starlings, chickadees, yellow-bellied sapsuckers—nesting, laying their eggs, raising their young, starting again. And then there are all the wars the oak has lived through: World War I and the second one, too. Korea and Vietnam. CambodiaLebanonIran. And the long string of U.S.-infested wars in just the past thirty-one years since Rin was born: GrenadaSalvadorHondurasNicaraguaPanamaGulfOneTheBalkansAfghanistan. And of course her very own war with its looking-glass name: OIF, Operation Insane Fuckers. Yes, quite an achievement, all those wars, not to mention the many little ones the U.S. fostered in between. Ah, what a waging of death upon the soil of others this American oak has seen, along with its cousin, the DoD, Dear old Democracy, Dead on Delivery, for whom Rin gave her faith, her body, her daughter's eyes, and . . .

And where were you when I needed you, sister-comrade-soldiers mine, that night of the . . . where were you, where were . . .

❖

Juney is crouching where her mother left her, head up and swaying, absorbed now in listening for birds, not boys. Over by the feeder she can hear the rough croaks of jays and crows, who never seem defeated by anything, but she is worried about how the tinier, light-boned birds fared in the storm. She knows how vulnerable they are, having held newly hatched chicks in her palms, their claws as fine as thorns, their feathers light as a tickle. How many of those little birds, the finches and sparrows and tufted titmice, lost their nests and eggs and fledglings to the hurricane? How many were beaten to the ground and drowned, like poor little Hiccup, or struggled in the wind only to be dashed against a tree? Her heart contracts at the thought of such flimsy creatures snatched up by the same force that knocked her and her mother into all that pounding water and mud.

At night, Juney sometimes dreams about the storm. The cry of limbs being torn from trees, the splintering of glass, the human shrieks. But more often she dreams of birds, the scratch of their feathers in her hands, the throb of their pinpoint hearts, their songs guiding her, like the stony path beneath her feet and the scent of her mother's lilacs, from the vegetable patch to the feeder. She dreams, too, of the music around her: the ten steps up to her bedroom, each stair creaking with its own woody tune; the fourteen across the living room, six shuffling over the warmth of carpet, eight slapping against the chill of bare floor. The rhythmic pant of the wolves as they move toward her through the woods, their breath heavy and hungry and yet as comforting as home; the moan of a cat in heat; the yearning cry of her mother's call. The warm lick of the sun, cool brush of a shadow, the sting-sharp lash of winter at her neck . . . She dreams of all the eddies of scents and sounds and sensations she must sort out day and night, asleep and awake, to make sense of the world.

"Hi."

She starts and turns up her face. "Tariq?"

"Yeah. I came to see how Hiccup's doing. That okay?"

"Sure." Too shy to show her pleasure, Juney wipes her grassy hands on her shorts. "I'm worried she's lonely, even with the flower. Come look."

Drifting off the ground, she walks down the path to the new bird feeder, without her cane today, feeling her way along the row of lilac bushes with one hand, the petals tickling her palm, while Tariq follows. He looks down at the grave, a small heap of earth marked now by a triangle of pebbles. Juney holds the feeder pole, waiting for his words.

"I don't think she's lonely," he says. "She's got the birds now and all those flowers and plants right here."

Juney considers this. "I guess. And she's got the maggots. I forgot about them."

Tariq raises his head and examines her in a way he wouldn't dare with anyone else. His mother is always telling him not to stare, but when a person can't see, you can stare for as long as you want. Juney's face is as white and small as a dab of paint; her body so slight it's almost as if he is dreaming her, especially with her flaxen hair braided and wrapped about her head like a crown. She reminds him of something, but he cannot remember what. Then it comes to him: a picture he saw long ago in one of the library books his mother used to bring him to teach him English; a book of folktales from a land far, far away and about as different from America or Iraq as a land can be. "You should know about the cultures and stories foreign to us," she said, and opened the page to show him illustrations of pale, white-haired girls in a forest. They weren't human girls. They were like the djinns in his grandmother's stories, only good instead of malicious; magical creatures of the forest whose bodies were half tree and half girl and ended in wisps instead of legs, which is why he was so drawn to them. Their hair was long and floating, their eyes blue-water clear. Just like Juney's. Maybe he could take a book like that to his mother in the hospital. Read it to her the way she used to read to him. Help her get better by making her remember happy things.

"I can hear you thinking," Juney says. "But I can't hear what the thoughts are."

Tariq takes a moment before he can answer. "I'm thinking about these magic girls I saw in a book once. They live inside trees and they can fly. I don't know what they're called."

"Dryads."

"They are?"

"Yup. I read a book about them once. Each dryad protects her own tree. And if the tree dies, she has to die, too." Juney listens for her mother, whom she urgently wants not to intrude right now, while Tariq tries to imagine how she reads. He is about to ask when she says, "Where's your name come from?"

"What? Oh, home. Me and my mom are from Iraq."

"Is that where you were in the war?"

"Yeah." His eyes drift toward the woods and the wolves.

"That's the war my daddy died in." She raises her head to listen again. "Can you see my mom anywhere?"

He glances around. "Nope. I think she's over by the barn."

"Good." And as if Juney can hear his thoughts after all, she adds, "You want to see our wolves?"

"Yes! Oh yes." He doesn't even say it; he breathes it, his yearning is so intense.

"Okay. But don't tell Mommy or anyone else. She wants us to keep the wolves a secret. Promise?"

"I promise."

"Really and truly? It's a super-important promise."

Tariq wishes now he had never said anything to Louis. "I really and truly promise."

"Good. Hold my hand so I don't trip. I don't have my cane and there's a lot of storm mess still in the way."

He wraps his fingers around her hand; a tiny, light hand, as soft as a kitten paw. "Your hand feels like Hiccup," he says, because with Juney he knows he can say what he wants.

And that makes her laugh.

❧

Rin has no heart left to tackle the trees for now, the oak's spin-bad memories having drained her of it, so she turns away from the barn to look for Juney. But then another carcass way-lays her, this one of a hen. Once a pretty cinnamon, she is black and bloody now, smashed by a branch, feathers mud-soaked and torn. She stinks, too, so Rin can't cook her for soup or even feed her to the wolves. Wolves don't eat carrion—in the wild, they leave that to the ravens that accompany them like camp follow-ers, bold enough to perch on their backs, heedless of snapping jaws. This is the fifth dead hen Rin's found since the storm, leav-ing only six. She raised each of those ladies herself, right out of their mother's warm, enfolding eggs, all fluff and beak and pinprick blinking eyes.

Rin grabs the hen by her scaly legs, pinching up her face at the stench, and carries her over to the compost bin, stuffing her in with a little incantation against foraging bears. She doesn't want Juney finding the hen; it's been bad enough with Hiccup and—Rin finally told her—Twigs the goat.

As she's scrubbing off the hen's death ooze under the outdoor faucet, she catches sight of Juney and Tariq strolling hand in hand across the yard with all the blitheness of *Babes in the Woods*.

She stares at them. Stares a long time. Then she tells herself to quit being paranoid. The boy is only ten, for god's sake, whatever his origins, and she should let her daughter have a moment with a friend without "hovering," as Juney so kindly put it. So, she forces herself to turn away and head back to the barn after all.

There, she takes a closer look at her trees. The storm snapped the poor willow into three pieces, the main trunk falling just clear of the back wall, the rest of it closer to the stream. At least it's done no harm. But the oak has inflicted serious damage. The wind split it clean in two from top to bottom and threw half of it against the barn wall, badly mangling the roof. Now the trunk is lying pressed up against the barn like the corpse of a giant. Rin will need chains to get it out of here, and a truck. Or better still, a BFV. Otherwise known as a tank.

Inside the barn, she pulls down her chain saw from its hook and up-armors in readiness to attack: gloves, eye goggles, her old Kevlar helmet. Rubber boots to her knees, despite the heat. (Last thing she wants is more shrapnel in her body, even wooden shrapnel, having taken plenty from that IED in Tikrit.) Carrying the saw back around, she starts it up with a roar, spreads her legs strong and steady, and prepares to buzz the old oak and all its history into ineffectual lumps.

Maybe, she thinks as the blade bites into the oak's flesh, rattling her body with the vibration—maybe she should chainsaw her way out of her sinkhole of a past, too. Her parents and their suitcases. Her brother. The shitpit of war. Maybe she should chainsaw them all out of her bones, her brain, her womb. Chainsaw Jay out of the oak as well, carve him out like a life-size voodoo doll and bury him for good—it's long past time she did.

She met Jay down at Fort Dix in New Jersey, right after Shock and Awe, when their unit was set to mobilize any minute, although which minute or to where, the army hadn't cared to say. All the two of them knew was that they were twenty years old and wanted to drink and fuck as much as they could before they got blown to the everafter. So that's exactly what they did.

She and Jay had been jammed-up stuck in their lives until then. That was the year his family farm had failed, leaving him with nothing to do but sell the cows and watch his father's eyes turn dark and lost. She was spinning in place in the industrial North, her parents having died driving drunk when she was nineteen, big bro rotting his teeth out on meth, no idea what to do with herself, aside from trying and failing to save him and hanging out in bars getting trashed and laid.

Then President Shrub declared war on Iraq and they were saved. The rest of the world might have been slapping its cheeks in horror, but America was still giddy over 9/11, intoxicated with patriotism spiced with a nice little pepper of fear, and she and Jay were no different. They were both ready to go blow up some bad guys and do their bit for American Democracy in the hope American Democracy would do her bit for them.

Instead, the army turned them into a delivery service. Attached them to a transportation unit, Jay a driver up front, Rin a gunner in the rear, and sent them to spend the war in long, roaring convoys barreling back and forth across the Kuwait-Iraq border, carrying everything from ammo to poop paper. They would deliver to bases in Baghdad and way up north to Mosul, and then drive south again for refills, down the whole IED-salted spine of Iraq. Up and down, up and down. Humvees, gun trucks, and two-tons nose-to-nose, long, deadly dragons hurtling along the wrong side of highways in a cloud of diesel stink and dust. Gray sand all the way to the horizon, pocked with rusting military vehicles, plastic bags, animal ribs, charred cars. Vultures pulling out strings of guts. Children fighting over food. Dogs under their wheels. Nothing to think about but thirst and needing to piss and how much you hated the guy on your right and how all you wanted was to shoot some motherfucker down so you could feel like a soldier instead of a sitting duck.

But those war years were the best of her life anyway, thanks to Jay. The two of them glued together from that very first night they fell into bed at Fort Dix. They married before they left, and she never appreciated how much that protected her until he was gone and it didn't.

Jay and his long stretch of a body, breath warm as a wolf's. He would lie beside her talking for hours those rare times they had a whole night together, trying to convince her that her shitty behavior before she'd enlisted hadn't been so shitty after all. And when her methhead brother, who had at least tried to look out for her after their parents died, joined them in the Great Beyond, leaving her with no relatives at all, Jay said, "Don't blame yourself, Rin. I know you will, but don't. Your brother was beyond saving by anyone, even you."

Nothing went for them the way a deployment marriage was predicted to go. They were supposed to split up after that one pie-eyed night at Fort Dix. They didn't. They were supposed to cheat on each other when their deployments mismatched. They didn't. They were supposed to grow apart as war made them grow up. They didn't. Only one thing could separate them, and that it did.

Did you know an RPG was what killed you, Jay? Did you see it fly into the window of your Humvee and explode right there, a little black bird of death? Did you have a moment—maybe holding it in your hand, maybe watching it smoke on the Humvee floor—a split second when you looked that death skull right in the eye sockets and knew? Did you think of me then, Jay? Or of our child, already listening inside my womb?

The Ghoul Squad found him in teeny-tiny shreds, like a

Dear John letter. They put as much of him back together as they could: the fingers and toes, the jagged squares of his head. But they never could piece together his lovely long legs. Rin had seen him leap over a fissure as deep as a canyon on those legs, whistling with his hands in his pockets, easy as if he were crossing his own kitchen. Still, those were brave women and men, those Ghouls, dropping him shred by bloody shred into a bag so they could reassemble him on a mortuary table: a man-sized, three-dimensional puzzle missing oh so many pieces. They worked hard to give her something to bury.

And all the while those others, her so-called comrades in arms, brothers in battle, were waiting.

They didn't wait long. Three of them, over and over. Held her down and took their turns with their dicks and the barrel of a rifle, too, knife to her throat, pistol to her head. As she left her body, watched it lying there splayed and bleeding, the body that had once been hers but was now the property of others, all she could do was pour every shred of her will into praying her baby would stay alive.

Nobody lifted a finger to stop them. Not one of the women she thought were her friends. Not one of Jay's self-proclaimed buddies, either. So much for Band-of-Brothers-and-Sisters. For Battle-Buddy. For Bear-True-Faith-and-Allegiance-to-Your-Unit-and-Other-Soldiers.

And then the consequences. Leaving the war as a medevac case because of what those men had done to her. Nearly miscarrying. Juney born blind as a cavefish, both the VA and the military refusing to help or even to research what took her sight and how. The months of trying to find a cure for her, of latenight weeping over all she would never see. Missing and needing Jay, the dark space his death left inside of her burning black as an oilfield. Both his parents dying of cancer, one after the other, neither having the will or the desire to outlive their only child.

Coping. Not coping. Scared every second that those men, each one of whom is alive and free, are going to come back to get her. Or to get Juney.

❖

Tariq leads Juney around the fallen branches and clumps of mud still littering the yard, watching the ground to ensure she doesn't trip. He takes her past the apple orchard, the trees as gnarled and hunched as fairy-tale witches; under the generous spread of a copper beech glinting red and blue in the luminous afternoon light; and finally over the dandelion-studded grass to the fence.

There they wait in silence, Juney's soft hand curled in his. He peers into the thick stand of trees before him, their trunks speckled with verdigris lichen, leaves heavy with summer dust. Then, without any warning, she lifts her face and calls, "Gray-eee! Silverrrr! Eboneeee!"

The call is high and eerie and not at all loud, yet he is sure it carries all the way through the woods—he can almost see it weaving between the tree trunks like a trail of silver dust. His skin tingles.

"No talking," she whispers, and grips one of his fingers.

They stand as still as they can, listening so hard Tariq can hear the hum of blood in his head. Now that Rin's chain saw has fallen silent, no other sounds are audible, not even the timorous peep of a titmouse.

But then a slight breeze kicks up and with it a faint rattle. The rasp of bark against bark. The scrape of dried leaves shifting over the ground. And finally, as quiet as snow, the wolves appear, trotting up on their wide, webbed paws, all three openmouthed and panting. Legs long and shaggy, heads enormous, eyes aglow, ears pricked forward—the most magnificent creatures Tariq has ever seen.

He knows not to move; only to stand and look, as he did before. And then he remembers Juney can't see them, and, for the first time, he pities her. Not to be able to see the luxuriant thickness of their coats, the sheen in their eyes, the wildness of their beauty! But she can smell them, and so she raises her head and sways, inhaling in a kind of rapture—a rapture Tariq is close to feeling himself.

He looks at them as though he can never look enough. Silver, the smallest and only female, her coat bushy and white, eyes the yellow silk of honey. Ebony, as black as his name, his jade green irises darkening to onyx in the shadows. And Gray, the biggest and most majestic, his neck ringed with fur as thick as a bear's. His cheeks and muzzle are white, his face framed by a line of charcoal, his arched eyebrows bold and black. His eyes are much brighter than those of the others; a gleaming, eloquent, burnished gold. When Tariq looks into those eyes, he feels as if he isn't looking into a wolf's eyes at all but a man's. And before he even realizes it, he is whispering, *"Al-salaam Alakum Ayoha al The'b al'deem."* Peace be with you, oh mighty wolf.

In a breath, the wolves turn and run away so fast and soundlessly it is as if they were never there at all.

"I told you not to talk. They need to get to know you better first," Juney says, but she doesn't sound angry. She lifts her face to the sky, her water-blue eyes drifting. "Tariq, Mommy will never tell me, but what do they look like?"

He can hardly bring himself to answer. His heart is too filled with the certainty that before Gray vanished, the wolf murmured directly into his head, *Wa Alaykum al salaam ayoha al-insan al-sagheir.* And may peace be with you, too, little human.

"They're beautiful," he finally whispers. "Their fur is so deep and thick you want to bury your face in it. They're like your dogs, but with bigger heads and ears and longer legs and . . . they're the most beautiful creatures in the world!"

"I know," she replies with no surprise at all but clearly pleased. "They smell like the earth and the sun and whatever they eat. And when they howl, they sound like the moon."

8

DEVOTION

Up the hill from the flattened clinic and sodden Main Street of Huntsville, on the fat-housed, lush-lawned side of town, Beth is sitting in a lotus position on her couch in front of the television, dressed in a black leotard from work and drinking her fourth glass of white wine. She gazes absently at the screen, filled with tiny figures scuttling about looking fraught, and re-crosses her legs to stretch the other side. What is she watching anyhow? The figures are in some kind of uniform and a long red lump is lying on a table in the background. The camera zooms in to show a woman with a slit throat.

"Oh for Christ's sake!" She grabs the remote. "My husband's fighting real people who bleed real blood and you serve me up this crap as entertainment? You're sick, you know that? We're sick. . . . We are a sick frigging country!" She clicks to another channel.

"Mom? What's the matter?" Flanner is peering at her from the top of the staircase, bending forward to see her around the wall. The rest of his body is hidden, so he looks strangely dis-torted: a neck sprouting directly from a pelvis.

"Sorry, honey. It's just me yelling at the TV again."

"If you hate it that much, don't watch it."

"Good point." She nods, not only with her head but her entire torso. "I was hoping for more news about the storm." For a few feverish days after the hurricane, Huntsville, Slingerlands, and even little Potterstown were all over the local news, along with the other upstate villages devastated by winds and floods. Videos showing raging red waves slamming up against barns and tearing down bridges. Cars turned upside down. Whole trees floating through fields, dragging their roots like squid. Reporters sounding urgent and important. Windswept politicians bellowing earnest promises into cameras. And now, a mere ten days later? Not a peep from any of them.

"Go to bed, honey." She takes in her son's anxious face. "You're not worried about those wolves, are you?"

"Shit, Mom, I'm not a baby." He heads back upstairs. She fails to chase after him and scold him, as she once would have done. She fails because she doesn't want to move. She wants to stay right here, drink and dream.

Falling back against her creamy velvet cushions, she tunes out whichever show the TV is blaring at her now and lets the wine float her back to her favorite year of her life when she was seventeen—no, eighteen—and the queen of Huntsville High. Long hair swinging, figure sleek, a face the envy of all the other girls. It was 1998, Bill Clinton and Monica Lewinsky were in the headlines, the economy was strong, and America was feeling good about itself, unless you were a Republican, which Beth wasn't. A sexy time with a sexy president. Todd was sexy, too. Rich brown hair flopped over his brow. A wide, boyish face. Big chocolate eyes, vague but tender. He had the build of a football player, but he didn't like football; he liked Nirvana, to whom he listened endlessly, sitting earphoned in front of his Kurt Cobain shrine, which was why he was picked on by the popular jocks at school. And so Beth, with the same instinct that made her rescue sparrows from cats and pluck frogs out of roads, was drawn to tall, shy, musical Todd McAllister.

What she had not foreseen was that by dating Todd, she would grace him with the very status that had eluded him before. Thus, in only a few weeks, he was invited to play football with those jocks after all, taking on their swaggers, their tattoos, their lingo, and, above all, their aspirations to join the Marine Corps. "Why do you want to learn to kill people?" she asked. But she knew why. Todd wanted to be an American Man; the kind of man people admired in Huntsville, New York.

He married her before he went off to boot camp, giving her an excuse to avoid college, much to her parents' disgust. And soon it wasn't 1998 anymore or even the nineties at all. It was 2001; the towers had been brought down and the Afghanistan War had started. And then she wasn't waiting for Todd to get back from Parris Island or any other home base anymore—then it was real and concrete and terrifying and she was waiting for him to return from those godforsaken rock piles, where he was being shot at by ruthless warlords with AK-47's and a history older than the Bible of warfare, torture, and revenge.

Todd, syrup-eyed, Nirvana-loving Todd. Each time he comes home now, he is deeper inside his armor than the time before. Edging around the streets, darting looks over his shoulders. Making her close the window shades even on the prettiest of days. Throwing her off the bed in the midst of a dream. Sobbing his apologies, begging her not to leave him.

"Don't worry," she always says. "It's not you hurting me like this; it's the war. I won't leave you, I won't."

Sighing, she stretches out her legs, takes another swallow of wine, reaches for her phone, and gets back to the business of being a parent.

"You got a minute?" she asks when Louis picks up, trying not to let the words stumble tellingly around in her mouth.

"Sure. I am watching a movie with Tariq, though. What's up?"

"I found out more about Rin Drummond's wolves. Guess what? It's against the law to keep wolves as pets in New York."

"Beth, nobody has any wolves."

Pulling her left leg farther up her thigh, she examines the gold nail polish peeling off her big toe. "I don't know about that. If what Tariq said is true, it means she's keeping illegal, dangerous predators inside our own woods. Don't you see how crazy that is?"

Louis takes a moment to reply. "Look, we've all got enough on our plates right now with the storm damage. I heard it was a tornado as well as a hurricane. Did you?"

"Yeah. I guess that's why it tore up the clinic so bad." She picks up her glass and drains it.

"Right. So try to relax, okay? See you later." And, to her surprise, he hangs up.

She stares at her phone a minute. "Screw you, Louis!" Tossing the phone down, she empties the last of the wine into her glass.

❧

At the top of the stairs, Flanner is glaring down at his mother. His dad would never let her drink like this night after night or talk like that at the phone. Where is the mom she was only a short while ago? The mom who made Flanner proud of his family, a Marine Corps family, the most important family he knows?

"Fuck," he says under his breath. "Shit, ass." He storms into his room. "Dick."

He paces the floor, restless, miserable. Seizing his pillow, he hurls it as hard as he can at the window. It only falls with a soft and maddening puff to the floor. So he takes his shoes out of his closet—his sneakers and baseball cleats, dress shoes and flip-flops—and throws every one of them with all his strength through his bedroom door, making them slam against the far wall and ricochet down the hall, leaving black marks all over the yellow paint.

Still not enough. He races around his room, yanking open doors so he can slam them shut, pulling out drawers and throwing them to the floor with a bang. Bang and bang and bang! He stops to listen. No response.

Giving up on his room, he runs into the bathroom to look for something big to break. There he sees it, the perfect target: a jumbo-size bottle of blue mouthwash. He picks it up, raises it above his head, and, with a great heave, flings it into the tub.

Thud.

The bottle lies there unaffected, the neon blueness inside barely foaming.

"Mom!" he screams, pounding through the hallway, almost tumbling down the white-carpeted stairs. "Mom!"

Beth has fallen asleep on the couch, the TV still on. She is slumped sideways, mouth dangling open. Lips wet.

"Mom, wake up!"

Flanner pulls back his arm and slaps her as hard as he can across the face.

9

FOG

On the morning Tariq is finally allowed to visit his mother, he cranes forward to peer through Louis's windshield at the crowd of hospital buildings looming in front of him. One gray monolith attached to another, they look as big as a city, glittering under a sky bright and hard as tin. A great stretch of asphalt spreads around them, not a tree or flower in sight.

"You ready?" Louis asks.

Tariq unbuckles his seatbelt and climbs out, the air so humid it drops over him like a blanket. Shoulders hunched, hands in his pockets, he shuffles after Louis across the parking lot, the heat rising from the ground in waves, enveloping his face in the stink of hot tar and rubber. When they reach the three revolving glass doors flashing in the sun at the entrance, he stops.

Louis rests a hand on his back. "I'm right here, bud, don't worry." He guides him into the dark gape of a door, which whips around, catapulting them from the blaze of the day into arctic air and whiteness.

Tariq shivers, a gallop of panic in his chest. If his mother were here beside him instead of lying in a bed somewhere in this giant refrigerator, he would let himself hold her hand. He almost reaches for Louis's before remembering he's too old for that now.

Louis walks over to a tall counter, more wall than desk, and murmurs to a man dressed in blue scrubs. He returns to attach little tags to both their chests. His says VISITOR: MARTIN. Tariq's says VISITOR: CHILD.

"You all right?" Louis bends to look into his face.

Tariq fixes his eyes to the floor.

Once more settling a palm on his back, Louis ushers him into an elevator and they rise with a series of sickening glides. Up and up. Tariq stares at the row of large black buttons, each rimmed with orange, each lighting up then dimming, one after another. "How high are we going?"

"Twenty-two. Almost there."

Finally, the door says *ding*, opens with a whoosh, and they step onto a floor exactly as white and frigid as the one they just left. Tariq shivers again. "Mama isn't dead, is she?"

Louis darts a look at him. "Of course not." He pauses. "She is probably asleep, though."

"I hope Mustapha's not here."

Louis, too, harbors less than charitable feelings toward Mustapha Rasheed, Naema's suitor and fellow Iraqi. The man has been pursuing her for longer than Louis has even known her, a fact that keeps him tossing in a particular anguish for much of every night.

"Here we are," he murmurs as they approach a room labeled 2204A. "She has a roommate now, so we have to be quiet."

He pushes open the door and they step inside, where they are confronted by a wall of murky green curtains. He leads Tariq past them to a second set by the window. "In here."

Parting them just enough to slip through, Louis moves up to the bed and gazes down at Naema. Tariq hangs back, squeezing his lips together. He tries to ignore the beeping machines around the shape of his mother, the tubes snaking from her arms, the ache gathering in his throat.

A long moment passes before Louis speaks again. But finally he whispers, "I'll wait for you in the hallway," and leaves.

Tariq eyes the high white bed for some time, waiting for his courage to appear. Then he forces a step forward. And another. One more. Slowly, he tiptoes over and peers down.

That can't be his mother. Her face has no expression at all under her mask. Her skin is a sickly waxen color, her body so thin it looks as flat as a leaf.

He leans closer. Her breathing sounds like the rattle of stones drawn under a wave.

"Mama?"

She shows no sign of hearing him.

"Mama!"

Still nothing.

"*Mama!*"

Her eyelids flutter. And then, at last, she opens her eyes, her beautiful eyes, their irises a deep gold flecked with green; the exact color of Gray's.

She turns those eyes to Tariq and smiles. He can tell because they crinkle at the edges, even though he can't see her lips under the mask. She can make no noise—her lungs aren't strong enough for even a sigh—but she does manage to slide her hand across the bed and open her fingers for him.

"Mama," he says with a sob, laying his forehead on her palm. He reaches across the bones of her hips and holds her as tightly as he dares. "You'll be all right, won't you?" He looks back up at her.

She caresses his cheek and, with the slightest of movements, she nods.

Out in the hallway, Louis is straining to hear what he can from Naema's room. He longs to be in there with her but knows not to intrude, so rests his hands on a windowsill, gazing through the grime-streaked glass into the tinny sky beyond. Below, a jumble of buildings and parking lots. Above, a smear of cloud. In front, a shimmer of his own reflection.

If Naema fails to survive this—if she fails to rise to her feet, sweep her braid over her shoulder and resume her previous self—how will he ever look at Tariq without weeping?

That evening, while Louis is rifling through his refrigerator for something to make for dinner and Tariq is reading upstairs in the spare bedroom, Beth calls again. Seeing her name, Louis is tempted not to answer. But his manners, along with his promise to her husband, get the better of him.

"I found out more about Rin Drummond," she says without preamble. "This friend of mine at city hall looked up her property lines for me and he said she inherited a hell of a lot of land from her husband's family. It reaches way back behind the hill—my hill—right across the township line. Those wolves are scarily close, Louis, just like I thought!"

Louis shuts the fridge, glancing at his watch. He should call his store before it closes. As manager of S&A Lumber, the biggest retail shop in Huntsville, it is his job to make sure everything is in order for the fall rush this weekend. His customers have been frantic lately, in a panic over fixing all they can of the hurricane damage before the cold weather sets in.

"Louis? You there?"

"Yup. What were you saying?"

"I'm saying I decided to do something about this before those wolves attack someone. So I reported Rin to the cops."

"What? Oh shit, Beth. Why?"

"I told you why."

"But you don't even know if she has any wolves." Feeling in need of a breeze, Louis crosses the sweltering kitchen and opens the back door to his deck, still in splinters from the storm.

"Of course I do! Flanner said he heard them in the woods with Tariq and I don't happen to think my kid is a liar. Tariq isn't, either, from what I know of him. Why can't you admit how dangerous this is? Jesus!" She hangs up.

The phone rings again.

"I'm sorry, I shouldn't have spoken to you like that. I'm just stressed right now."

Louis pictures her standing alone in her kitchen, a drink in one hand, phone in the other. Hair disheveled.

"We're all stressed. Don't worry about it." He leans wearily against the door frame, watching a hornet drag its bulbous abdomen up the wall. "But what did you tell the cops? I mean, Rin Drummond is on her own out there, raising a kid by herself like you. And she's not ... well, wouldn't it better just to leave her alone?"

"I only asked them to check on her, that's all." Beth pauses. "Listen, I don't suppose you feel like swinging by for a drink, do you?"

Louis knocks the hornet down and steps on it. "Thanks, but I can't. I took Tariq to see his mom this morning and he's too upset to see anyone. I should stay here with him."

"I'll come by your place, then. Just for a quickie. Why don't you ask him about the wolves again while I'm on my way?" And she's gone.

Louis closes the deck door and rubs his forehead. Then he

mounts the stairs, knocks on Tariq's door, and pokes his head in. "Can we talk a sec?"

Tariq glances up from his book. He is stretched out on the single bed in the corner, sitting up against the pillows, his prosthetic leg lying on its side nearby, and he has that faraway glaze in his eyes of someone dragged out of a dream. His face looks particularly small and pinched at the moment, particularly young.

Louis sits on the end of the bed. "You okay, bud? Want to talk about this morning at all?"

Tariq drops his eyes back to his book.

Louis waits a beat. "Listen. Flanner's mom is coming over. Not Flanner, just her. If you want to stay out of the way up here, I'll cover for you."

Tariq riffles the pages. "Thanks."

"What're you reading?" Louis takes the book from him. "Oh, *White Fang*. I remember that. Like it?"

"Nope. I think it's dumb. It makes wolves sound so mean."

Louis hands it back, seeing his opening. "You've gotten pretty interested in wolves, haven't you? Is it 'cause of the ones you saw at Mrs. Drummond's?"

Tariq flashes him a look of alarm and then lowers his eyes again. "There aren't any wolves."

"You sure? That's not what you told me the other day."

"I know." Tariq scrapes a spot on the book's cover with his thumb. "I was just pretending."

"I figured. Still, a game is one thing, a lie another."

"I know. I'm sorry." Tariq pulls on his leg, and taking the book with him, leaves for the bathroom.

Louis stands to go, too, but first he runs his eyes over the room. White walls, forest green rug, single bed with a pale yellow coverlet. It was Melody's study once, but her desk is gone now, as are her books, her shelves, her apricot curtains, even her

satin cream wallpaper, Louis having ripped out all her belongings long ago. Every chair and rug, picture and vase, hairpin and
sock. The result is a home as soulless as a chain motel and an
absence that hangs in the air like a fog.

Melody spiraling down and down. Her young face lifted to
him, eyes black with pain. He too absorbed in himself to see.
"I'm in your way," her note said. *"My own too. Don't go into the
bathroom, just call the cops. I love you."*

When Beth arrives wearing a clinging summer sheath of electric blue and matching earrings, Louis is embarrassed. She looks
dressed for a date, not the early-evening coffee he is determined
to serve, and he worries he has misled her. "I'd invite you to sit
out on the deck but it's still a mess," he says awkwardly, and tells
her about the tree trunk and garage door.

"No problem. It's muggy as hell outside anyway." The humidity
is indeed pressing against the windows like a hot-breathed dog.

They move to his living room, it beige furniture and café au
lait walls just as self-effacing as the rest of the house. She takes
the sofa, he an armchair, a fan clacking noisily in the window.
He gives her a glass of ice tea—she turned down the coffee—but
she doesn't look exactly happy with it. He can smell the alcohol
on her like a stale perfume. It is long past time, he thinks, for
Todd to come home.

Shaking off her high-heeled sandals, she stretches her legs
out on the dark wooden coffee table, which Louis has waxed
to a gleam, and gets right to the point. "So what did Tariq say?"

Louis moves his eyes to the curtainless window, the blanched
sky filling its frame. "He says he made it up about the wolves."

She tosses back her hair, loose today despite the heat, and

rubs her bare feet together, flexing them like the dancer she was, her toenails a sparkling silver this time. "Well, I'm sorry, Louis, but he's lying. I asked Flanner about it again and he said that they not only heard the wolves loud and clear but that Rin *told* them she has wolves. Three dangerous, wild wolves right here in our own woods! That woman is out of her mind." She takes a swallow of tea. "Where is Tariq anyhow?"

Louis is more inclined to believe Tariq than anything Flanner might say, but he's not going to pick a fight about it. "At a friend's house."

"He is? I thought you said he was too upset to see anyone. Who is it? A kid from school?"

Louis refrains from telling her this is none of her business. Instead, he blurts in some desperation, "Want something stronger than ice tea? We could probably both use it."

She brightens at this, suddenly looking extremely pretty. Her eyes are not only a luminous jay-feather blue but enormous and long-lashed, if overly laden today with makeup. She has that classic, commoditized, white-girl face you see on supermarket magazines, Louis decides; the kind of face Melody used to insist on admiring more than her own, no matter how much he tried to persuade her otherwise.

"So anyway, I called the cops again," Beth continues when he comes back from the kitchen with two cans of beer. "This time, they told me it isn't always illegal to keep wolves after all; you just need a special kind of license. I asked them to look into whether or not Rin has one. Bet she doesn't."

"Seems to me it'd make more sense to call the ASPCA about something like that." A fresh wave of anxiety for Naema washes through him. He wishes he hadn't offered Beth beer. He wishes she would go home.

"Maybe. But I thought I'd start with someone I know first,

this state trooper I was in high school with. Mike Flaherty.
Know him?"

Louis shakes his head.

"He'll do whatever I want." And reaching for her beer, she
sends Louis a wink.

10

KNOT

It has taken Rin the entire morning to finish sawing the old oak and all its memories into chunks, and now she is glossed with sweat. The weather is still eerily hot for the last week of August—almost as hot as the Sandbox, only humid instead of skin-desiccatingly dry—so she heads to the kitchen for water. Filling her glass at the sink, she looks up and catches sight of Juney through the window, stepping along the lilac path in her usual weightless way, cane swinging, feet careful but sure. But her brow is in a pinch and her mouth pulled into a thin, unhappy line. Rin sets down her water and goes to the back door to meet her.

"Hey, little bean, something wrong?"

Juney only says she's thirsty and hot, so Rin pours her some water, too. Taking the glass in both hands, Juney sits in her usual chair and starts up her humming again. Her moods have become so changeable that Rin wonders if some female hormones are kicking in, young as Juney is. She still looks like a stick, but lately she has been wistful and withdrawn in a way that is entirely new. If she isn't building up hormones, she is certainly building up secrets.

"Mommy?" she says after a long silence, her hands still around her glass. "You think wolves can understand human languages?"

Rin loves questions like this. She leans against the sink,

settling in to answer. "Some, yes. Their names, of course, and tones like affection or anger—but you know that. They aren't as good at it as dogs, though, 'cause they haven't been bred to—"

"Do they understand Arabic?"

Rin frowns. "Is this something that Hajji kid told you?"

"Don't call him that. He's got a name." Juney pulls herself up in her chair, posture as severe as a drill sergeant's.

Rin examines her hands: meaty, rough, the lines in her palms etched by chain-saw grease, nails caked in oak dust. "Have you been talking to Tariq about our wolves?"

Juney declines to answer. She only looks haughtier than ever.

"How many times have I told you? Never, ever tell anyone about our wolves."

"*You* did—you told those boys. I heard you."

Rin scrapes the dust off a fingernail. "That's true. I was trying to scare them. My mistake. But it doesn't mean you can repeat it."

"Why not?" And then Juney asks for the first time ever, "What's wrong with telling?"

Rin cleans another nail. "Because folks won't like the idea of wolves living around here. They're ignorant and prejudiced about wolves. They think they're much more dangerous than they are. . . . They hate them."

"Like you hate people?" Juney lifts her chin, her water-pale eyes swiveling to the ceiling.

"I don't—" Rin stops. She may have to hide certain matters from her child, but she won't tell her a bald-faced lie. "That's my problem. I know it isn't healthy. I wasn't always this way. But yes, a lot of folks are like that about wolves."

"Maybe . . ." Juney starts swaying again, her voice sliding into one of her singsong tones. "Maybe you don't hate people, Mommy. Maybe you just want to keep our wolves all to yourself."

Rin shakes her head, which of course Juney can't see. A nine-year-old shrink she has here. "No, it's just that I don't want anyone taking them away. They're the only family we've got, aside from each other and the mutts, right? So we have to protect them, just like they protect us." What else has she to offer this child who has never known her father, her uncle, or any of her grandparents—who has been raised by a lone woman and her crowd of ghosts?

She moves over to Juney and embraces her, kissing the top of her head, silk-soft and damp. "I need to take a shower. But tell me first, little bean, are you feeling sad?"

Juney sways back and forth on her chair, humming again. Raising her hands, she fingers the air as delicately as if she's catching a sunbeam. She hums and hums. But she offers no answer.

In the shower, Rin turns the conversation over, worrying the mama worry that won't stop boring into her bones. Is it that curse of a boy troubling Juney—that she misses him when he's not here? Or has his intrusion opened a new door through which she has glimpsed something bigger than she has at home? Rin has built such a careful world around her: Their farm. The school where Juney has her own specialist to help her in class and where everyone has learned to accommodate her needs. Her field trips with other sightless children. Were Rin to draw a map of this world, there would be a knot in the middle—their home—and maybe three paths looping out of it and back again, like a bow on top of a present. But she has always known the day will come when Juney will want more than this. And when it does, when she is ready to venture into the universe alone, that is when it will hit her, the fact that Rin has worked so hard to protect her from—the irrefutable blastwall of a fact that she can't see when most of the world can, and nobody will give a damn.

11

ENEMY

For two weeks now, Tariq has refused to return to baseball camp, preferring to go to work with Louis at S&A Lumber. The days can be dull, but he does like the way he gets to command the seasons. Banishing summer to the ON SALE corner in the back by tucking away leftover mosquito torches and barbecue chef hats. Ushering in autumn with rakes and pumpkin-colored garbage bags. Preparing for winter by following the orders Louis barks at his staff like the squad leader he once was. "Stack the firewood against the west wall!" "Roll out the snow shovels!" Best of all, he likes arranging the decorative items in the middle aisle: doormats saying *Oh Crap, Not You Again*; mailboxes the shape of gaping fish; a clock he wishes he could buy for Juney showing twelve different birds, each trilling out its song on the hour. He knows his mother would find these objects absurd and wasteful, but he would love to fill their house with silly things like this. To be able to look at them and simply laugh.

It is on one of these mornings that Louis suggests taking him to see Naema again. "Slow day today so I can stay longer than usual. What do you say?"

Tariq hesitates. What if she is no better than last time, waxen and silent?

"It's been a while, bud," Louis adds. "I think you should come."

They drive to the hospital sunk in the same wordless anxiety as before, Tariq's stomach drawn so tight he can scarcely breathe.

As soon as they spin through the revolving doors, they run into Mustapha Rasheed, his blocky, square-shouldered figure hurrying toward the exit. He avoids looking at Louis altogether, but he does address Tariq. "Nice to see you, dear one," he says in Arabic, patting him on the head. "How is my little man today?"

Tariq mumbles at the floor.

"It's good you are coming to visit your mother like this. A dutiful son."

Tariq shrugs, eyes still down.

"If you want me to bring you here anytime, call me and I shall. All right, my boy?"

Mustapha waits a long moment for an answer while the air fills with Tariq's silence.

"Well," Mustapha says, clearly disconcerted, "I won't keep you. There's a surprise for you upstairs. *Salaam.*" He bends to kiss Tariq on each cheek while Louis watches. Louis knows from Naema that Mustapha was a military interpreter like Khalil and was kidnapped and tortured for his efforts, barely escaping with his life. But knowing this only makes Louis feel ashamed.

After Mustapha straightens up, pats Tariq on the head again and strides out of the hospital, Tariq hurries to the elevator with obvious relief. Once he and Louis reach Naema's room, though, he balks again. "I don't want to go in yet. Can I just wait?"

Louis looks at him. "What's wrong?"

Tariq clutches his stomach, huddling into himself like a cornered mouse. "I need to go to the bathroom."

"Want me to go with you?"

"No, I know where it is." He hurries off, Louis watching in concern.

Taking a deep breath, Louis pushes open the door. Walking past the first bed, its occupant eerily silent, he steps through Naema's curtains and stops.

She is sitting up. Her head is turned toward the window. Her hair, freshly washed and brushed, is draped over her shoulders like a shawl. Her thin wrists are clear of all but one IV line. And, at last, she is free of her mask.

"Naema!"

She looks around. The two of them gaze at each other a moment. And then she breaks into a smile.

He pulls a chair over, too overcome to say more, searching her face for the Naema he knows. The sweep of her high-boned cheeks, her swallow-shaped eyes, her neck as slender as a girl's—these stir the old longing in him as powerfully as ever. Yet she is still drained of color, the white star even whiter.

She holds out a hand to him on the bedspread and he wraps his three fingers around it, barely able to stop himself from covering her palm with kisses. Her wrists are bruised from the IV needles, her hand cold and dry.

"How are you feeling?" he finally manages. "God, it's good to see you awake."

Removing her hand, as she always does if he holds it too long, she inhales with an audible effort. "I am . . . much better." He can hear her struggling to draw in air between every other word. "I was going to call you . . . as soon as I awoke. But Mustapha, he came." She inhales again and points to a plastic tube beside her, fat and translucent, a Ping-Pong ball nestled inside it. "They tell me I must . . . breathe into that. Blow and blow . . . all day. Like a child . . . with a balloon." She smiles, her chest heaving. "Where is . . . Tariq?"

"He's coming. He went to bathroom. This place makes him nervous."

"Yes." She inhales again. "He is afraid . . . of hospitals. Before he comes back, tell me . . . has he been all right?"

Louis longs to take her hand again but doesn't dare. "He's fine. You've got a resilient little guy there. He's staying at my house and coming to work with me. He's been a great help. You don't remember him visiting you?"

"I remember nothing but dreams. But why is he not with Flanner and going . . . to camp?"

Tariq steps through the curtains at that moment, sparing Louis the necessity of answering. "Mama!" he shouts. "Mama, you're better!" He runs over, about to fling himself on her when Louis stops him.

"Careful, bud. Your mom's not quite strong enough to have a big guy like you jump on her."

Tariq leans over the bed instead and wraps his arms around her waist, burying his head in her ribs. "You're better! You're better! You're better!"

Naema caresses his curls, her eyes moistening. "Your hair, *habibi* . . . it has grown so long . . . I can't see you," she says in Arabic, lifting the tangle off his brow. "Ah, there you are!" He looks up at her with a grin.

Louis pulls his chair closer. "I'm so sorry this happened to you, Naema. I'm so very sorry."

Her gaze lingers on Tariq a moment before she looks up. "Thank you . . . but do not . . . be sorry. Not everything is . . . your fault, my friend." She knows about Louis's tendency to blame himself, just as she knows about Melody.

"But this shouldn't have happened to you," he protests. "Nobody else in the clinic—"

Tariq interrupts. "Mama, can you come home now? Can we pack your stuff and leave this creepy place? Please?" He is speaking English, as he always does these days, no matter how much she objects.

"No, not yet, my love," she murmurs in kind. "But soon . . . *inshallah,* soon."

He picks up a strand of her hair and winds it around his fingers, a habit he's had all his life. "But when you do come home, will you be completely better?" He looks at her anxiously. "I mean like you were before?"

"I shall try . . . to be, yes."

Louis stares down at his hands.

"Good." Tariq is smiling now. "Because when you are, I want you to meet my new friend."

"You have a new . . . friend?"

"Yes. She's the best I've ever had." He studies the strand of hair entwined in his fingers and then looks back at his mother. "Her name is Juney and she's blind."

❊

Flanner is standing at his bedroom window, pressing his forehead against the glass as hard as he can. Now that the excitement of the hurricane is over and everything is more or less back to normal, he is sick of summer. Sick of the long, hot evenings dragging vapidly by. Sick of the boys at his YMCA baseball camp, most of whom are city kids here on vacation and too snooty to play with locals like him. And sick of spending the end of every day like this with nobody better than his mother.

He grinds his forehead against the window just to feel its

cool surface imprinting his flesh. An ATV roars past, driven by that snarling teenager up the road, but the ensuing silence only makes the afternoon emptier than ever.

Flanner's world is shrinking. The walls of his room are closing in, the ceiling lowering down on his head, the yard looking smaller and dingier by the day. Even the meadow, the one that was full of pink sea during the storm and used to seem boundless and filled with possibilities, has shriveled to nothing but a patch of weeds. His sole avenue to a larger world, other than TV, is his laptop, on which he has taken not only to playing war games but to looking up war pictures and videos: Soldiers dancing like strippers in a tent. A boy screaming armless on a stretcher. A marine with a face like ground beef. A woman sprawled dead in a market street, an infant girl in her arms, her head torn off like a pulled tooth.

Flanner's eyes catch a movement. Someone is crossing the meadow—a kid—moving fast . . . Tariq! He runs downstairs and into his yard, completely forgetting their feud. "Tariq!" He waves his arms. "Wait up!"

Tariq glances his way before flickering out of sight behind a tree, then appearing again. He looks oddly ethereal in the late-afternoon light, half swallowed by waist-high grasses and rose-tinted milkweed. Flanner waits for him to come over, smiling eagerly, hands in his pockets. But Tariq only keeps going. He ducks under a barbed-wire fence, clambers up the freshly hayed field beyond, and vanishes into the woods.

Flanner stares after him, bewildered. Why would he do that?

He decides to follow him. Track Tariq the way a marine scout would track an enemy. And maybe confront him, too.

Tariq is so far ahead by now that Flanner has to run to catch up. He bounds up the stubbled field, reveling in the sensation of moving instead of being trapped in the house. By the time he reaches the woods, Tariq is out of sight, so Flanner stops to listen. Before long, he picks out the crunching and twig snaps of a human tread. He follows, matching his footfalls to Tariq's.

The deeper they penetrate the woods, the harder it is to see, the trees only allowing the sun to break in here and there with a shaft of brassy light. When he and Tariq were friends, Flanner used to find it pleasingly spooky to walk among the vast and ancient trees of these woods, the pine and beech, oak and hornbeam and hemlock, their trunks patched with moss, branches netted with vines. It was like being surrounded by the legs of giants. Now, the woods only seem dark and endless.

Tariq is humming and talking to himself now, believing he is alone, which makes Flanner feel smug. But as time crawls by, flies dive-bomb his eyes, burrs creep into his shoes, and he grows increasingly itchy and thirsty, the game loses its thrill. Sneaking up on someone for a few minutes is quite different from doing it for nearly an hour, and playing with someone who doesn't know you're playing is no better than playing by yourself. Several times he almost calls out to Tariq to put an end to it. But having no idea how to explain his presence without looking like a loser, he continues to trail him in silence, feeling more miserable by the minute.

Flanner has long since guessed where they are headed, and, sure enough, after what seems like forever, they reach the same towering fence as before. He slips behind a tree and waits to see what will happen.

Tariq walks up to the fence and stands there a moment, perfectly still. Then he lifts his face, cups his hands to his mouth and cries out with a sound so penetrating and inhuman that Flanner drops to a crouch in fright. He dares to peer out only when he hears Tariq talking. Tariq is leaning into the fence now, mumbling something guttural Flanner can't decipher. And there, pressed up against the other side, is a long-legged, huge-headed, hulking gray-and-white creature that can only be a wolf. Even worse, Tariq has poked his fingers right through the fence.

Get your fingers out! Flanner is about to yell. But it is so clear that Tariq isn't afraid that Flanner only creeps out from behind his tree to see better. The wolf isn't eating Tariq's fingers, as he feared, but sniffing them—and all the while Tariq is talking to him in his private language. And then Tariq squats by the fence, pushes his face against it, and actually lets the wolf lick him. Flanner gapes as the huge pink tongue slips out, pokes through the holes in the fence and slobbers all over Tariq's nose and mouth. Why isn't he scared the wolf will bite him? Take off an ear or even his nose? But Tariq only giggles while the wolf keeps licking, and as Flanner watches, he is seized by a longing to have that, too. To be able to talk to wolves like that—to have them lick you and not even be afraid!

Then, in a flash, everything changes. The wolf stops licking, pulls back its lips and emits a growl so deep and hair-raising that both Tariq and Flanner leap back with a cry. In the next instant, Mrs. Drummond pops up out of nowhere.

"Get your ass out of here!" she bellows at Flanner.

Flanner reels away, turns, and bolts.

❖

Closing her laptop slowly, Beth walks downstairs to the kitchen to finish making dinner. A chicken is already roasting in the oven; she has only to snap the beans. She fills a large tumbler with red wine and puts Fleetwood Mac on to play, needing both for their soothing effects. The e-mail she just received from Todd is a shock. "Get Flanner ready 0200 hours EST. 8/26. Skype."

She takes a long swallow. And another. If only Todd would agree to limit their communications to e-mail and letters and the occasional phone call, the way they did during his first deployment. Computer cameras are so cruel: the time delay, the face-to-face focus, the way the picture both distorts and yet impels you to look. She glances at her watch and finishes off the wine. Pours another. Eight and a half hours to go.

Decapitating the string beans with practiced speed, she sweeps them into a frying pan, adds a wad of butter, and is just about to turn on the burner when Flanner comes hurtling into the kitchen. "Mom! Help!" He flies into her arms.

She holds him close. His knobby back; sharp, little-boy shoulders. "What happened, honey? You okay?"

He shakes his head, too out of breath to answer.

Pushing him off her gently, she bends to look him in the eye. "Did somebody hurt you?"

"No—yes! She screamed at me. And that wolf wanted to—"

"Are you talking about Rin Drummond? Did you try to see her wolves again?"

He nods, his breath shuddering. "I did see one! It was right there, a great huge one, big as a bear! It growled at me—it wanted to kill me!"

"Oh, my poor guy. Come here." Beth leads him to the living room couch and sits him down next to her, where she holds him until his breath steadies. For once he allows this, even though she stinks of wine again. "I can't believe that woman!" she says. "I'm calling Mike Flaherty about this."

"Yeah. But don't tell Dad, okay?" Shame is oozing into Flanner now. Tariq wasn't scared, either of the wolf or of Mrs.

Drummond. He wasn't even scared that time she pointed a gun at them.

"Mom," Flanner adds, "when your cop friend arrests that mean-ass lady, get him to shoot her wolves, too!"

Later that night, much later, Beth rouses herself from her wine and the television and heads upstairs to dress for Todd's call. Stomach watery, head thick, she pulls on a flattering turquoise tank top, brushes her hair, and reapplies her makeup: shimmering pink lipstick, a thick streak of eyeliner on both lids, two coats of mascara, and peacock blue shadow to bring out her eyes. She peers into the laptop camera, trying to see herself as Todd will see her. But her face looks blotchy and her eyes are too washed out to show blue of any shade. Todd will see what he wants to see, she supposes, and beyond that she can do no more than she has done.

"Flanner?" She opens his door. It is ten-thirty A.M. in Afghanistan, two in the morning in New York, an absurd hour for him to be up, but he would never forgive her if she let him miss this. "Honey?" She shakes him until he blinks. "Time to talk to your dad."

Pushing himself out of bed, he follows her groggily, his hair mussed and his favorite NASCAR pajamas drooping down his whippet-thin hips. He squeezes in beside her on the wooden chair at her bedroom desk, his body as sharp against hers as a bundle of bones.

"Flan, remember now, we don't want to upset Dad, so not a word about the car or what happened to you in the woods today. Deal?"

He nods. She connects to Skype and the two of them wait, staring at the screen in silence.

Soon they hear an electronic whoosh and the sound of popping bubbles. The screen flickers and, after an excruciating moment, reveals a face so gaunt and worn that for a second Beth has no idea whose it is.

"Jesus, are you all right?" she blurts.

"I'm fine, babe. Chill out." His voice sounds hoarse, as if he's been shouting all day.

Beth knows Todd is training Afghan troops at Camp Leatherneck in Helmand Province, the last U.S. Marine base still operating in this thirteenth year of the Afghanistan War. She also knows he is barracked with dozens of other men in a giant, tunnel-shaped tube, no privacy, no solitude, in what appears to be a sprawling complex of airplane hangars at the bottom of a giant dust bowl—she's seen the pictures. But that is all she knows; Todd having been forbidden to tell her more.

"Is that Flanner I see there?" he says.

"Hi, Dad!" Wide-awake now, Flanner pushes his face closer to the camera. Beth looks down at him: the coppery flop of hair, the pale skin behind his freckles.

"How you doin', sport? Still playing baseball?" Todd rubs his eyes with the heels of his hands. Beth can just make out a white wall behind him, the backs of shaven heads, the occasional face whose youth still startles her.

"Yeah, at camp. The kids suck, though."

"You getting to catch at all? You were always good at that." Todd leans closer, filling the screen with his new face.

"Some. Coach says he might make me catcher next season."

"Cool. Wish I was there to practice with you. Get your mom to play. She pitches pretty good."

Flanner is of the opposite opinion but keeps this to himself.

Todd squints. "What else are you up to? Any new music you like?"

"Nah, not really." Flanner rarely listens to music, even though he knows his dad wants him to. He squirms on the chair, poking Beth with his elbow. "We had this humungous hurricane a couple weeks ago. They're calling it Hurricane Meg, like it's a girl. You hear about it?"

"Nope. What's the damage?" A sunburned hand claps on his shoulder and moves away.

Beth intervenes. "Nothing we haven't been able to take care of. But are you all right, honey, really and truly all right?"

"I still got both legs and arms, don't I? Balls and a cock, too."

"Flanner's still here," she reminds him, slipping an arm around her son's narrow back.

"I know he's here." Todd's eyes move to a spot just above Flanner's head. "Built any more forts with Tariq this summer? I remember that last one you showed me. Awesome."

Flanner looks at his mother. "Uh . . . not really. Things got kind of messed up after the storm."

"Like what?"

"Oh, people's homes," she interjects again, eager to avoid any questions about the boys' friendship or the end of it. Todd took long enough to come around to Flanner's having an Iraqi amputee as a friend, grumbling about returning home from one war only to be reminded of another. "Everybody's busy cleaning up. Some houses got so wrecked the families had to move out."

"Sounds rough." Todd rubs his face again.

"Sure was. It still looks like a war zone around here."

"Babe, you got no fucking idea what a war zone looks like."

Silence.

"Dad?" Flanner says then. "I'm starting fifth grade soon. It's in a different building and everything."

Todd drops his hands. "Shit, you're growing up fast. I should be there. Fuck."

"You can't help it," Beth says quickly. "It's so great to see you. We miss you so much, you know that?"

Todd glances over his shoulder, lowers his voice. "That's good to hear, babe. I think about you every day, every minute. You and Flanner both. Miss you so bad." He pauses, and she hopes he might say something nice now about the way she looks. "Listen," he says, "I got news. I'm coming home. They finally granted me that leave I'm owed. Haven't given me a date yet, but it'll be within the next couple weeks or so. Two weeks R&R, babe! Flan, we can play ball, and you and me, Beth, can have us a fucking good time."

"That's fantastic, honey!" A chill slithers through her. "I'll tell Louis. He'll be pleased to see you again, too."

"He looking after you like he promised?"

"Some. He helped me haul a bunch of branches out of the yard."

"Huh." Todd's hollow-cheeked face stares at her from the screen.

"What?"

"I don't want you hanging around that dude too much. Understand?"

"But you—oh. Oh! Don't worry. He creeps me out. It's you I love. We both do, don't we, Flan?"

"Uh-huh." Flanner isn't listening. He is busy trying to memorize every inch of his father's faraway face. The deep-set eyes. The thin nose. The crisp jaw jutting out to a big chin. The new lines curved around his mouth like parentheses. Flanner doesn't remember this face. He doesn't remember it at all.

"Flanner, did you say 'uh-huh' to your mom? What kind of an answer is that?" Todd's voice is rising but then he seems to catch himself. "Guess you're used to me being gone, huh?"

Flanner shrugs.

Beth looks into Todd's pixilated eyes. "He's just a kid, Todd. Of course he loves you."

But Todd's face, already so visibly filled with tension, tightens further. "Fuck this. Call the FRO for the ETA." And he pulls away, stretching into a broken streak of pink and brown until the screen blinks into black.

Part Two

SEPTEMBER

12

FENCE

Juney keeps telling Rin not to worry about Tariq and the wolves. "He loves them just like we do, Mommy, so he's not going to give away our secret." She says, too, that the wolves have taken a shine to him in return, Gray in particular, who even goes so far as to lick him. But Rin worries anyhow. Children have loose lips when it comes to secrets, and although wolves have their likes and dislikes as much as anyone else, they are also capricious and excitable and rough, which is why she has never allowed Juney to so much as touch them. Even if Gray doesn't lose his temper for wolfish reasons of his own, what he may intend as a friendly frolic—a playful nip here, a nuzzle there—can be like taking a cheese grater to human skin. Not to mention a wolf's ability to snap through an arm with one bite. No, if Tariq is going to insist on playing licking games with Gray, Rin needs to teach him a lesson.

The children are in school now that it's September, so Tariq doesn't come by until after three. But when Rin hears him yakking it up again with her increasingly unknowable daughter, she closes the chicken coop, stows her basket of warm, freshly laid eggs high on a kitchen shelf, out of reach of her greedy mutts and wantonly destructive cats, and goes out to collar him.

She finds him sitting in the vegetable patch with Juney, helping her weed, his prosthesis lying on its side beside him. As he

121

seems to like doing chores and is surprisingly strong for a stringy smartass with one leg, Rin has been putting him to work lately, figuring she might as well find some use for him other than letting him bewitch her daughter. She's had him repair the deer netting, mulch the compost, haul the remains of the flood wood out of her yard, even help her fix some of the dangling shutters on her house. She also has him regularly check the perimeter of her wolf fence to make sure none of it is uprooted.

To hold wolves securely, a fence must extend two feet below the earth as well as eight feet into the sky because wolves can not only jump as high as flagpoles; they are spectacular diggers. They dig lairs, after all, to have and hide their pups in—to die in, as well—and they can root out a rabbit even when the hapless furball is cowering deep underground. If Rin weren't careful, her wolves would dig a nice little tunnel under the fence and take off, only to be shot as coyotes or run down on roads, like all those dim, maladapted deer.

She built her fence out of a nine-gauge chain link she bought from a military-supply outlet, along with a series of olive drab stakes to hold it up. Around the base, she laid sharp, paw-piercing gravel to further discourage her wolves from digging, and at regular intervals installed two-foot-high lean-in arms so they can't knock the whole thing down, no matter how high and hard they hurl themselves against it. She also uses padlocks for the doors, wolves being highly adept at undoing latches—they would only have to watch her open one once to know how to do it themselves. As she was trying to tell Juney, wolves might not be bred to communicate with humans, but their brains are 30 percent bigger than those of dogs and 40 percent in the hippocampus, which is where mammals store and organize most of what they learn. In other words, compared to a wolf, a dog is a mere infant.

Rin is just about to tackle Tariq when the telephone rings back in the house. She almost never gets phone calls. Juney's teachers, the social worker, that's about it. She hasn't even listed her number.

"Phone's ringing," Juney tells her as if she's deaf.

Heart flapping already, Rin wipes her hand-sweat off on her pants and returns to the nook adjoining the living room, which she has made into her office. She eyes her old black desk phone warily before picking up the receiver.

"Mrs. Drummond?"

"Who the hell is this?"

"Officer Flaherty. I'm calling about a license?"

The flapping turns into a banging, making it hard to breathe. If Rin hates people, she hates cops even more. "What license? Driver's?"

"No. DEC. For keeping dangerous wildlife? In your case, uh, wolves?" He says the word as if he's never spoken it before. "It's been reported to me that you keep wolves. If that's true, I'm sorry to say, ma'am, but there's no license on record for you."

Rin drops into her chair, sweat breaking out over her chest and back, cold as pond slime. She has been dreading this ever since she brought Gray and Silver home as pups. "I don't have wolves. All I've got is huskies. People are always making that mistake."

Flaherty pauses. She can hear him breathing asthmatically down the line. "I'm sorry, ma'am, but I was told loud and clear that you have wolves."

"This is harassment," she tells him, summoning her emergency calm and crispest sergeant voice. "I don't mean you, Officer. I know you're only doing your job. But my neighbors are a bunch of cranks and they're always trying to find ways to bother me. I'm a veteran. I served to protect our country. I don't break its laws."

"I know you're a veteran, ma'am, and I thank you for your service. But I'm afraid I'm obliged to follow this up anyhow. That means you either file for the license or send us proof you got huskies. Otherwise, me and the DEC pay you a visit. Which is it gonna be?"

"What kind of proof?"

"Photos, ID, dog licenses."

She squeezes her eyes tight, rubs them hard with her free hand.

"Ma'am?"

"When do I have to get this done by?"

He hesitates, and she can hear him relishing his bitty bit of power. "I'll give you a week."

After she hangs up, she stares at the telephone a long while before she can move. Its rows of sinister buttons, its maleficent receiver. She looks down at the body to which she is somehow attached. Hands dangling limp as seaweed. Boots rooted to the ground.

Betty runs up. Noses Rin's thigh and whimpers. *Come on, do something.*

Rin takes a deep breath and drags herself to her feet. She follows Betty out to the vegetable patch, where she stands over Tariq, legs apart, fists tight against her waist. "Tariq!"

He looks up at her with a start, and she sees Juney's face change from the blissed-out expression she keeps for him to the new wariness she has been trying on lately for her. Somewhere along the way here, Juney seems to have taken his side against hers—if there are sides.

"Yes, Mrs. Drummond?" he says in that formal Arab way Rin doesn't like at all. He peers up at her from under his curls.

"Have you told anyone about our wolves?"

He rolls up the left side of his track pants and pulls on his leg, wishing again he hadn't blabbed to Louis. "Only Flanner. He's that kid who followed me here the other day. Why, has something bad happened?"

Rin is about to say, *hell yeah, something bad's happened,* when she stops. Because maybe it hasn't. Maybe she can head this off at the pass. It's true she holds her wolves illegally—her little secret from Juney. She never could face registering them or following any of the other rules involved. She doesn't like rules, not after the army. But she could get herself over to the library, download the damned license application, and send it in before that meddling cop and his DEC buddies stage an invasion.

"Mommy, don't be mean to Tariq," Juney chimes in, clambering to her feet.

That startles Rin. "Tariq, I want you to come with me," she says more gently. "You need to learn a few things about wolves."

"Yes, Mrs. Drummond," he says again. She scowls at him. There's something about his unflappability that makes her want to shake him up. On the other hand, that's probably why her wolves like him, just as they like the calmness in Juney. Sly kids, jittery kids, like that sneaky tattletale who trailed Tariq—those are exactly the type to set the wolves off. Wolves can smell nervousness. Bad intentions, too. Just as they will in those cops if they come.

"You need to understand something about pack mentality and dominance," Rin says as they walk to the house. "Now Gray, the big timber wolf out there, he's the alpha male. He chooses who the pack befriends and who it doesn't. He protects them and he bosses them. Which means he has to be the boss of everyone, including you, me, and Juney. You following?"

She hopes she doesn't sound the way she used to with her

soldiers; not her favorite part of herself. Back in '05, when she was promoted to sergeant at the ripe old age of twenty-two, she became known as Dragon Drummond. She was tough as boot leather and mean as a rattrap, but you had to be to get any respect as a female NCO, especially one as young as she was. Boss or be bossed, that's how it is in the military, just as it is for the wolves.

"Yes, Mrs. Drummond, I'm following."

"That means you show submission," she continues.

"Roll on your back with your belly up!" Juney crows.

"Enough sass out of you, young lady. No, it means don't stare into his eyes—look away if he's staring at you. A stare is his challenge, and it's your job to reassure him that you're not challenging him, you're a friend."

Tariq nods so calmly Rin suspects she hasn't told him a single thing he doesn't know already. But then he says, "That's funny. Me and Gray stare at each other all the time."

"Well, don't overdo it," she says testily. "It might mean he's accepted you or it might mean he's competing with you for dominance. Just don't push it."

"I won't." But he sounds unconvinced, so she decides to up the ante. "Come with me."

She leads him into the pantry behind her kitchen, a narrow corridor lined with zinc shelves where she stores her homemade pies and bread, canned fruit, stews and vegetables, jarred pickles and preserves. She and Juney live almost entirely on what they make and grow themselves, although Rin has also stockpiled water and batteries in case of power outages or more hurricanes, along with a couple of extra M4 carbines and a supply of magazines in readiness for a terrorist attack, an FBI siege, or, most urgent of all, the sudden appearance of any of the men who raped her.

"Open that," she tells Tariq, pointing at the long chest of a freezer she keeps against the back wall, hoping he will be at least a little bit squeamish.

He lifts the lid and peers inside, Juney hovering behind him. She follows him everywhere now, like an overeager puppy. "Yuck, what's that?" he says, which gives Rin some satisfaction.

"Deer. Frozen. I've got chickens, rabbits, squirrel, and fish in there, too. All dead," she adds unnecessarily, still wanting to shake him.

"Gray likes fish best," Juney comments. "He rolls around in the scales and bones to make himself extra stinky."

"This is for when we can't get fresh meat," Rin continues, ignoring her. Then she explains the deal she's made with local hunters: They give her the parts of the deer kill they don't want: legs, hearts, livers, kidneys, and all the other organs they normally throw away, along with whichever little critters they murdered for fun, all of which she's told them are for her dogs. In return, she gives them a home-baked berry or apple pie. She makes them leave their plastic bags of deer guts, their fresh-shot squirrels and rabbits outside her gate, while she leaves their pies in an old metal milk box. That way, she doesn't have to talk to those knuckleheads any more than necessary, and they don't have to talk to her.

"How come you don't hunt for the wolf food yourself?" Tariq asks. "You've got all those guns." He blinks up at Rin, all wide-eyed and innocent. Which, she has to remind herself, he is.

"I had enough of killing in war," she tells him before she can stop the words. Hoping he doesn't think through the implications of this too closely, she pulls three squirrels from the pot on the back shelf, where they've been thawing, bushy tails, beady eyes and all. "This is the appetizer. Let's go." Carrying them by those tails, she leads him outside, Juney holding his hand and trotting along beside him.

A rain has started up, a light but gloomy September spittle. Charcoal clouds layering on top of one another like sheaves of hay, trees bursting into rustles as if shuddering at a bad dream. Rin doesn't like this weather. It makes her think of the long stretch of the school year ahead, the lonesomeness that shadows her while Juney is gone.

The wolves don't care about the rain, of course. They are focused like bullets on one thing only: food. By the time Rin and the children are in sight of the fence, all three of them are already there, whipped into a fever by the odor of freshly thawed squirrel. The closer the food gets, the more frenetic they grow, tearing back and forth, mouths open, saliva streaming. Soon they are leaping and snarling, snapping at one another and throwing themselves against the fence with great, rattling thuds.

Tariq watches them, holding his breath, eyes big. Rin knows he has never seen them as agitated as this. "You're going in there?" he asks her.

"You tell me." She opens the little hatch she cut high into the fence and drops in the squirrels one by one, imagining them as Officer Flaherty and his DEC cronies. A blur, a flash, and the wolves are ripping them to pieces amid snorts and grunts and the unmistakable squelch and crunch of fangs rending flesh.

"Guess you don't want to get in the way of that," Tariq says, taking a step back.

"Guess not," Rin replies.

13

BARGAIN

When Tariq wanders rain-soaked into Louis's house later that afternoon, his head still humming with the snarling murmur-growl of feeding wolves, he discovers Louis scrabbling through a kitchen drawer. "Where have you been all this time?" Louis says. "I've been waiting and waiting. We have to go!" He slams the drawer closed and yanks open another. Like the rest of his house, his kitchen is as spartan as a barracks, its walls an unyielding beige, its meager collection of spices lined up like saluting recruits, its pots and pans buffed and hung in perfect alignment. But inside every drawer dwells a secret mayhem: Can openers tangled with buttons and thread. Pliers, paper clips, and spoons jumbled into a metallic stew. Wads of expired warranties and never read manuals layered atop essential items, such as the car keys he is searching for now.

"At my friend's. Why, where are we going?" Tariq squints up at him. Louis looks taller than usual—maybe in contrast to little Juney and her bulldog of a mother. He looks big and warm, and despite his agitated mood, reassuring.

Louis turns around, holding his keys aloft in triumph. He is calmer now, his eyes, the color of sunlit grass, smiling into crescents. "Your mom's being released. We can get her right now!"

"Now?" Tariq drops his sopping backpack to the floor. "Does that mean she's all better?"

"Not all better, no. That'll take some time yet. But better enough. Go change—you're drenched. Then we can leave."

During the entire circuitous drive to the hospital, which seems to take twice as long as usual—too many potholes and stop signs, too many hay carts and slowpoke tractors that won't get out of the way—Tariq jiggles about in the passenger seat, barely able to contain his impatience. Just this past Labor Day weekend, he and Louis spent every minute they could with his mother, watching her blow into that plastic tube, unconsciously blowing with her, and she seemed so weak Tariq was afraid she would never come home at all. So as soon as they reach the hospital and enter the elevator, the same orange-rimmed buttons lighting and dimming, the same *ding* ringing out at each floor, he runs down the corridor and bursts into her room with a whoop.

"*Habibi!*" She is sitting upright and ready on the edge of her bed, dressed in an embroidered white tunic and blue jeans instead of that pale blue hospital gown Tariq so disliked, her hair once again in its braid, her hands held out to him. "Come, give me a kiss." He does, wrapping his arms around her thin shoulders and hugging her with all his strength.

"So, my friend, they are letting me out at last," she says to Louis, laughing at Tariq's exuberance and then having to catch her breath. Louis is standing in the door, beaming. "I feel as if I have been trapped in here for—"

"Mama, stop talking. Let's go!" Tariq tugs at her braid. "I'll carry your bag." He picks up the lumpy green sack at her feet, filled with books.

"Thank you, little one. Yes, I long to be out in the air again. Louis, will you help me up? My legs, they feel like noodles."

With Louis's arm supporting her, she shuffles to the door, Tariq following. He hefts the bag higher up his chest like an overlarge baby, rocking under its weight. But it disturbs him to see his mother leaning on Louis like this, as if she is an old woman, and he is suddenly convinced that a doctor or some other demonic figure will pop out of nowhere and stop her from leaving. "Hurry, Mama!" he cries.

She turns to assure him there is no need to rush, but then she sees the fear in his face. It is the same stricken expression he wore in the Baghdad hospital the day after the bomb, the day he was trying to grasp in his three-year-old way that it was his own father and grandfather he had just seen atomized into a cloud of blood; his own leg that had just been sawn off at the thigh.

"Do not worry, little one," she says in the murmuring Arabic of a mother soothing her child. "There is no need to be afraid. We are safe."

But Tariq feels anything but safe. So he begins a frantic series of bargains with fate: His mother will get out of here *if* he reaches the elevator without dropping her bag ... *If* the elevator comes before he counts to five ... *If* he doesn't speak a word till they reach the ground floor ... *If* Louis doesn't say anything about the wolves ...

The bargaining works. They reach the lobby unharmed. Cross its cold, hard floor under its even colder and harder lights. Enter the revolving doors without mishap. And finally, they are successfully ejected, one by one, into the warm, wet, September evening.

"You're free, Mama!"

"Yes, I am, my sweet one," she says with a smile, folding him again to her side. And although he knows she doesn't understand what he means, it is good enough.

It takes only thirty minutes to reach their house, which is nestled at the intersection of two tree-lined streets bordering Huntsville and Potterstown. Louis helps Naema out of the car while Tariq wrestles her bulky bag from the trunk. "It is so good to be here again," she says, stepping gingerly onto the sidewalk, its flagstones buckled by grass and weeds. She looks up at her house. "Oh! What happened?"

The edge of her roof is smashed, two windows are cracked, and a fair bit of vinyl siding is missing. Louis fixed what he could while she was in the hospital, but now, looking at it through her eyes, he sees his efforts have not amounted to much. Her house looks as beaten up as his own.

"The hurricane made the whole town like this, Mama," Tariq tells her quickly. "Some people's homes are much worse than ours. And Louis mended a lot of the broken stuff. You should've seen it before."

"You are always so kind to me, my friend." She pats Louis's hand. Her house is only a modest two-story cottage, squat as a cake box and painted pale green, a row of narrow windows squinting beneath its roof, but it is the first true home she has had since fleeing Baghdad; the first she has owned since she was turned into a refugee.

She was sitting beside Tariq in Saint Raphael Hospital only two days after the bomb when Khalil's fellow interpreter, Salim, came to snatch them away from their lives. "You must leave Iraq now," he whispered. "There are informers everywhere. It could be only a matter of hours till a militia finds you."

She gazed up at him, barely able to comprehend. "But I can't move my son. He's just had an amputation."

"I'm sorry, Umm Tariq, you must. Umm Khalil will accompany you. She's waiting in my taxi. Come!"

Naema looked about in a daze. Before the war, this hospital had been the best in Baghdad. Now patients were strewn all over the floor, covered in filth, and only two doctors were left to treat the hundreds of people streaming in by the day. "But where is my mother? Is she still at our house?"

"No, she went to her uncle in Basra. We are only authorized to fly out Khalil's mother, not yours. I'm sorry."

"Who is 'we'?"

"Sergeant Donnell and me. Hurry!"

Lifting Tariq into her arms, blood seeping through his bandages, Naema followed Salim out, the whispers of gossips trailing them like spies.

Over the next hour, Salim drove them to the airport through the chaotic streets of Baghdad and one terrorizing checkpoint after another. No traffic lights or police, but plenty of blaring horns, screaming drivers, and huge military vehicles with soldiers bristling from them like aliens. Tariq moaned in her lap, his face ashen, his blood staining her skirt. She held him as still as she could to protect him from the jolts of the car, trying to ignore the burning in her freshly stitched cheek while she prayed they would not be stopped, not be caught, not be killed. Hibah sat mute beside her, too numbed by the loss of her husband and son in a single instant to speak. They had nothing with them but the passports and visas hastily procured by Sergeant Donnell, the single bag Hibah had managed to pack in a panic, and the money and jewelry she had sewn inside Naema's sanitary pads and the soles of their shoes.

"Stay in touch with me in Damascus and I will tell the sergeant what you need," Salim said at the airport. "He'll to try to help you get visas to America, but it might be many months before that happens. *Fi Amanhallah.*" And he hurried away, taking their last tie to Baghdad with him.

On the airplane, Naema sat in silence, the multiple shocks of all that had happened breaking over her like wave upon wave of frigid water, each slap icier than the last.

Once they landed in Damascus, they stumbled out to the taxi line, Naema clasping Tariq, Hibah dragging their lone suitcase, their ears battered by the unfamiliar sounds of Syrian Arabic. "Please, uncle, will you take us to an inexpensive hotel in Qudsiya or Jeramana?" Naema asked the first driver, naming neighborhoods she had heard were full of her countrymen escaping the war.

"Can't do it, sister, too far," he said, averting his eyes from her torn face and the mutilated child in her arms.

She tried a second and then a third driver, only to hear more excuses. "I'll pay whatever you want," she finally pleaded with a fourth. "Can't you see my son needs a bed?"

The driver glanced at Tariq: the stained bandages around his stump, his eyes clouded with shock. He named an astronomical fee, enough to live on for two weeks. Naema knew this was robbery, but she was too desperate to bargain, as the driver had clearly surmised. Yet even then he hadn't finished taking advantage, for once he had dumped them at an overpriced hotel in Qudsiya, he snatched their money and, before they could demand change, roared off in a cloud of dust.

Not knowing what else to do, they entered the stone archway leading into the hotel lobby, a grand affair painted scarlet and lit by dim, multicolored lanterns. They crossed the polished mosaic floor to the reception desk, where they asked for a room. The proprietor swept his eyes over them and declared he would allow them to stay only if they paid for two nights there and then. "*Yah Allah,* what is the matter with these people?" Hibah wailed once they had shut the bedroom door behind them. "Have they no pity?"

Naema laid Tariq down on the bed and prepared to change his bandages. "A thousand of us arrive in this city every day," she replied. "Their pity must be used up."

The next morning Naema borrowed one of Hibah's black abayas and stepped out of the hotel in search of food, still benumbed by all that had happened. Instantly, she was swept into a maelstrom of noise and color. Shrouded women and spry, kaftan-clad men barking their wares as they batted away clouds of flies. Street vendors barbecuing *shwarma* under plumes of smoke. Carts heaped with purple figs and sweating oranges. Stands crammed with sacks of lentils, rice, and tea, their scents spicing the air. It was so like Baghdad before the war she felt a strange, shifting sensation, as if she had slipped out of her body to melt into the past. And for the first time since the bomb, she wept.

Wiping her eyes quickly, she forced herself into the street, walking for half an hour, afraid talk to anyone until she realized the neighborhood was so full of her countrymen that most of the shop signs were in Iraqi Arabic. This gave her the courage to enter a small bakery. "Peace be upon you," she said to the baker, a skull-faced man with hooded eyes and a tightly trimmed mustache dusted with flour. After paying for her *samoon*, she added timidly, "I and my family arrived from Baghdad only last night. Do you know, uncle, where I might find work?"

He raised his powdered brows. "Refugees are not allowed to work here. Don't you know that?" His eyes dropped over her, making her feel as if a snake had slithered between her breasts. "You must seek an underground job."

She stepped back, drawing her hijab farther over her wounded cheek. In Iraq, she had resented being forced to wear a head scarf, never having worn one before the American war had brought conservative imams to power. But at that moment, she was glad of the anonymity it gave her and even for the cover of Hibah's heavy abaya. Under the insinuating eyes of the baker, she almost wished to be hidden from head to toe in a burqa. "What sort of job, uncle?"

He glanced around before leaning his dough-crusted hands on the counter and lowering his voice. "Go to the hairdresser over the road and ask her."

Naema picked up her bread, uneasy about what he was implying, and dodged through the barreling traffic to the far side of the street. The hair salon was nothing but a wardrobe-size shopfront containing two chairs, a sink, and a long and tarnished mirror split from top to bottom by a zigzagging crack. A heavily made-up woman clad in a lavender hijab and matching abaya was leaning in the doorway, her big arms crossed. Her lips were so thickly painted they appeared to be made of vinyl. In the light of the baker's words, Naema could not help but wonder what else this woman did besides dressing hair.

"You are newly arrived?" she said after Naema greeted her. "I can always tell." She looked Naema over quickly, taking in the wound on her cheek and Hibah's baggy abaya, nowhere near as elegantly cut as her own. "Tell me about yourself." Naema complied, although in the barest of terms, leaving out Khalil's death and the bomb, neither of which she could bear to speak of aloud. "The best jobs for you, in that case, are private nurse or seamstress. But such jobs are scarce and none are legal."

"But with all due respect, auntie, you have this salon and the uncle across the street has his bakery. Are these illegal?"

"No, but the baker and I have been here many years and we have families here, connections. Do you have connections?" Naema had to admit she did not. "In that case, *barak Állahu feek.* May the blessings of Allah be upon you."

"What about a place to live?" Naema asked, her voice trembling. "Do you know where I might find a cheap apartment? We cannot afford to stay in our hotel."

The woman shrugged, sending a powerful waft of sandalwood perfume her way. "There is a three-month waiting list for even the most dismal of places. So many refugees from the war are pouring in every day, my dear, I've heard the government is about to close the doors to our people altogether. There'll be a rush, so hurry." She reached into her pocket, extracted a stumpy pencil, and scrawled her name and an address on a scrap of paper. "Go to this building, tell them I sent you, and put your name on the list as soon as you can. But I can't promise success."

"May Allah reward you for the good," Naema told her, ashamed now of her earlier suspicions, and returned to the hotel. "Why do they take us into this country if they won't let us work?" she cried to Hibah. "How do they expect us to survive?"

For the following six weeks, Naema went out every morning to stop anyone speaking Iraqi dialect and ask if he or she knew of a job. Day after day, she haunted Iraqi cafés, restaurants, and beauty salons, finding nothing but requests for medical help paid for by promises never kept, or offers to buy her body. But at last, she came across an acquaintance from Baghdad, also now a refugee, who was willing to pay her to care for his dying grandmother. Later, she also found piecework trimming hijabs with lace and beads. Hibah tried to help, but her hands were too arthritic, so Naema spent her nights by the grandmother's bedside, trying with little success to sew the trimmings on straight until the woman needed a bedpan, her bottom washed, her clothes changed, or her toothless mouth spooned with watery soup or tea. And when the night was over, Naema would return to the hotel, sleep for a few fitful hours, play with Tariq for a few more while Hibah took her rest, and then go back out to search for more work or to take him to a doctor.

After staying at the hotel for three months, Naema's earnings draining away on its bills—even with the money Sergeant

Donnell sent them, they could scarcely afford to eat—they finally reached the top of the waiting list and were able to move into a single-room apartment. The ceiling was greased with nicotine, the air filled with the cries and quarrels of neighbors, and they had only one bed between them, but there they lived for two and a half more years, filling out forms, gathering documents, undergoing interviews and medical examinations, and waiting for hours in this line or that, whether to register with the UN refugee office, fulfill Syria's requirement that they renew their visas four times a year, or apply to go to America. And when, at long last, the American visas arrived, spurred on by Donnell, and Naema and her little family were delivered to Albany in 2010, it was only to live in another single room, this one in the back of Donnell's house with the knowledge that he was always there on the other side of the door. Then came the slum she found with Louis—and finally, after years of saving and searching, this cake-box house with two bedrooms and an actual backyard.

Naema unlocks her front door, Tariq and Louis standing behind her, and steps inside, kicking off her sandals and standing on the bare wooden floor a moment just to bask in the relief of being home. Having lost a house and all her property twice, she is averse to accumulating belongings, but she likes her simple abode: the combination living and dining room, its walls the color of old linen; her comforting sofa and armchairs, plush and red; her crimson carpet woven with the tree of life. A row of potted ivies line the back windowsill, and her beloved fig tree stands waiting in a corner, its broad leaves splayed like the offering hands of a father, as if to say, "*Alhamdulillah*, you have returned once again, a phoenix from the ashes."

"Ah, I see someone has been watering my little garden," she says.

"Yes, me," Tariq replies proudly.

"You are a wonderful son. Now, I must rest."

Making her way across the room, she sets herself carefully down on the sofa, tucks her bare feet beneath her, and flicks her braid over her shoulder.

"Can I do anything for you?" Louis asks from the doorway.

She looks at him and smiles. Louis and his anxious hovering. "No, you have done enough. Come sit and relax."

Piling his shoes among the others on a shelf by the door, he takes the armchair beside her, leaning forward with his elbows on his knees, so happy to be here with her again that he hardly knows what to do with himself. If only he could lift her up and dance her about the room. But the few times he has tried even a hug, she has backed away.

"Now," she says, "tell me what happened in the storm. I realize you have been protecting me, but I am home now and strong enough to hear. I know my nurse, Wendy, she is the one who took me out of the flood and called the ambulance. But I remember none of that, only water and screams."

Louis glances at Tariq, who is standing by the kitchen door, listening gravely. "I've no idea what happened, except that something must have knocked you out when the clinic was collapsing. Wendy said there was a lot of debris crashing around in the water. It's amazing no one else got hurt."

"Ah. The luck of the immigrant, no?" Naema is joking, but Louis can hear the bitterness in her words.

"Yes, but now you're home again and you'll be getting stronger by the day." He looks over at Tariq. "It's great having your mom back, huh?"

Tariq nods, yet a sadness is shadowing his face. Naema turns and sees it, too.

"My love, I am all right, I promise," she says, her voice soft. "Will you brew us some chai? You are so good at it." She gazes at him a moment and then looks back at Louis. "That is another thing I missed in the hospital. You Americans, you know nothing about how to make tea. A cup of lukewarm water and a tea bag on the side. Imagine if you served coffee like that! A teaspoon of grounds on a saucer." She looks again at Tariq. "Will you do that for us, little one?"

"Of course, Mama." He hurries off to the kitchen. "I'm going to be like Gray," he tells himself, picturing the ripping fangs and glorious ferocity of his favorite wolf. "I'm going to protect Mama like an alpha male so she never, ever has bad luck again."

14

HOME

Beth pulls herself as upright as she can in her white, spike-heeled sandals, the tarmac burning her feet through their flimsy soles. The Family Readiness Officer told her to come to Albany airport this afternoon to meet Todd after he had been "processed," a word she had always associated with sliced cheese until she married a marine. So here she is, corralled inside a roped-off area on the runway with other military families, like a groupie awaiting a rock star, her nails pressing into her palms.

Flanner is equally upright beside her, dressed for the occasion in his best chinos and blue button-down shirt. His eyes are narrowed, his teeth gripping his upper lip. She rests a reassuring hand on his shoulder, but he shrugs it off and moves away. She wishes he didn't have to wait for his father like this, as nervous as if he has to pass an exam. She wishes Todd had never done this to him. Or, for that matter, to her.

She glances at the people clustered around her. Jacked-up children. Girlfriends in too much makeup and shorts so tiny they reveal crescents of buttock. Teary-eyed wives and husbands clutching American flags and clumsily spray-painted banners: WELCOME HOME MY HERO NOW YOU HAVE TO KISS ME. Ragged mothers and fathers, faces drained, eyes darting, as if awaiting a ghost. As bad as it is for us spouses, she thinks, it must be much worse for the parents. Todd's tall, nicotine-skinned mother, for instance, who is so noticeably not here. Who regressed a long time ago into a second adolescence that came with widowhood and a new husband. How does even a mother like her bear up under the knowledge that her child is at war?

Pushing back her sunglasses, which are making her face hot and her nose ache, Beth tries to distract herself by surveying the landscape. Acres of steamrolled macadam, oily and glittering. Airplanes squatting in the distance like colossal seagulls. The roar of planes rising and falling, rising and falling . . .

A new roar, a blast of hot wind and diesel, and one of those planes thumps onto the tarmac and rolls to a stop in front of the crowd. A whoop bursts from the families around her. Her heart slams up against her collarbone.

The plane growls. Falls silent.

A second explosion of cheering and squealing, followed by a collective holding of breath while a back door opens like a mouth and a set of metal steps is rolled slowly and clankily across the tarmac.

And then, it begins, the parade Beth has seen so many times before: the marines appearing one by one at the top of the steps. Bodies clad in splattered sand-colored uniforms. Matching rucksacks humping their backs. Eyes scanning the crowd. Young faces wary, eager, and scared all at once—exactly the expression she used to see on Flanner when she picked him up from kindergarten.

A drip of sweat runs down her back. Her nails dig deeper.

"Isn't Dad coming?" Flanner asks after some fifteen men and two women have descended the steps to be embraced and kissed and vacuumed up by their families.

"Yes, he's coming. Don't worry."

And finally, there he is. Stepping out of the plane and

pausing on the top step like a president: tall, tight-knit, and broad-shouldered. Head shaved. Face bony.

The families are screeching louder than ever now, jumping up and down, waving their flags and banners. Beth only stands stiff and silent, her eyes fixed on Todd, searching for the man he once was and the man he might be.

"Home at fucking last" is the first thing he says when he finds them. Scooping Flanner up with one arm, he hugs him so long and tight he squeezes the air out of him. With the other, he pulls Beth into his chest, knocking her nose against the hard plate of his breastbone. "It is so good to be here," he says hoarsely. "So goddamn good."

Face mashed into him, sunglasses knocked askew, she can scarcely breathe. He may be shaven and fresher-looking than he was on Skype, but he reeks of anxious sweat and something else, something metallic and sour. She waits for him to release her, fighting for air against his chest and already feeling in the wrong.

"Welcome back, honey," she says with a gasp when he at last lets her go, rescuing her sunglasses from the back of her head. "There's a celebration for you all at the high school. Interested? Or do you just feel like heading home?"

He isn't listening, too busy searching the crowd for his buddies, grinning at them, pulling faces.

"Todd?" She hears her voice rise high and thin. "Want to go the party or not?"

He shouts a joke to someone and only then switches his attention back, dropping his eyes over her: hair brushed to curl around her breasts, shirt his favorite cornflower blue and cut low, skirt white and tight, matching heels. "Looking good, babe." He scans her face. "Tired, though."

She glances away. "Where do you want to go?" she asks for the third time. "Welcome party or home?"

"Home. I've had enough of those fucking parties. Just wanna be with you and Flan."

Beth, too, has come to dread those celebrations. The marines turning drunk and dangerous. The families trying so hard it hurts. The jealous suspicions clogging the conversation.

"Okay, let's get your bags," she says. "Flanner, come on."

Flanner follows them to baggage claim, unable to tear his eyes from his towering platoon sergeant of a dad.

Once they retrieve Todd's duffel bag, patterned with the same splatter of brown and tan as his uniform, Beth leads them with mounting dread to the parking lot and over to the white Honda Civic she managed to pry out of the insurance company. "This is us!" she calls, trying to sound chirpy.

"Where's my Camaro?" Todd looks about in confusion, his naked head taut and veined.

"Um, that hurricane we mentioned?"

"Answer my question."

"I am. It blew a gigantic branch off the maple and . . . well, it crushed the car. I'm sorry, honey." She peers into her purse.

"You're kidding." She can feel his eyes on her. "You know what that car meant to me. When was this, a month ago? Why the fuck didn't you tell me?"

"I didn't want to worry you. Please don't get upset."

"And you didn't think to move it out from under the tree before the hurricane hit?"

She looks up. "I had the store to close, Todd. And two kids to pick up from camp and get down to the basement. I had a lot to worry about."

"So it's completely fucked? Can't be salvaged at all?"

"Afraid not. They took it to the junkyard."

Todd rubs his face, and she remembers he is exhausted. "Insurance is covering it, though, right?"

"Yes. Well, some of it anyhow."

"Shitheads! I'll deal with it then. I'll call tomorrow and give 'em hell. They damn well better replace that car, or else."

"I already did deal with it, Todd. I already gave them hell."

"Yeah, right."

"I did! I've been doing it all while you've been gone, like I always do. I've dealt with everything, including the storm damage. I even got the company to cover renting this Honda till the payments come through."

"Gimme the fucking keys." Snatching them from her, he opens the trunk and flings in his bags. She stands there, shocked. In all the fifteen years he's been in the Corps, he has never spoken to her this roughly before. Never.

He barely waits for her and Flanner to get in before he takes off with a screech, careening out of the parking lot and down the road as if he were on a racetrack. His neck is running sweat. Jaw clamping and unclamping.

"Slow down!" she gasps, clutching the dashboard.

"What?"

"You're going too fast! You'll run into someone!"

Todd looks at her as though he genuinely has no idea what she is talking about. "Oh," he says. "Yeah." And slow down he does.

As soon as they reach the house, he jumps out of the car and lets himself in, yelling something she misses over his shoulder as he heads for the shower. So she hauls his bags inside for him, lugs them up to their bedroom, and drops them in a corner, where they lie sagging in their war colors: dusty, faded, foreign. She stares at the duffel, its bulk and length reminding her ineluctably of a corpse.

Down in the kitchen, she has the same meal ready to cook that Todd always wants on his returns: T-bone steak, mashed potatoes, green beans. Red wine, for what he calls her sophisticated streak, but plenty of beer, too. A surprise for dessert.

As she sets the steak to broil, she tries to ignore the ice seeping under her skin. After all, she has been through Todd's homecomings before: twice for leave and three times at the end of his previous tours. She knows he is always on edge, teetering between the hostile moonscape of Afghanistan and the tree-cluttered streets of Huntsville, the tight-knit company of his all-male infantry platoon and his demanding family of two—the adrenaline high of war and the dull routine of home. She knows also that he is usually too jet-lagged to finish his first meal, wanting only to shower, drink and collapse. All this she expects, along with the thrashing while he searches for sleep, the night terrors she is determined to endure, the apologies that inevitably follow. Why should this return be any different?

By the time he emerges, dressed like a frat boy in jeans and a short-sleeved plaid shirt in brown and green, which only make his shaven skull and sunken cheeks look more alien than ever, she has dinner on the dining room table. She set it before he came, with his favorite candy-striped tablecloth and his grandmother's silver, along with a vase of expensive yellow roses to complement her decor.

"Wash your hands, Flanner," she orders, and pulls out the chair at the head of the table with the flourish of the restaurant hostess she once was, trying to clown away her nervousness.

Todd sits without a word while Flanner runs to the sink, so eager to be at his father's side he returns with his hands still wet. He takes the chair next to his father while Beth gives Todd his meal first, opening his beer before pouring her own glass of wine. Then she serves Flanner and herself and sits on the other side; a family triumvirate.

Todd says little while they eat. Asks nothing about their nine months without him, says nothing about his nine without them. Beth watches him, his hefty shoulders hunched over his dinner, his gaze flitting from his plate to the windows and back again, his eyes flat as paint. She wonders how long it will take him this time to truly understand where he is.

Flanner, meanwhile, is talking nonstop about the summer, his first week in fifth grade, and his new after-school football program. He tells Todd again about the hurricane knocking down all those trees, about the flood rerouting the creek and destroying the clinic—about everything except his loss of Tariq and his encounter with Rin and the wolf, which still fills him with a skin-crawling shame.

Todd stares at him glassy-eyed, nodding in all the wrong places. Then, with a yawn, he shoves his half-eaten meal away. "This was great, babe, but I can't stay awake another second." Picking up his beer, he stands. "Sorry, Flan. We'll hang tomorrow, okay?"

"Wait," Beth says. "Honey, just wait a sec. We've got a surprise. Flan?"

Todd sits back down.

Flanner runs to the kitchen and comes back bearing the cake he and Beth baked that afternoon: a heavy, lopsided chocolate layer as big as his chest, adorned with Marine green frosting Flanner made himself and his carefully chosen words, *WELCOME HOME DAD. Semper Fi.*

He places it in front of Todd with a shy smile and stands beside him.

Todd peers down at it. "*Green?* Are you kidding?"

"Flanner made that specially for you." Beth gives Todd a pained look. He ignores her, pushing the cake aside and downing a long slug of beer. He stretches his big arms above his head with a second loud yawn. The skin under his left bicep is newly tattooed with a spread-winged eagle perched on a globe and the logo *USMC*. Beth wonders how many other new tattoos he has acquired since she last saw him. His back and chest, shoulders and upper arms are already a gallery of military symbols, American flags, and weapons. Tucked just above the inside of his right elbow is the iconic crossed-out eyes and smiley face of Nirvana.

"Flan, I couldn't eat that now if you paid me," he says once the yawn is finished. "But tell you what. Stick it in the fridge so this summer heat don't ruin it and we'll make it a midnight snack. Okay? I'll come wake you up. Special treat."

The tightness in Beth's throat eases a little, as does the misery in Flanner's face. "That'd be great, Dad!"

"Good. Come here, sport." Todd gives Flanner a squeeze. "I missed you so much, know that? So what d'you wanna do tomorrow, huh? Go fishing? I been waiting a long time to go fishing. Or practice some of that catching we were talking about?"

"Both!" Flanner says happily.

"Cool. Go get my rucksack. I got something in there for you."

While Flanner is upstairs, Todd leans forward and finally rests his eyes on Beth. "How's he been doing?"

"So-so." She decides not to mention the shoe scuffs she had to scrub off the wall. The shoes all over the hallways. The slap. She lowers her voice. "Tariq stopped playing with him, though."

"Why?" Todd sits back, brow knotting.

She is about to explain Naema's near drowning when Flanner reappears, gripping his father's bulky rucksack. "Here," he says with a grunt, heaving it onto Todd's lap.

"No, you open it. Look for the plastic bag."

Flanner thumps the rucksack onto the floor and struggles with its straps a moment. Inside, he finds a new baseball mitt, supple and leather and just the right size for his hand. He looks up, flushing with pleasure.

"We'll break it in tomorrow, deal?" Todd says.

"Deal! Can we play down in the park?"

Todd pats him on the back. "Sure thing, sport. But now it's time for you to scoot. Off you go to bed."

The pleasure fades. "But Dad, it's only six. It's still daytime. Look." Flanner points at the sunlight filling the picture windows around the room. "I can't go to bed now."

"Then watch TV or whatever the fuck you do with yourself these days. I need some time alone with your mom."

Flanner scowls and hangs his head. "Why'd you want to be with *her*? She's useless."

"Flanner—" Beth begins, but Todd interrupts.

"I said go to bed."

"But Dad, she never helps me with homework or plays ball with me or takes me anyplace anymore!"

Todd turns his desiccated face from Flanner to Beth and back again. "What the hell is this?"

"It's true!" Flanner yells. "All she ever does is sit around getting drunk as a pig!"

"Flanner!" Beth gasps.

Todd grips Flanner's stick of an arm. "You don't talk like that about your mom, understand? Ever! Now haul your ass upstairs and not another word."

Flanner's eyes fill, but he says nothing. Head down, he trails across the butter and cream dining room, which Beth dusted and vacuumed and polished for Todd's homecoming, and soon they hear him stamping up the stairs. A door slams once, then again, louder. *Slam, thump. Slam, thump.*

"What the fuck was that about? First the Camaro and now this. Can't a man come home from war to a little goddamn peace and quiet?"

"Of course he can," Beth replies hurriedly, sick with the shock of Flanner's words. "Don't listen to him. He's always testing these days. It's puberty. It's creeping up on him now that he's almost eleven. I think I even glimpsed a little fuzz under his arm the other day." She is trying to sound jokey, but Todd doesn't react and he certainly doesn't smile.

"Well, you better not be hitting no bottle, not while you're holding up the home front. I need you to be strong while I'm gone." He frowns at her. "I need to feel welcome, too."

Beth looks at him. Where did he get such talk? He sounds like a movie cowboy. And she wishes he would clean up his language. "Listen honey, why don't you lie down awhile, relax? Remember how we spoke about this before?"

The old Todd would have understood, climbed down from whatever hopped-up plane he is on and paid attention. After all, they've read the homecoming manuals together, the military spouse websites. They've attended the family readiness sessions, too. Beth could quote the advice verbatim if asked: *Expect that intimacy and sexual relations may be awkward at first. Go slowly. Your time apart really has made you strangers to each other in many ways. Make an effort to be patient and charming, much as you did when you were first dating.*

But this Todd only stands and stretches with yet another yawn. "Hell with this. I'm going upstairs."

At twelve-thirty that night, long after Beth has slid under the covers, careful not to wake him, and long after she has lain there thinking about all the cumulative years they have been apart and how it's even lonelier to lie beside him like this than to be on her own, she awakes in a black panic, thrashing and gulping for air. Todd is pinning her down on the bed, one knee on her chest, a hand at her throat. And he is hurting her. Yanking violently at her nightgown, making the armholes cut into her as he pulls it off. Pushing her chin back and back until her neck strains to snapping point, his fingers pressing down on her trachea. Her head spinning, vision sparking red and yellow and black . . .

It is the worst that has ever happened. Worse than anything he has ever done to her. It isn't even sex, what he does. She pleads with him to stop, tries to push him away, pry herself out from under him and escape. "Todd, I'm Beth, stop!" But the more she pleads and resists, the more vicious he gets, until she gives up, crying silently while he tears and tears at her, all the while sobbing under her breath without even knowing it.

After he is done and has flung her away from him, she curls up on the far edge of the bed, racked and bleeding and sick with shock, and tries to reach him again. "Todd, don't be like this, *please.*"

He raises himself to an elbow and looms over her, his jaw so tight it looks about to crack. She shrinks away, expecting another blow. But then something passes over his face, a lifting, as of a shadow flitting and gone. He drops onto his back and throws his arm over his eyes.

"Oh Christ, Beth, fucking Christ." And he begins to sob.

15

ELBOW

Ever since Juney has been back in school, Rin's days have turned just as hollow as she feared. She keeps busy enough with all her plenty to do, but an ache walks around with her now, instead of the quietude that accompanies her when she knows Juney is nearby. She feeds her still-unlicensed wolves, deticks the mutts, collects the eggs and apples, milks the nannies, cleans the house and barns, hammers and fixes, digs and weeds, harvests, cooks, and preserves. ... But it all feels as though she is doing it for nobody at all.

The ache begins the minute the school bus picks Juney up in the morning and spirits her away to go through who knows what (she will rarely say), bringing her back only after Rin has had way too many hours to fret and imagine. Rin doesn't believe Juney is being bullied or teased—her classmates are too used to her by now, having grown up with her from the day Rin walked her into kindergarten, clutching her hand as if someone were about to steal her. But she can't deny that Juney is mostly alone. She will sometimes mention a few friends from her field trips, and one or two kids from class, but her silence about her regular days speaks volumes, as does the fact she's never invited anywhere. *Unless*, Rin thinks, *that's because of me.*

Recently, though, the ache has been persisting even when Juney is at home. Rin knows this is largely to do with her dread of Officer Flaherty, but it is also Tariq. He comes to see Juney just about every day after school now, and once they've visited the wolves together, they lie on their backs in the living room and talk for hours. Rin assumes they're telling stories, but she can't be sure because as soon as Juney hears even one creak of a floorboard under Rin's feet, she whispers, "Shh," and they both shut down quiet as thieves till she leaves. Then they do their homework together, Juney with her computer and voice record-ings, Tariq with his laptop or old-fashioned workbooks, after which he insists on sticking around even longer to help with the chores, instead of leaving and finally giving Rin some time alone with her daughter. "Don't you have your own chores to do at home?" she keeps asking. But he never gets the hint. "I'll do them later," he tells her, and carries on as if he lives here.

Juney being away at school all day also forces Rin to cope on her own when she needs to go into town, for even she, with all her self-sufficiency, must shop for supplies once in a while, or visit the braille library to catch up with the latest technology for the blind. She is further obliged to show up at the Depart-ment of Vanquished Ambitions and persuade her doctor to check off all the right boxes on all the right forms so she can qualify for the disability checks on which she depends. This entails calling a dozen times to make the appointment and then having to muster the patience of a turtle to get through the ensuing wait. And even when she is granted an appoint-ment, the doc only offers the same solution to her problems every time. Flashbacks? Take a pill. Nightmares? Take another pill. Hallucinations, misanthropy, rage? Take a whole sackful of pills. She throws the dingbat's prescriptions away as soon as she walks out of there, damned if she'll let him turn her into another of those zombied-out headcases she sees sad-sagging around his office. All she wants is the money she's owed and justice. If she could get genuine recognition from the army and its boss, the DoD, Dealers of Death, that they not only sent her to a pissass pointless war but rape-trained the guys she served with and poisoned her daughter, too, then she's sure a lot of her so-called problems would simply get up and walk away.

Stop, Rin. Just stop.

Today she needs to apply for that cursed license, the deadline Flaherty gave her being tomorrow. So, while Juney is still at school, Rin bundles Betty into the backseat, piles her invisible wolves up front, and, heart pressing against her tonsils, drives into Huntsville.

When she reaches the library, one of those glum federal buildings, redbrick smooth and symmetrical, white cornices like old-man eyebrows, she dresses Betty in her service apron, leaves the invisible wolves in the car, and takes her inside. Librarians don't normally allow dogs, but they can't do anything about service and Seeing Eye. It's the law.

They know Rin at the Library for the Blind, but they don't know her here. They don't know how she walks into a new place. How she stops in the door, Betty a pace ahead on her leash. How she scans each shadow and corner of the room, body shaking, teeth clenched.

She looks down at Betty. The silly bitch is wagging her tail. She is too damn friendly for a service dog. Gray would be better. He would scare the bejesus out of anyone, ill-intentioned or not.

It's a library, Rin. Shape the hell up.

Rin used to love libraries. In every new town or city her father dragged her to as a girl, the family bearing one fictitious name after another, she could at least find consistency in its library. The books were reassuringly the same everywhere, of course, but so were the librarians. The lonely young women still pudged with hope and baby fat. The withering divorcées smelling of dust and paper. The aging gay men forever locked in their closets by the small-mindedness of their small towns.

Betty, who has clearly decided everything is just dandy, wags her way into the room, pulling Rin with her. She looks so matronly in her service apron. If she were human, she'd probably be a librarian herself, one of those elderly, stern types who scold restless children and chase out the pervs jerking off under their raincoats.

Rin croaks a request for a password and sits at her assigned computer, not having one of her own. Juney is forced to take a laptop to school every day, the trend in the blind world now being to do everything through computers, but Rin refuses to have anything to do with it. She doesn't like it spying on her. She doesn't like it leaking the evil of the world right into her own house, either. The news. The ads. Facebook. E-mail.

Parking Betty beside her, she tells her to lie down. She won't, insisting on sitting upright instead, snout twitching. But then, she is on guard duty. Rin has to respect that.

Wishing she had a lead apron to protect her from the computer's spying eyes, Rin types in "Department of Environmental Conservation/Wolf License" and waits. The first words that hit her are these:

Illegal to keep wolves as pets.

She rests her eyes on Betty. Rin saved her wolves. Kept them just as wild as Jay wanted. Spent months studying up on how to raise and doctor them. She has treated them well, and they have returned the favor. And now the Department of Environmental Catastrophe tells her she should never have done any of this at all?

Betty stands up and licks Rin's knee. *Get back to work.*

Rin returns to the screen and reads the next line. *Only*

exceptions are for three purposes: Scientific, Educational, Exhibition. See Endangered/Threatened Species License.

Her hope spirals up. *Scientific* she likes. *Endangered*, yes, alas.

Scientific: This tells her she would have to have a project. A grant. A team. Maybe even a degree and a little white coat . . .

Next.

Educational: This one says she would have to turn her property into a school. Allow gangs of yapping kids to swarm over her yard, trample her vegetables, snoop in her barn. Sit their little butts down on benches and let them watch her feed her wolves like a clown while they ooh and ahh. . . .

Next.

Exhibition: But this one is the worst of all. She'd have to make her home into a zoo, her wolves into specimens. Crowds of strangers—not only kids—would come to laugh at them, show off by posing with them for their endlessly snapping "selfies," rile them up by howling at them like idiots. . . .

Rin stares at the screen, hands clammy as jellyfish, the words flying around her like clouds of gnats.

I can't do this, Jay. I can't do any of this at all.

❧

"What do you see behind your eyes?" Tariq asks Juney while they pick apples after school, Rin back from the library and brooding in the house. He pulls one off a low-slung branch and hands it over. Now that September is halfway through, the trees are licked with the first flames of fall and the apples red and ready.

Juney runs her fingers over it to feel for wormholes. "This one's been munched." She drops it to the ground.

"I mean, do you see all black? Or white? Or maybe just a kind of invisible color, like air?" He picks another and gives it to her.

She approves this one and adds it to the others in the wide pockets of her green windbreaker. "Try seeing out of your elbow."

He does.

"It's like that." She gropes the bulges around her legs. "I've got enough now." She buttons her jacket, its sides strained and drooping with the weight of the fruit. "I smell winter coming, do you?"

Tariq sniffs. The strongest scents are grass and the cidery sweetness of decaying apples. But just beyond those, he does catch a new tang in the air, the tang of coming bonfires and ice. "I think so, yeah."

"You want to feed some of these to the wolves?"

"Wolves eat apples?"

"Of course. They eat all kinds of stuff. Come on."

Taking each other's hands, the children duck under the wizened branches of the trees and make their way to the edge of the woods, Juney tripping twice, Tariq catching her. She giggles. "I do this better with my cane," she tells him.

Once they reach the fence, she raises her face and again cries out her skin-prickling wolf-call, so startling a chipmunk it darts away with a shriek.

The wolves run up in no time, eager as always to feed, although not as frenzied as when they scented Rin's squirrels. Soon they are rubbing their ribs and heads against the wire, ears pricked, tongues out, faces ardent. Tariq's chest opens in a bloom of love. Now that winter is closing in, their coats are thickening, rendering the wolves more majestic than ever. Ebony's coat is showing a new touch of silver at the tips, as if he has been brushed by stars. Silver's is growing whiter and bushier by the day. And Gray's coat, patterned in black and white and charcoal, with the bold stripe of the alpha running over his shoulders and along his spine, is so thick that were Tariq to sink his hand into it, it would disappear to the wrist.

Tariq squeezes his eyes shut and tries again to see out of his elbow, concentrating on the wolves this time. And finally, he understands what Juney was trying to tell him. Just as she will never see what he sees, he will never see what she doesn't.

She pulls an apple from her pocket, the size of a grapefruit in her little hand, and gives it to him. Her cheeks are pinker than usual, flushed by the new crispness in the air, her hair a loose spill of sunlight down her back. "Throw it over the fence."

"You sure?" He assumed they would push it through the same hatch Rin had used for the squirrels.

"Yes. Go on."

He steadies himself on his false leg and, with his best baseball pitch, lobs the apple over the wire. Instantly, Silver leaps up so high she catches it in midair. He gasps. "Silver's an acrobat!"

"Quick, throw the next one and tell me what they do."

He throws another, this one snapped up with equal alacrity by Gray. "They jump from just standing and spring way up above my head!"

"Do it again."

He lobs a third apple over. "Ebony did it, too. Higher than ever!"

"Do it some more."

He does, again and again, the wolves leaping and snatching, never missing once.

"They're flying, aren't they?" Juney says happily. "You made the wolves fly!"

❈

At home with his mother that evening, Tariq finishes the last of his schoolwork and settles onto his bed to read more of *White Fang*, disappointed with it though he is. He chose the book because he wanted to learn how Gray and Silver and Ebony think and feel—to learn about their souls—something none of the articles he has found online have told him. But the deeper he reads into the novel, the more he finds that its wolves don't think or feel at all. They are no more than bundles of instincts and rote behaviors, living out the brutal laws of *kill or be killed* and *oppress the weak and obey the strong*. They don't even express any loyalty, aside from mother to pup, and that only lasts a month or two. Even White Fang himself fails to feel anything beyond anger, fear, pain, and hunger. He certainly possesses nothing like what Tariq would call a soul.

He closes the book over his thumb and studies the cover, an old-fashioned illustration of a scrawny black wolf baring its fangs. This book is all wrong. This isn't what wolves are like—it isn't even what they look like. When he gazes into Gray's amber eyes, he sees much more than raw instinct and aggression. He sees a rich and complicated being in there, a being with whom he can speak his secret language, boy to wolf, wolf to boy.

"Hey, sous-chef, you ready to make the salad?"

It's Louis, knocking on his door. He has come to dinner with the understanding that Tariq will help him cook, neither of them wanting to make Naema work.

"Sure." Tariq throws *White Fang* aside and pulls on his leg.

While he and Louis maneuver deftly about the compact, white-tiled kitchen, Naema sits at a tiny round table in the corner, her hands resting with uncharacteristic docility in her lap, watching them with affection. Louis has been making dinner with them for so many years he knows this kitchen as well as his own, and Tariq is equally practiced at dodging around him, trying as always to disguise any awkwardness in his step. It pains Naema to see the effort her son puts into defying his disablement. Even when he was small and had to rely on heavy wooden crutches to move, he taught himself to swing on them faster than his friends could walk and to cast one aside to race across the ground with the swooping motion of a finch in flight. In the rough streets of Damascus, he also learned to use a crutch as a weapon. But even so, he has never been able to shield himself entirely from those who look at him with pity, treat him as incapable or, most cruel of all, as an aberration. How she wishes her leg had been torn off rather than his; how she wishes she could absorb all his suffering.

"You think I should use these onions?" Louis asks her, gesturing to the vegetable basket by the sink. "They look kind of shriveled."

She pulls her eyes from Tariq. "They will be fine once they are cooked." She pauses to seek a breath. "I have some good news to tell you, Louis. I telephoned Children's Hospital yesterday and they said I can go back to working in the emergency room. I begin next week. So now we can celebrate that I am a doctor again instead of a patient, yes?"

He turns to examine her face, lovely as ever but still drained by illness. "You sure you should go back to work so soon? Maybe you shouldn't push yourself yet. Lungs are delicate."

"I must earn a living, no?"

"I suppose."

"Come, don't look so worried. You should see your expression, all crumpled and scowling." Chuckling, she reaches up to pin her hair in a haphazard bun, the grace of her movement making him catch his breath. Patting her hair to make sure it holds—it is so long and heavy it tends to fall out of any clasp she can find—she folds her hands again in her lap. "See? I am being quiet, just as you wish." She smiles as only she can, warmly and with humor, but with the unmistakable message that he better cease meddling, and cease now.

Once dinner is ready, Tariq dims the lights and they sit at the dining room table, which Naema has decorated with a red silk cloth and matching candles. She takes the head, Tariq and Louis on either side of her, and serves them each the halal burgers Louis made and a helping of Tariq's salad.

"A toast to your being a doctor again," Louis says, eager to make up for his earlier tactlessness, although he is far from happy about her news. He lifts his glass of cranberry juice to her. Even after her four years in America, and even though Naema's faith is more private than traditional, she maintains her ban of alcohol in the house.

She raises her own glass. "Thank you. But I am going to miss my clinic patients very much."

"Why? Their parents were so nasty to you."

"True. But you know how much I care about working with children hurt by war. There, at least I could do that. And children are not responsible for what their parents choose to do." She twists her glass around on the tabletop with her long fingers, watching the candlelight blaze over its beveled surface. "Anyway, the last time I worked at the hospital, my colleagues were hardly more polite." She glances at Tariq and says no more.

"Well, perhaps they'll treat you better this time. After all, you were only a resident then, and now you're nearly a full physician." Louis is phrasing this as carefully as he can, knowing how hard Naema worked to complete the training and residencies required to qualify here, her degrees and achievements as a doctor in Iraq counting for nothing.

"If I had stayed home, I could have helped so much more," she murmurs, as if talking to herself. "Only a handful of my colleagues had the courage to stay. I wish I had been one of them."

"No, Mama!" Tariq looks at her anxiously. "Then you would have been killed and I'd be an orphan!"

She doesn't answer him at first, still wrapped inside her thoughts. But then she reaches out to stroke his face. "Perhaps you are right, little one. I am sorry."

Louis's cell phone buzzes just then, startling them all. He pulls it from his pocket. "It's Beth," he says in surprise.

"Answer, I do not mind," Naema tells him. "We cannot talk over that thing droning like a bee anyway."

"Can you hear me?" Beth whispers when he does. "I can't speak any louder."

"Is something wrong?"

"I need you to come. . . ." Her voice is shaking. "Todd . . . he's not . . ." She falls silent.

"Beth? What's going on? Beth?" But she's gone.

"What is the matter?" Naema asks.

"I don't know." Louis hesitates before pushing back from the table. "I hate to leave in the middle of dinner like this, but I think I better go see. It sounds bad."

"Of course. Go, go. And if I can do anything, tell me." Naema rises to bid him good-bye Iraqi-style, with a kiss on each cheek and a press of both hands. She does not hesitate to touch the stubs of his missing fingers, as so many do, and if he presses back a little too fervently for a little too long, she never seems to notice. Still, he wishes he had a second self, a shadow self he could leave behind to watch over her.

16
HOODLUMS

On the way to Beth's house, a mere twenty-minute drive up the hill, Louis tries to prepare himself for whatever he might find there. He doesn't much care for Todd McAllister, or his chameleonlike eagerness to conform to whomever his companions want him to be, but he tries to retain what empathy he can for the man. After all, he knows something of what Todd is going through, just as he knows that coming home for two weeks while your redeployment shadows you like an assassin is enough to unglue anybody, even a gung-ho marine. He also knows who bears the brunt of this arrangement: the parents, the spouse, the children, anyone you've taught to love you.

He pulls into Beth's driveway and parks by the now-lopsided maple tree in the spot once occupied by Todd's Camaro. Turning off the engine, he gazes for a moment at the gaudy yellow house, its white porch fringed with latticework as intricate as lace. He pries the car key off its ring, slots it back into the ignition, and climbs out.

Flanner opens the door the instant he knocks, his ginger hair flaring in the early-evening light, eyes avid. Louis guesses he's hoping to see Tariq.

"Hey there, Flan. Your parents home?"

The boy nods and stands there, not making a move. Louis studies his face. "Want to tell them I'm here?"

"Tell 'em yourself." Squeezing past him, Flanner runs outside and around the corner, Louis gazing after him. Flanner is usually polite to adults, in that crisply disciplined way military kids are so often polite.

"Todd? Beth?" Louis steps into the sun-yellow hallway. "Can I come in?"

"Oh, hey, bro." Todd appears holding an open beer bottle. Louis is struck by how drawn he is; skin dry and tight, cheeks so hollow the bones look like little wings. Only his arms, bare and tattooed beneath his green T-shirt sleeves, are as bulked as ever. He has aged a decade since he was last home.

Todd raises the bottle. "Want some?" He is clearly half-plotzed, even though it's barely past six.

"Maybe later. So, welcome back. What've you got left now, a week?" They bump fists, slam shoulders.

"Less—been nine days already. I was wondering when you were gonna show up." Todd takes a swig. "Hey, Beth," he yells up the stairs. "Come down here! We got a visitor."

As soon as she appears, Louis knows. She is wearing sunglasses and a pink scarf around her neck and he can see rows of little blue circles imprinted on her arms. His hands clench. She flashes him a look of warning. "Want something to drink?" She leads him into the kitchen and opens the fridge.

"Yeah, take that beer you said no to before," Todd insists, coming up behind him. "It's stuffy as a dog's asshole in here. Beth, open some windows."

"You said not to."

"So now I'm saying different."

She pulls out a bottle of German beer and twists off its top. When she gives it to Louis, he sees that her hand is shaking. He turns his back to Todd and mouths "CAR," shifting his eyes to the front window. Aloud, he says, "I saw Flanner just now. Kid's taller every time I look. He scooted out the door mighty fast."

"I'll get him—he needs a shower before dinner." Beth hurries outside and Louis knows she's read him.

"Let's sit on your deck," he says to Todd, standing to block the window. "I like it out there—great view of the mountains you got."

"Nah. Too cold."

"Come on. There's a warm breeze—I felt it on the way here."

Todd shrugs, extracts another beer from the fridge, and follows Louis out. They each take a lounge chair and kick their feet up on the railing, facing the meadow and the distant humps of the Helderbergs, which look misty and insubstantial in the evening light, more like billows of lavender smoke than mountains.

"You should've seen that meadow of yours out there in the storm," Louis says in a near shout. "Did Beth tell you? Said it was like an ocean. Waves. Whitecaps even."

Todd frowns. "What're you blathering about, Martin? And pipe the fuck down. I'm not deaf."

Louis lowers his voice, but only a little. "Never mind. So how's it feel being home?"

Pause. "Ah, y'know. Seeing my boy's good. Food, too. Sometimes. Beth ain't much of a cook, really. But on the whole, yeah, it's bullshit."

"Know what you mean. I used to look forward to coming home like a kid waiting on Christmas. Counted the days. Got here. Counted the days to go back."

Todd nods, lids drooping, eyes glassy, but he doesn't reply. Louis hears his car driving away up the hill.

They sit in silence a long moment after that, Louis relieved, Todd staring out at the sleepy meadow beyond. Leaning forward, Louis rolls his beer bottle between his hands, his phantom fingers sensing the cold glass with their own aching memory. He decides to take a gamble.

"Listen, bro, be careful with Beth, okay? Treat her right. She's a good person, real loyal to you."

Todd gives him a grip-jawed glare. "What the fuck do you know about how to treat women? Didn't do so good with your own, did you?"

Louis jerks his head back as if he's been pistol-whipped. He takes a long slow breath, summoning the self-restraint he's practiced for years. "You can say whatever you want, but I never hit her, never left bruises all over her. I saw what I saw just now."

"You fucking my wife, Martin? That why you're so concerned?"

Louis raises his eyebrows. "Don't be an asshole. I've got eyes in my head, that's all. Look, I know you've been through shit; it's written all over you. But you can't take it out on Beth or Flanner. They're innocent. Don't add to your crimes, man. You hear me?"

Louis braces himself for a fight even as he's speaking. He grips his bottle and a scene flashes through his mind of the two of them going at it with jagged glass, slashing at each other like street hoodlums. Todd might be built like a fullback with a body pumped with Marine muscle, but Louis is big, too, and just as combat-weathered, and he'll be damned if he's going to be afraid of someone as obviously war-fucked as Todd McAllister.

But Todd doesn't fight. Todd doesn't even argue. He only blinks at Louis with the helpless eyes of a wounded dog. "You got me all wrong, Martin," he mumbles, and he slowly folds over his knees and drops his head into his hands, his beer dribbling splash by splash to the deck floor.

❧

Setting a CD player on the windowsill above her kitchen sink, Naema inserts one of the discs of Iraqi oud music Hibah brought with her to America. Hibah had never been easy to live with, demanding and irascible as she was, but were it not for her help with Tariq, Naema has no idea how she would have survived their life in Damascus or her years of working for her medical degree here. "Cast no dirt into the well that gives you water," Hibah would admonish when Naema complained about their dependence on Sergeant Donnell. "One hand cannot clap by itself," she scolded when Naema insisted on breaking free of him. No, Hibah was not easy, but even so it is only now, a year after her death, that Naema is able to listen again to the oud's rippling notes without her heart contracting in sorrow or her mind turning to the dark side of her memories.

Tariq wishes she wouldn't play the music at all. The slow songs make him ache and the fast ones agitate something deep within him he does not even want to understand. He prefers the Rihanna and Kanye West his friends play at school. Still, he puts up with the oud for his mother's sake, just as he once did for his grandmother's.

He and Naema are cleaning up after the meal Louis had to abandon, she by washing the delicate dishes, he by carrying the heavy ones in from the dining room. Neither is in the mood to talk, Naema needing to save her breath, Tariq too full of thoughts of Gray, so they are content to remain silent, lifting their heads now and then to gaze through the window at the evening sky flaring from salmon to smoky blue.

When her cell phone leaps to life on the corner table, she reaches over to turn the music off. "See who it is, will you? If it's Mustapha, I won't answer."

"You know he'll call back a zillion times till you do."

"True. You want to tell him I'm out?"

"That won't work, Mama. You can't be out with cell phones."

"I suppose you're right." Were she not a doctor, she would throw the tiresome device away.

Tariq hands her the still-ringing phone, and seeing the caller is indeed Mustapha, she carries it with resignation to the living room sofa and lies down to catch her breath. She refuses to pity herself for what happened in the hurricane, but she does wish her lungs would allow her to breathe freely again. They feel as clogged as if she had been smoking for years. In medical school, she spent an entire week dissecting the lungs of smokers, which were riddled with oozing tar as thick and black as that used to build roads, and once she squeezed a pair to see what would happen. Instead of springing back like a sponge as healthy lungs would, they stuck together like a wet and shriveled balloon. This is how she pictures her lungs now: two wads of gluey black rubber.

"Mustapha, *salaam*," she says in Arabic, her voice weary.

"You sound worse than usual. Have you been overdoing it again?"

This irritates her. "If you believe that eating dinner, standing up, and sitting back down is overdoing it, perhaps I have."

"I'm sorry. It must be so frustrating."

"How is Saba?" She would rather talk about his elder sister, a widow and mother like her, than hear his overbearing, solicitous tones. He behaved like this each time he came to see her in the hospital, too, telling her what she could and couldn't do until she was forced to send him away. Louis is never like that—or almost never. He knows her too well.

"She's fine and sends you her wishes. But may I come by? I have something for you."

"I'm very tired, Mustapha."

"I won't stay long. Has . . . has Louis Martin been to see you today?" Mustapha's jealousy is so manifest, Naema is embarrassed for him. The two men often cross paths on her doorstep, eyeing each other like rival dogs.

"Yes, he just left. And yes, I suppose you can come."

Mustapha does come, and so quickly she suspects he called from around the corner. Tariq opens the door for him, sullen in a way he is with no one else. He runs down the hall to his bedroom before Mustapha even has his shoes off.

When Mustapha is in her presence, though, sitting on an armchair and leaning toward her in concern, his square face and thick shoulders exuding reassurance, she wonders why she is so hard on him. Ever since they met at the Refugee Center during her first month in America, he has never been anything but kind to her. And she admires the way he refuses to complain, either about all he suffered in Iraq or his life here, where he works in a factory making window shades, and keeps applying over and over for more suitable work he never gets—he, who was an accomplished engineer at home. Yet, whenever she is near him, she feels buried under stones.

"Here," he says, once he has finished interrogating her about her health. He pulls a packet the size and shape of a pencil box out of his pocket and hands it to her. "May Allah the Gracious and Merciful wash away the sorrow with the sweet."

She opens it to find a double row of plump Iraqi dates. "Where did you get these?" she asks in delight. "The only dates I can find here are all hard and dry as toes."

He smiles. "My mother brought them back from Baghdad last winter."

"She was able to visit home safely?"

"She was, *Alhamdulillah*. Although I doubt she would dare now."

Naema's mouth fills with a taste as bitter as brass. "Yes, and I thought our home could get no worse after the Americans."

Mustapha shakes his head. "We have no home, Naema. It has been parceled out between the corrupt and the fanatic. There is no Iraq, not as we knew it."

Naema has said this often enough herself, yet the old yearning tugs at her like a hungry child. Nearly seven years have passed since she last saw Baghdad—how she longs to go back! But this is impossible, not only because of the newest wave of thuggery and extremism, the Syrian civil war and floods of refugees in and out of Iraq, but because, as the widow of an interpreter, she might still be marked for death. And then, even if she could return, whom would she find there? Her father and thirteen-year-old brother, who had opposed Saddam and yet were arrested by the Americans anyway, were killed in Camp Bucca, a U.S. prison made of nothing but tents and razor wire in the middle of the desert. Khalil was blown up by one militia or another—nobody knew which. And even her mother, who survived all that, died of heartbreak soon after Naema was forced to leave her behind by the rules of her American visa. Most of her other relatives are gone as well, the Sunnis from her father's side hunted down or exiled, only to find themselves shunted from one war to another; the Shia from her mother's killed or scattered to live the marginal lives of refugees everywhere.

"I wish I could go home like your mother," she says to Mustapha. "But if I did, it would be only to visit graves."

❋

Louis gazes out at the shadowy row of the Helderbergs, watching the remains of the same salmon sunset Naema and Tariq were admiring while he waits for Todd to get a grip on himself. Out in the meadow, three cinnamon deer lift their heads of one accord, alerted by a sound he cannot hear, and bound away in alarm. A crowd of goldfinches, bright as butter, loops over his head to bed down in a tree. A chipmunk emerges from the tall grass behind Beth's bird feeder, clambers up the pole with the furtive speed of a practiced thief, and stuffs its pouch with seed. Only when the sun has stretched the last of its light over the land, glazing it in a gilded haze, does Todd finally lower his hand and right his dripping beer bottle.

Louis turns his eyes back to him, this bulk of a man still slumped over his knees, thick neck bowed. The veins in his muscled arms are knotted and blue, and his older tattoos—the rifles, the Stars and Stripes, the Nirvana face—are already blurring at the edges; memories sliding out of focus.

"You okay?"

No answer.

Louis tries again. "You got five days left, you said?"

Todd grunts without moving, his scalp exposed and fragile under its stubble.

Louis persists. "Why don't you come stay with me? Leave it with Beth for now. Let the dust settle—"

"Mind your own fucking business, Martin." Todd sits up at last, throwing back his shoulders. "The hell you think you are, my mother?" He wipes his arm across his brow and stares into his bottle.

"You look like shit, you know that?" Louis says, but he tries to keep his voice kind.

Todd shrugs. Shuffles his feet. Stares into the distance.

"Oh, fuck it, why not?" He stands and moves toward the kitchen. "Me and you can have a good time—bros together and all that crap. Hit some bars or whatever."

This is not what Louis has in mind at all, but he keeps that to himself. Putting down his own beer, he rises, too. "I'll wait while you get your stuff."

Todd rests his eyes on him a moment. Nods. Runs upstairs.

Louis sends Beth a text warning her not to choose his house for refuge. Where she will go, he has no idea—not too far, he hopes, given she has his Camry. He also hopes she doesn't choose to turn to Naema, who has had more than enough drama lately. But just in case, he writes her a text, too.

Within minutes, Todd is downstairs again, rucksack on his back, duffel in one hand, a new six-pack in the other—Beth seems to have laid in quite a supply; not, perhaps, the wisest of decisions. "You seen Beth and Flanner?"

"Yeah, they went to get something from the basement." Louis hopes there is a basement.

"Huh." Todd follows Louis outside and looks around. "Where's your car at?"

"In the shop. Transmission trouble . . . I walked here."

Todd looks confused. "Oh. Guess we'll have to take this piece of crap instead." Unlocking the door of Beth's rental Honda, he flings his gear in the back and looks over at Louis. "Let's move. I don't wanna have to explain anything. Beth can find another car, since she wrecked up mine." He tosses over the keys and drops into the passenger seat, prying the cap off a new bottle. "You drive. I feel more like drinking." Slapping the dashboard, he shouts, "Drive on, soldier."

Louis casts him a curious glance. Todd can't seem to speak without sounding as though he is imitating somebody. Maybe it's ordering all those Afghan trainees around, but he never used to talk like this and it doesn't sit right on him. Louis knows plenty of Joes, jarheads, too, who can carry off this machismo act convincingly. Todd is not one of them.

"So, are you healthy?" Louis says after they have been driving a few minutes. "Any aches, pains, Afghan bugs, or sucked-up wounds? 'Cause I have a plan if you are."

"I got Taliban grit up my ass and everything here looks phony as fuck. Otherwise, I'm fine."

"Good. How would you like to go hiking? I'm owed a few days off of work. We could head up to the Adirondacks. Swim. Camp. We could even rent a canoe." Louis braces himself for mockery, but he is determined to make this happen. He doesn't expect Todd to open up about whatever he's been going through—it's too soon, and Louis doesn't need to hear it anyway. He can guess. Todd could have shot a kid in the face. Watched a buddy explode and get picked over by dogs. Screwed up a command and caused a whole squad to be blown to pieces. All the events of war bleed together into one long parade of savageries that gouge the soul and befoul the heart. . . . Yes, Louis knows all this, so why talk about it? But if he can get Todd away from town, away from those bars he's pretending he wants to go to, and, most of all, away from Beth, perhaps the man will at least take the chance to think.

"It'll be cool and green, nothing like that pile of rocks you've been stuck in," he adds. "Pine trees. Birds. Lakes."

Todd looks at him as if he's speaking Martian. "What? I come home from war and you wanna turn me into a fucking Boy Scout? Are you out of your mind?"

17

MANTRA

On the far side of town, Beth is hurtling through farms and up and down hills in Louis's car, panic clutching her chest. She keeps checking the rearview mirror for Todd, expecting him to loom up behind her at any second, ram her off the road and drag her out. . . . She shakes her head, jerking the car out of its lane.

"Mom!" Flanner cries from the back.

"Sorry, honey, sorry." She grips the steering wheel tighter.

"Where are we going anyhow?"

"I don't know. I need to think." She scans the darkening landscape, trying to calm herself enough to recognize where they are. Hills shading from green to gold. Farms sprinkled with a horse or two, cows and mud. Fields running to weed. Caved-in barns, abandoned silos. A lake covered in algae, a lone swan drifting across it like a puff of cotton. If only she could go to relatives, but her parents have retired to Miami, her brother lives in California, and her cousins have long since scattered. As for her friends at work, she doesn't know any of them well enough for a humiliating moment like this. Still, she has to decide on somewhere. She can't drive forever.

She glances in the mirror at Flanner, who is glaring out of the side window, a long, sharpened stick across his lap, his freck-led face brooding. "Flan, you okay?"

"Dad's a shithead."

Beth knows she should stand up for Todd, tell Flanner his father will get better once he's over the war—that's what the military parenting sites would advise. "What if we go to Tariq's house?" she says instead. "His mom's back from the hospital now, and you could play with him and get your mind off of . . . things." Yes. Todd has never met Naema; he isn't likely to think of tracking her there.

Flanner's mood does lift at that, but only for a second before the anger at both his dad and Tariq comes boomeranging back, along with the memory of Tariq watching him run like a rabbit from Mrs. Drummond and her wolf.

"We don't *play*, Mom. We're too old to play. Can't we just go someplace for dinner? I'm starving."

"I don't have any money on me." Beth left her purse in the house, along with her driver's license and everything else she owns, aside from the cell phone in her pocket—maybe even her entire life. She draws in a long, thin stretch of air to steady herself. "I'm sure Tariq's mom will give you something to eat. But you sound like you don't want to go. Don't you want to see your friend? I know you've been missing him."

Flanner fingers his stick, refusing to answer. He hates his mother now—for being hurt instead of angry, for crying all the time, for acting scared and weak and for not killing his dad. He hates Tariq, too. But he hates his father the most. That's what the stick is for, carefully sharpened just the way he sharpened it for the wolves. He's going to stab it into his dad when he's asleep, right through the heart. Exactly the way you kill Dracula.

When Beth knocks on Naema's door, Naema opens it without surprise. "Ah, I thought it might be you. Louis sent me a message. Please, come in. Hello, Flanner. Nice to see you again. You will find Tariq in his room."

Flanner looks down at his feet. "I'll stay out here." He plods off into the yard, trailing his stick behind him.

Naema is too struck by Beth's appearance to notice. She only asks Beth to remove her shoes and ushers her inside. Mustapha has just left, his box of dates still on the coffee table. "Sit down, please. Would you like some water or tea?"

Beth shakes her head, glancing behind her to make sure the front door is firmly closed. Sinking into an armchair, she covers her face with her hands. "I'm sorry, I just didn't know where else to go. Oh, Naema. Oh God, I'm sorry, but would you mind locking your door?"

Naema hesitates, thinking of Flanner, but then she complies, understanding the need for locked doors more than Beth could know. Carrying a chair over from the table, she sits opposite her. "It is good you came here to me. Now, let me look at you as a doctor." She tilts a lamp to shine on her and leans forward.

Beth shrinks back. Her domestic life, her marriage, and, above all, her failures are matters she has always kept to herself. But this luxury, like her dignity, seems to have been snatched away from her now. With a cold wash of shame, she removes her sunglasses, unties her scarf, and raises her face to the light.

Naema examines her gently, lifting her eyelids one by one. Beth's eyes are bloodshot, the left one swollen, its socket radiating red and violet. Her neck is chafed and streaked purple, her arms marked with the same rows of blue circles Louis noticed. "Your vision, is it blurred at all?"

"A little, yes." A dry sob wrenches out of Beth. To be touched gently like this after this past week feels like a kind of sleep, even a kind of forgiveness. It is all she can do not to collapse under the release of it.

"And your throat? Can you swallow?"

Beth wonders the same about Naema, her voice is so hoarse. "Yes, but it hurts to eat anything solid."

"Your esophagus, it is bruised, I suspect. Do not worry. It will recover." Naema fetches an ice pack from the kitchen, gives it to Beth to hold over her eye, and then sits down again, folding her hands in her lap. "Please do not be embarrassed, but it would be best if you tell me, as a patient to a doctor, if your husband has hurt you anywhere else. I must make sure you are all right. You understand?" Naema has worked with the women and wives of the military for long enough to have guessed more or less what happened.

Beth nurses her eye, equally unable and unwilling to answer. What Todd has been doing to her in the bedroom is not something she can even face, let alone talk about.

After a tense silence, Naema changes tactics. "Come." She rises to her feet. "You can put the ice down now. I will take you upstairs for a sleep. You need to rest."

"Thank you . . . but . . . you will keep the door locked, right? And get Flanner inside? In case . . . you know."

"I will. But you and Flanner are safe now. Louis has promised to stay with your husband and he will not let him come here. Follow me."

She leads Beth upstairs to her low-ceilinged bedroom, where the twilight seeping through its row of squat windows has draped the room in shadows. There, she feeds her a sedative, helps her change into a pair of soft, fern green pajamas, and tucks her under a bedspread she brought from Damascus, patterned in the lustrous oranges and reds of a pheasant's breast feathers. Dimming the lamp, she sits beside her, stroking her hair. "Try to go to sleep now."

Beth squints up at her, the sedative already loosening her tongue. "I couldn't leave. I tried, but he hid the car keys. . . . I should've called Louis before but . . . crying and saying sorry . . . I should've tried. . . ."

"Shh, it is all right. None of this is your fault. Quiet now. You are safe."

"He followed . . . wouldn't let me . . . I don't . . ."

Beth's words tumble out in a frantic tangle, bumping up against one another, slurring and overlapping until, at last, they begin to subside, first to whispers, then to mumbles, and finally to whimpers. Naema remains by her side, stroking her head until she can see the sedative taking its hold.

Rising carefully so as not to wake her, Naema gazes down at Beth's bruised face, thinking how very long the reach of war turns out to be. The day she fled that Baghdad hospital, she assumed that, painful as it was to leave her country forever, she was at least leaving war as well. But instead, it has followed her everywhere. First to Syria. Then to the resettlement center in Albany with its refugees from all over the world, their faces emptied of joy, eyes drained by loss. Then again to the clinic, her patients sickened by the toxins their parents absorbed at war, or harmed by the violence those same parents brought home. And now it has followed her all the way here to her bedroom in Huntsville, New York, and her very own bed.

❖

Tariq is so absorbed in his latest book about wolves, he has no idea that Beth is upstairs or Flanner out in the yard. The book isn't *White Fang* this time, Tariq having finished it in disgust—he couldn't bear the way the wolf succumbed to servile dependence on that white man at the end—but another book, lent to him by Mrs. Drummond, full of pictures of wolves from all over the world. Snowy ones like Silver from Alaska. Small red ones from Europe. Timber wolves like Gray from Canada. Right now he is reading about the pups, their noses stubby, eyes deep blue, ears the shape of teddy bear ears, fur as fluffy as down. How he would love to have a wolf pup like that to take into bed with him on those nights when dreams tear at his sleep.

He reaches over to switch on his bedside lamp, time having dialed the twilight down to a moonless evening, and turns to the section about the social order of packs. The alpha male and female, he reads contentedly, are the only wolves in a pack to have pups because the female, who comes into estrus only once a year, bullies the other females so badly they either miscarry or never ovulate at all (being the son of a doctor, Tariq knows perfectly well what this means). Meanwhile, the rest of the wolves take on specific jobs. The nannies guard the pups, and teach them how to fight and hunt and howl. The omegas protect the pack by clowning to deflect fights and diffuse tension. And the rest divide into hunters and trackers. But it is the alphas who run the show, controlling who grooms whom and when, where they hunt, who gets to eat which parts of the prey, and how they interact with other packs. The alphas look after everyone in return for unhesitating obedience, just as Mrs. Drummond explained to him about Gray.

Tariq flips to the chapter about howling. Wolf pups practice howling from the minute they can stand, he learns, because howling is as complex as a language. There are howls to reach the rest of the pack when it has wandered away, howls to recognize family, howls to proclaim an alpha status, to court a mate, lead the pack on a journey, warn off rivals, defend one another. . . .

And each wolf knows a wide variety of howls, yips, and growls to frighten off enemies by making the pack sound bigger than it is.

A movement catches Tariq's eye and he looks up just in time to see something flit by his window. Dropping the book, he reaches for one of his crutches and swings over, poking his face out with caution. "Who's there?"

"Me."

He leans farther out. "Flanner! What are you doing here?"

Flanner ignores the question, so Tariq fits on his leg and heads out the back door. He still stings from the insults Flanner flung at him that day in the woods, so he approaches him with caution.

Flanner is crouched on the grass, pretending to have found something intriguing.

"What's up?" Tariq asks.

"Nothing." Flanner stands and shows him the quarter he planted there before Tariq appeared. "Found this, since you're so interested. And you can't have it."

Tariq peers at it through the dark. "Who said I wanted it?" He eyes the sharp stick in Flanner's other hand, which reminds him of their game about spearing wolves, and he feels a sudden gape of time between the kid he was then and who he is now, companion to Juney and Gray. "What are you doing with that stick?"

"Hunting."

"Hunting what?"

"Groundhogs. They've been digging holes in our basement, so Mom asked me to kill a few. I'm looking to see if you got any too."

This is such an obvious lie it only makes Tariq feel more distant from Flanner than ever. "Killed any yet?" he asks with a scoff.

"Fuck you, lameleg! You think you're so chill with your dumb wolves. I know. I saw. But just you wait."

The words are so unexpected, ripping into the gossamer veil over Tariq's secret world, that any possibility of a comeback deserts him. "What do you mean?"

Flanner grips his stick. "I know more than you think."

"You're lying. You don't know anything!"

"Yeah I do. I saw you talking to that evil wolf. You and that crazy lady."

"What are you talking about? There's nothing evil about Gray. And she isn't crazy!"

"Oh yeah, she is. But you and those wolves and that nutball are over for good, now. You'll see!"

"What are saying?" Tariq grabs Flanner's arm in fright. "Did you tell somebody?"

This is all Flanner needs. "Don't touch me!" he screams. And he swings his stick as hard as he can at Tariq's head.

The scream wakes Beth instantly, cutting through sleep and sedative. "What's that?" She sits upright, staring wildly at Naema. Before Naema can find the breath to answer, Beth is running downstairs.

Naema forces her maddeningly uncooperative body across the room to look out the narrow window. She sees Beth flying across the yard, her green pajamas only just visible in the dark, bare feet flashing. She sees Flanner kicking something on the grass. She sees a dark shape lying by itself some distance away. And only then does it dawn on her that it is Tariq being kicked, Tariq curled in a ball on the ground, Tariq's prosthesis torn off and cast aside. Turning with a cry, she pushes herself over to the door and stumbles as fast as she can down the stairs.

Beth is grappling with Flanner now, pulling with all her strength to get him off his friend. "Stop! For God's sake, stop!"

"I'll kill him, I'll kill him!" Flanner is shouting, fighting her hard, the sharpened stick in his hand grazing her cheek, nearly gouging an eye. She is forced to twist his arm violently—her own child!—to pry the stick loose. Throwing it out of reach, she seizes him by the shoulders and shakes him. "Stop! What's the matter with you? What are you *doing*?"

He struggles, still yelling, while she wrestles with him, panting from the effort, until she manages to pin his arms to his sides and hold his writhing, furious body tightly enough to control him.

Naema reaches the yard at that moment, white-faced from lack of breath. Running over to Tariq, curled and sobbing on the grass, she drops to her knees beside him and takes his head in her hands, which are instantly drenched in blood. "Allah help us, are you all right, *habibi*? What has he done to you?"

Although she is speaking Arabic, Beth understands. "Flanner hit him with that stick!" she gasps, still gripping Flanner tight. "I'm so sorry!"

Naema examines Tariq's head quickly. The blood is gushing from the top of his scalp. Quickly, she pushes apart his hair, searching for the wound. But it is too dark to see. Tears are mingling with the blood drenching his face and his stump is flailing in the grass. Naema pulls him onto her lap, cradling him and murmuring comfort just as she did when the bomb tore off his leg. She looks up at Flanner.

"Why did you bring that stick to my house? Did you come here to attack my son?"

Still writhing in his mother's arms, Flanner is sobbing

himself now, horrified at what he has done and yet still in a maelstrom of confusion and fury. "No," he chokes out. "It wasn't for him. It was for Dad."

But Naema is not interested. "You should be ashamed," she says, her breath rasping. "To hurt him like this and to be so cruel. How could you do such a thing to a friend?"

18

DAWN

Rin is spending as much time as she can with her wolves now that she's so afraid of losing them. Today is the deadline for the license application and all week she has been racked up tight, jumping at every clank of a truck in the distance, every shriek of a tire beyond her hill. She keeps stepping out to the porch or walking up to the gate to peer down the rutted driveway, waiting for the blade to fall. So at dawn, while Juney is still asleep and the school bus not due for another hour, she walks down to the woods alone. She likes best to visit her wolves when the day is still clean and full of hope like this, the sky a faint rosy gold, the birds singing their hearts out, the sun dawdling, and the rest of the world far away.

The walk to the fence takes her past the lilac bushes she planted to guide Juney, around the old orchard, and down a broad stretch of grass, right now crying out for a mowing. The trees rustle wetly as she passes, like a whispered welcome, and the sound warms her. She has always loved this place; has done since the very first time Jay brought her here. The disheveled buildings, unkempt fields; the way it looks both domesticated and rebellious. "Let's bring this farm back to life if we make it home from war," he said as he showed her around, as if he'd known he was leaving her a legacy.

When she reaches the fence, she stops a moment to gather

herself. A person needs to be calm to handle wolves. The dew, spangled over the grass like bejeweled cobwebs, is already evaporating. The sumacs along the edge of the yard are shuddering under a breeze, their branches heavy with the end of summer, their leaves flashing signals of red like flags of warning. A squad of grackles has stormed Juney's feeder to raucously gobble their breakfast.

Once Rin feels steady enough, she lifts her head and calls the wolf cry Juney invented. Then she unlocks the catch pen, which juts from the fence like a vestibule, walks through the inner door, and waits for Gray to arrive. If he doesn't want her around, he might growl or snap a warning and she will beat a hasty retreat. But today he only gives her a quick sniff and ambles off to lie some distance away beside Ebony, both yawning great yawns, all fang and tongue and glistening black lips. They rest their snouts on their front paws and watch her lazily. Two heaps of fur and muscle, faces sharp and watchful, bodies seething with vitality even as they blink away sleep. Rin is always careful not to underestimate her wolves.

Silver comes trotting up then, her thick white coat aglow in the early light, her face wearing the mild look she keeps only for Rin. Just as Gray has chosen Tariq and Ebony favors Juney, Silver has marked Rin as her own. Silver is the quickest of her wolves, too, perhaps because, like Rin, she knows what it is to be the only female in a pack. She moves like a streak of mercury. Flash, snap—there goes a rabbit. Whisk, crunch, there goes a fox. She is merciless and savage, exactly the way she should be. But with Rin she is gentle. She will nuzzle her hand through the fence the way Gray nuzzles Tariq. Press her white flank up against it so Rin can scratch her. And on the occasions Rin goes inside the pen and crouches down to play, Silver will rub against her while Rin massages the top of her head, Gray looking on protectively. Rin is not sure he approves.

Now Rin squats beside her, taking the precaution of staying on the balls of her feet, and scratches Silver between the ears, where she most likes it. Silver wriggles with pleasure.

Jay would have loved to see this. It was his dream to make wolves part of their family, which is maybe why Rin can sense him closer to her when she is with them than anywhere else. Jay, her wolves, and Juney. How it should have been.

The sun has drifted higher now, turning the grass and trees dry and bright. It is almost time to rouse Juney and send her away again to be whoever she is when Rin's not there. But first Rin whispers to Silver as the wolf closes her eyes under the bliss of Rin's caresses and flaps her long tongue over Rin's face.

"Silver, I don't know how, but I'm going to try everything I can to stop those cops taking you. Maybe I'll hide you. Maybe I'll pull out one of my rifles and defend the fort. Maybe I'll find a way to bundle you and Gray and Ebony into the basement till they go away. . . .

"Or maybe I'll lure the cops into your pen and let you do with them what you will."

19

VIGILANCE

Todd sits folded up in the passenger seat of Beth's rented Honda, his head brushing the ceiling, knees pressed against the dashboard, nursing an inky black coffee the size of a bucket. "This Jap car's made for fucking dwarfs," he grumbles, shifting irritably in his seat. His voice, Louis notices, is worn-out weary this morning, toneless and hollow. "If this was my Camaro, I could stretch out at least. And you could floor the motherfucker and streak up the other side. You're driving like an old lady, Martin."

Louis ignores this, already wishing for better company—namely, of course, Naema. But here he is, stuck with a truly unpleasant man, trying to give him some kind of nature cure for a matter that may be incurable, with no real idea of what he is doing aside from taking him away from his wife.

He and Todd drive for two and half hours, barely exchanging a word, while Todd hunches forward, scanning the radio for heavy metal or hip-hop, and turning the volume brain-crushingly high. Louis clenches the steering wheel, the stubs of his missing fingers paling from the effort. He does not appreciate having his ears commandeered like this, especially with a racket that sears his nerves and catapults him back inside an MRAP, blasting AC/DC and screaming "Highway to Hell" to stoke his killer instinct. But he tells himself to let Todd have his way. For now.

The farther north they drive, the brighter the trees become, until the woods flanking either side of the road are as gaudy as a paint-splashed wall. They stop to use the toilet in a tiny convenience store inaptly named Moose Manor, where Todd buys another tub of coffee and Louis stocks up on survival food and camping supplies. But during the entire journey, Louis can sense Todd on high vigilance, body taut, eyes scanning, veins pulsating in his tendon-tight neck. He grows especially tense each time they drive under a bridge, the flashes of shadow and light momentarily blinding them. Louis recognizes this, still feels it himself at times: that plunge in his guts when he remembers he's without his weapon, his armor, his team; alone and naked as the fleshy plug of a snail torn from its shell.

"Listen, relax, I got your back," he calls over the music, instantly feeling a fool. Todd neither answers nor looks at him. Louis is not even sure he heard.

When they reach the park, Louis pulls up to his favorite trailhead and turns off the engine, silencing the radio at last. The two men jump out and stretch, the sudden quiet making Louis's ears ring.

"Keys." Todd holds out his palm. Louis tosses them over and Todd opens the trunk. They each pull out a backpack, a sleeping bag, and a one-man tent provided by Louis, who had enough of sleeping beside the snores and secret groans of other men in the army.

"You ever been here before?" he asks, lifting his backpack onto his shoulders.

Todd shakes his head, eyes bruised by sleeplessness. "What's the goal?" He looks up from where he's bent over his pack, strapping on his sleeping bag.

"Goal?"

"I mean the fucking point, Martin. Where we going?"

"Oh. Well, I have this circuit in mind. Twelve to fifteen kliks a day. Sound good?"

"Sounds pussy-whipped. But what the hell."Todd stands and swings his own pack on as easily as if it weighs no more than a pillow. "Let's go."

Louis leads the way, Todd so close behind he is practically treading on his heels.

The trail heads directly into the woods, taking them past moss-furred rocks, pools of feather-duster ferns and birches growing like magic tricks out of boulders. The trees stretch up straight and dense, their canopy filtering the sky like a sieve, bathing the men in dappled green light. Louis inhales the spicy scents of pine and earth, and, even with his disagreeable companion breathing down his neck, feels the habitual gnarl of tension between his shoulder blades slowly begin to unfurl.

They walk for four hours that first day, Todd saying scarcely a word, although occasionally Louis hears him humming, wisps of tunes at times familiar, at times not. Louis says little himself. What can you say to a man who beats up his wife and won't even try to be companionable?

At three that afternoon, the wind drops and the forest falls into a hush so profound Louis can hear each leaf falling to the ground with a tap. Even their footsteps are silenced by the damp earth and moss of the forest floor, reminding him of walking across the Iraqi desert, the moondust carpeting the sand like powder.

They reach the rim of a cobalt blue lake, glossy as satin and ringed by trees. A breeze picks up, rumpling its surface and sending a series of little waves to lap at the shore. Louis tries to enjoy this the way he does when he comes here alone, breathing and looking and emptying his mind, but the bulky muteness of the man beside him is pressing against the back of his skull. He wonders again why he let himself in for this.

They march on, the woods thinning out in places, thickening in others, some of the trees still green, some like a fountain of golden coins, some a spray of scarlet. Todd has taken the lead, which, after a flash of annoyance, Louis decides is better. He can keep his eye on him this way, watch his wall of a back for whatever move he might make next.

They climb a steep hill, calf muscles flexing, and descend to the edge of a second lake, this one a deep indigo. Louis stops and calls out to Todd to stop, too, glancing a question at him. Todd shakes his head and sits down on the grass, crossing his arms and leaning against his pack. He shuts his eyes.

Louis peels off his clothes and dives into the water, the cold kicking the breath from him. Strong-stroked and fast, he swims out to the middle of the lake and back. No comment from Todd. No laughter. Just Louis's gasp at the first shock and the panting when he climbs out and dresses. They walk on, Louis damp, flushed, exhilarated; Todd silent.

The hours roll slowly away, the light shading into a brassy blue. Louis glimpses a pair of loons idling on the lake beside him, their bulbous heads, heavy black beaks and white collars distinct in the gilded air. "Look," he says, pointing, his voice startling after the long quiet. "Oldest bird in America. Go all the way back to dinosaurs, you know that?"

Todd says nothing. Once in a while he does stop to look, but he seems to notice only the big things: a squared-off boulder squatting in the water like a rhinoceros. a bluff as high as a fortress; a particularly thick and magisterial tree trunk, its pythonic roots humping over the ground. He is so incommunicative that Louis feels compelled to guess what is going on his head. He could be scanning every shadow for a sign of the enemy, as he was in the car. Or thinking about Beth and Flanner. Or simply counting the days and hours until he can leave this ill-fitting straitjacket called home. On Louis's returns, he always used to crave these hikes, the clean air a necessary medicine after the choking dust of the desert, the quiet an essential reprieve from the head-pummeling racket of war. The forest gave him a chance to think about his marriage and soul and faith in God and whether any of them would survive the brutality that had become part of him. But that doesn't mean it's the same for Todd.

"You all right?" Louis asks.

Todd glances at him. "Don't worry your pretty Latin head about me, Martin. It's just too fucking quiet, that's all." Yanking an iPod out of his jeans, he attaches a pair of earbuds and stuffs them into his ears.

And so it goes, not only during their first day but the second, too. When they stand at the edge of a lake, the water pink and crimping under a sunset, earplugged Todd says not a word. When they reach the top of a mountain, a view of nubby forest brushing the horizon, the air clear all the way to the sun, Todd only yawns, the veins in his forehead bulging as he nods to his private music. When they lie cocooned in their sleeping bags, the Milky Way a powdery veil over their heads, a loon wailing like a lost ghost across a nearby lake, Todd remains as silent as mud except for the tinny beat emanating from his ears.

The second night, as they sit in their usual bulging silence around a campfire, eating blackened hot dogs tucked into rolled up slices of Wonder bread, Louis asks him if he wants to go home.

Todd raises his eyebrows. "Why? Ain't you enjoying yourself?"

"Me? No, I'm fine. Thought maybe you weren't."

"Nah. This is just what the doc ordered. Music and nature. No fucking dumb chatter." He gazes at Louis a moment, his eyes a little less glassy and walled in than usual. He looks both young and as if he's never been young at all. "Good of you to keep me out of trouble like this. I wish Flan could've come. But I appreciate it."

The next morning, they awake to a fog as white as gauze, the sky and lake below blending together, as if the earth has dropped away. Louis longs to say something, but the silence of his companion has so infected him he can't.

By the time they have boiled up their campfire coffee, downed their instant oatmeal and broken camp, the sun has burned off the fog, leaving nothing but shreds of mist curling like unravelling bandages through the trees. Louis walks to the edge of a nearby bluff to look down at the lake below. The steam rising from its surface has formed a row of white columns, undulating like a troupe of ballerinas. Naema would love this, he tells himself. And such longing for her courses through him, the strength of it leaves him shaken.

"Hey, McAllister," he calls, needing to hear a human voice. "Come over here."

Todd thumps up beside him, yanking his earbuds out at last. The sun, still morning-pale, is sparking over the water now like surfacing diamonds.

"What?"

"Beautiful, huh?"

Without a word, Todd turns away, screwing his earbuds back in.

"Hey," Louis calls after him, annoyed. "What the hell are you listening to anyway?"

"Nirvana."

"This whole time?"

Todd swivels around. "Fuck, yeah. Why listen to anything else?" For a second, his face is more animated than Louis has seen it yet. "Cobain was a fucking genius. There'll never be anyone like him again. Day he died was worst day of my life."

Louis doubts this but seizes the opening anyway. "You were what, fourteen when that happened?"

"Thirteen. Heard it on my mom's TV. Sat and played his music all that day and night, and I don't mind telling you, I bawled like a baby. Built a shrine to him, everything. Fucking Courtney."

"It wasn't Courtney's fault. It was his stomach."

"Tell that to the Man on Judgment Day. Bitch is a notorious ball-buster."

"You got a favorite song?" Louis asks, hoping to deflect Todd from this train of thought.

Todd looks at him with scorn. "That's the question of a true amateur." Then he shrugs. "I like the raw stuff best. 'Territorial Pissing.' If you weren't such a tree hugger, Martin, I'd have you head-banging to it all over this pussy forest." And plugging his earbuds back in, he lopes off down the path.

Later that day, they reach the shore of a lake considerably east of where they started. The sun is licking the horizon by now, suffusing the air with a burnished haze, so they stop at the lake's edge to watch. The water is so still it reflects the trees in a perfect reverse image, filling the lake with umber and vermilion, fire and rust. A glistering path of sunlight stretches all the way across its surface and Louis feels a childlike entrancement at the sight. Again, he longs to show this to Naema. And that is the moment Todd finally speaks.

"Makes you want to walk on water, don't it? Right along that shiny path all the way to the end of this fucked-up world."

By the time they return to Louis's house after four days of wordless hiking, thigh muscles like steel, body odor like bear breath, it is the night before Todd has to report back to base. He springs out of the car, more buoyant than he has been all week, waits for Louis to unlock his front door, and accepts his offer to shower first. Then he washes his laundry, folds his gear, packs his bags, shaves his head and face, and comes downstairs in a crisp olive undershirt and clean camo pants, every inch a marine again.

Louis nods at him. "You look better. Much better. Guess all that free North American air did the trick, huh?" No answer. "It's your last night, so you choose where to eat. We could head into Albany if you like." He is not going to ask Todd if he wants to say good-bye to Beth and Flanner. That is not something he is going to push either way.

"Not hungry. You go out if you want. I'm gonna watch TV. Sleep. Get myself psyched."

"You sure?" Every time Louis was due back at war, whether after a furlough or to redeploy, he and Melody would splurge like newlyweds. A fancy dinner, all the whiskey they could drink, lovemaking long into the night. Melody tried her best to make it good for him. While she could.

But Todd only opens Louis's refrigerator and pulls out a can of beer. "This is all the dinner I need." Heading into the living room, he switches on the television. Loud.

With a powerful lift of relief, Louis leaves him and drives to Naema's, so eager to bask in her presence again he can hardly refrain from pushing the speedometer over ninety. But as soon as she opens the door, she steps outside, pulls it closed behind her, and says, "Shh. I do not want Tariq to hear us." And she tells him about Flanner.

Louis looks at her, shaken. "Damn, I should've told Beth not to go to you! I should've made sure—"

"Louis, do not be foolish. It is not your fault." She lays her hand on his arm, sending a tingle through his body. "Say nothing to Tariq, please. He does not wish to talk about it."

"Is he all right?"

"Come see for yourself."

When Louis returns at ten that night, aching from the sight of Tariq lying in bed, forehead stitched and discolored with bruises, gaze turned inward, he finds every dish in the kitchen washed and put away, every magazine in the living room stacked, every towel and sheet Todd used laundered and perfectly folded. Even the floors are mopped. Suddenly afraid Todd has run back to Beth after all, Louis tiptoes upstairs and cracks open the guest room door. But there he is, breathing the heavy sighs of the deeply asleep. He looks peaceful. He looks happy.

Part Three

OCTOBER

20

BOX

Beth lights a cigarette and props herself against the outside wall of DanceHi, shuddering under the new cold while three rumpled pigeons forage through the garbage at her feet. DanceHi is placed between a pizza joint and a Subway, and their debris tends to overflow all over the street: Paper cups and ketchup-stained napkins. Half-chewed crusts. Wads of foil. Still, she prefers to take her break out here with the garbage and other smokers than inside over stale gossip and doughnuts. She thought she had conquered the smoking habit long ago, but since Todd's last visit home she has needed nicotine the way she needs air.

"You got any plans tonight?" asks Roz, one of her coworkers, a giraffelike young woman who runs the yoga classes offered in the back of the store. "'Cause if you don't, a bunch of us are going to this cool bar I know over on Delaware."

Pinching her lips around her cigarette, Beth gathers her hair into a topknot and fastens it with the rubber band she keeps around her wrist. Enough time has passed to allow her bruises to fade; the wounds that hurt are all invisible. "Which bar?" she asks without interest, pulling up the collar of her denim jacket against the wind. Beth is at least twelve years older than the other women at DanceHi, and although two of them are mothers, she often feels as if she is working with high school kids.

Roz squints at her a little shyly, pushing back her own hair, a heap of black corkscrew curls that reminds Beth of Cher in *Moonstruck*. "The Slinger. But don't worry if you've got something better to do."

Beth takes a prolonged drag. What does Roz imagine her life is like? A long string of parties and men lining up to take her out on dates? Once she leaves work, it will only be to return home with Flanner, lock the doors and windows, and sit there jumping at every sound. Even after Louis shanghaied Todd to the Adirondacks and she changed all the locks, and even though Louis kept texting to say he had Todd under control, she could never shake the certainty he would return to beg and cry and blame his flashbacks, only to hurt her again. During all five remaining days of his furlough, she spent every night lying rigid in bed, listening for the creak or rattle that could be his footstep. And now, these two weeks later, standing outside DanceHi on a frigid Albany sidewalk, knowing he is back in the badlands of Afghanistan, she still feels as vulnerable as if he were waiting around the corner.

"No, I don't have any plans. I need to pick up Flanner from football practice at seven, so I can't stay long. But I'd love to come."

When she and Roz reach The Slinger that night, it turns out to resemble a low-life cowboy saloon more than anything Beth would call "cool," complete with a covered porch, swing doors, and windows festooned with neon outlines of naked women, legs spread, nipples blinking. Inside, a toadlike fellow with a face almost as wide as his shoulders is tending bar. Several obvious drunks are clustered loudly around the jukebox, a gang of

Box   201

workmen is clogging up most of the room in their telltale over-
alls, and there is hardly a woman in sight.

"You come here a lot, did you say?" she asks Roz as they
elbow their way through the men.

"Oh, only once in a while."

They find their three workmates waiting for them in a battered wooden booth and squeeze in beside them, Beth ending
up on the outside edge with her back to the door. "What's your
poison?" Roz asks after they've poked and joked themselves
into place.

Beth already wants to leave. She has never felt at home with
these women. Different generation, different lingo, different
problems. She feels old.

"They make amazing martinis in this place," Roz says. She
calls over the waitress, a woman of about fifty who is the height
of an eight-year-old, with an underdeveloped body and a wrin-
kled, mannish face. Her name tag says, HI! I'M GRETEL, but her
dour expression strikes Beth as closer to that of the witch. Beth
wonders where on earth this bar finds its staff.

Roz orders the drinks, which turn out to be served in globular
glasses the size of heads. "Holy shit!" the women exclaim, "Hey,
to Friday frigging night, right?" Each has to use two hands to
heft her glass to her mouth.

Beth can tell they are attracting attention from the men in
the bar, which isn't surprising. DanceHi hires only the fit and
pretty, and as it not only sells exercise clothes but offers Beth's
old people's dance classes and Roz's young people's yoga, the
boss insists the women dress accordingly, so they make quite a
sight in all their black spandex. She runs her eyes over her companions: Roz with her mass of curls, lips painted the same glaring red as Todd's dead Camaro. Terri, svelte and brown, eyes as
big as a doe's. Lynnette and Jen blond, pink, and blow-dried. But

their conversation is already turning her catatonic. Boyfriends, TV shows, exercise routines. And dullest of all, as Beth is lucky enough not to need one, diets.

Drinking down her martini faster than she means to, she wonders what she would rather talk about. Certainly not Todd. Not the hurricane or war or politics, either, all of which have come to feel like the same thing. But she does wish she could talk about Flanner. How moody he has been lately, how incommunicative and sullen.

Beth's shame over Flanner's attack on Tariq has so paralyzed her she has never been able to call Naema to ask if he is all right. She hasn't found a way to bring it up with Flanner, either, tell him how wrong he was or punish him. She can't even figure out what to say to him about Todd, or how to cheer him up or help him feel safe, feeling anything but cheerful or safe herself. She tried going back to the Family Readiness sites for advice, reading articles with titles such as "A Parent's Guide to the Military Child During Deployment." But the platitudes and obviousology only made her feel conned. And when another site recommended that she comfort her own military child with a Hug-A-Hero doll, she almost threw her laptop out the window.

"Did I tell you my son nearly got attacked by a wolf?" she blurts into the conversation, needing to defend Flanner now, make him seem less the bully she is afraid he has become and more the victim. The others stop talking and look at her.

"What?" Roz says.

"There's a lunatic woman who keeps wolves in the woods behind my house and one of them tried to attack my kid."

"She keeps *wolves*?" says Terri, who has a little boy of her own. "He must've been scared shitless."

"He was. I don't think he's been the same since. It really shook him up."

Box   203

"I bet. Did you call the cops?"

"I did, yeah." Beth polishes off her tub of a drink.

"Another, anyone?" Roz asks so quickly that Beth suspects she doesn't believe a word she just said.

"Why not?" someone replies, and Beth feels a skip of mood at the prospect.

Roz waves Hi! I'm Gretel down and orders a second round and a bowl of chips, while two furred and tub-bellied men amble over. Soon they are squeezed up on the other side of the booth, facing Beth. "Hey, what'd you do with Hansel, lost him in the woods?" one of them says to the poor waitress when she brings the drinks, guffawing and plunging his fingers into the chip bowl. She looks at him stonily and clumps away.

Beth buries her face in her fishbowl of a martini and stops listening, mesmerized instead by the man's fingers plunging again and again into the chips. Short and thick, patches of hair beneath the knuckles, nails grimy and ragged—the fingers of a mechanic. She glances at her own hands, slender and clean, their nails shaped into perfect almonds and freshly polished hot pink. Todd used to say he thought her hands were "beauteous" in the days when he still said such things.

"Hey, Beth?" Roz says after a stretch, the first time anyone has addressed her for at least ten minutes. Beth looks up. "Has your husband gone back to Afghanistan yet?" Roz looks at the men importantly. "Her husband's a marine. War hero. He's got all kind of medals. So Beth here, she has to be real strong. Run the home, work, raise her kid all alone while he's away. I admire her, truly do. You don't mind me bringing that up, do you, Beth?"

Beth feels the heat rush to her cheeks. "No, it's all right." She drops her eyes again to the chip bowl. "I did have to learn to be strong, it's true. Had to learn how to wait, too." She falls silent. Why is she even saying this? She is grateful to Roz for not mentioning all the sick days she took while the bruises faded; the telltale sunglasses when she returned. But she doesn't want to go into all the things she's had to do for Todd. Ever.

Her phone chimes in her purse at that moment, a chirpy little jingle she picked this morning to lift her spirits that is already irritating as hell. She fishes among the tangle of Kleenexes, tampons, comb, wallet, lipstick, and compact to pull it out.

Three missed calls. All from Flanner.

"Crap!" She slaps it to her ear. "Flanner! I forgot!"

"Mo-om! I been waiting and waiting and calling and calling. All the other kids went home hours ago and it's dark and cold and I'm hungry!"

"Oh Flan, I'm sorry. I got—delayed and I didn't hear the phone, it's so noisy where I am. I hope you're not alone?"

"No. Coach is waiting with me, but he's fucking mad about it."

"Don't say that word. Can't he just drive you home?"

"He says it's not allowed if you aren't there. When can you get here? It's been hours and hours!"

Beth looks at her watch. "It's been one hour, honey. But I'm sorry. I'm coming right now. Tell Coach I'll be right there. Okay?"

"Mom, you suck." Flanner hangs up.

"I've got to go," Beth says, jumping to her feet and dropping both her phone and her purse to the floor, the martinis hitting hard. She sways and grabs the back of the booth. "Whoa."

"You gonna be all right to drive?" asks one of the men, rising.

She narrows her eyes at him. "I'll just get a quick coffee at the bar." Picking up her bag and phone, she leaves.

Box   205

Flanner is waiting for her by the school gates, looking small and miserable in the dark, a grumpy coach by his side. Beth pulls up to the curb and rolls down her window, apologizing and hoping neither her breath nor her enunciation will give her away. The coach grunts and frowns and gets into his own car while Flanner climbs into the back.

"I'm sorry, honey," she says again. "We'll order in some pizza for a special treat, okay?"

"I'm not hungry," he mutters.

"Of course you are. How was practice?"

"Fuck practice," he replies, and refuses to say another word.

The next morning, Beth sits alone in the kitchen, pressing a cup of hot coffee to her chest and letting its steam mist her face, having already downed three Advil and a pint of orange juice in an attempt to scour her head of the martinis. She closes her eyes, the lids like flaps of sand. The cartoon voices from Flanner's TV are needling into her temples like dentists' drills. At least she managed to drive home without either an accident or a police encounter—unusually lucky, given the predilection of local cops for hanging around places like The Slinger to pick up people like her. Still. Weaving along like that, Flanner yelping in the back, cursing . . . She opens her eyes, wincing against the light, and shifts uncomfortably in her chair. *What the hell is the matter with me?*

Pulling her blue satin bathrobe tighter around her with a shiver, she rubs her feet together, so cold and sandpapery they don't seem to belong to her at all, and stares into the swirl of her coffee, trying not to let the prospect of the Saturday ahead sink her into an even darker mood. As much as she dislikes the tedium of her workweek at DanceHi, the weekends are worse. Nobody to call, nobody to see. How did this happen? A short while ago she had truckloads of friends, not only from her Huntsville childhood but from her queen bee days in high school, when every boy in town was panting after her. Beth of the dancer's body and swingdangle hair, Beth of the blue-jay eyes, Beth of the swish and sway. . . . She smiles wistfully. She had more recent friends, too: military wives, workmates from her old job as a hostess at a fancy restaurant in Albany, mothers from Flanner's school. But over the past year or so, they all seem to have melted away. Quite a few, she knows, dropped her because they couldn't stand Todd, for which she can hardly blame them. Naema, whom she has always liked, she lost thanks to Flanner, now forever banned from Tariq's company. But the others? Is it just that she has been so overwhelmed she's neglected them? Or is it—and this thought sends a corkscrew of misery through her—that Todd has turned her into a person nobody wants to be around anymore? Whatever the reason, she seems to be reduced to no friends at all now, aside from Louis and those girls from work, who, she might as well face it, are so brainless she cannot abide them for longer than it takes to gulp a cocktail. Her life has become as boxed in as a closet. Flanner scowling and withdrawn. Nothing to look forward to but TV and her wine. And lurking beneath it all like an underground oil spill, the knowledge that one day Todd will be done with war and come home for good.

She takes a sip of coffee, burning her tongue, and raises her head to look over her kitchen: its buttery surfaces, bee-splattered curtains, ornately framed cake recipes. *I have to get out of here. Out of this house and out of this town.* But to go where? Not to her parents, sunning it up in their retirement condo in Miami—God forbid. Not to her brother, Billy, either, who is busy cultivating

Box   207

so-called medical marijuana in Sonoma County and hasn't spoken to her for years. So where?

Hearing a car pull up outside, she carries her coffee to the window, assuming it's Louis, who has been checking in on her now and then ever since he rescued her from Todd. Even his company, taciturn as it is, would be welcome right now, although she would prefer that he not see her like this: hair unkempt, yesterday's eyeliner smudged down her cheeks, breath martini-bad and mood even worse.

But it isn't Louis. Rather, an unfamiliar polished black car is parked by the remains of the maple tree. She watches as both front doors swing open and two men climb out, bodies as stiff as surfboards, bald faces blank. They are wearing the dress uniform of the Marine Corps, which she hasn't seen since she attended Todd's induction ceremony fifteen years ago. Perfect red stripes down the outsides of their pressed blue trousers. Immaculate gold buttons. Gleaming white belts tight and straight. Equally white caps precisely aligned atop their shaved heads, their glossy black brims like little shelves.

She watches the men pull down their jackets until they are smooth and crisp. She watches them settle their shoulders and lift their chins. And she watches them advance, side by side, in a slow and even march across the yard, up the steps of her porch, and to the threshold of her sunny front door.

21

FIRE

Rin is sunk deep into one of the dog-haired armchairs in her living room, looking through her favorite wildlife veterinarian book for reasons why a wolf might lose its appetite. Silver has been eating less and less this past week, and instead of bounding up eager-eyed when Rin calls, she only slouches over now, head hanging, tail down. Rin wonders if the problem is her teeth. Perhaps she has started chewing the chain link again, as she did when she was younger, or maybe her gums are decaying—after all, Silver is nine years old, a senior citizen in the lupine world. But there are other possibilities, too. She could be diseased. Or she could have absorbed the visceral stink of Rin's dread.

Flaherty called again last week. Just as Rin was beginning to hope he had forgotten all about her—that he had better things to do with his law-enforcing time than bother some harmless woman in the woods about her animals—the phone rang and there he was, pointing out that his deadline had long since passed and he hadn't noticed anything resembling either a license application or proof she has huskies coming in from her direction. She did her best to summon all her indignation and hard-earned veteran arrogance again, but he was clearly unimpressed. It made her want to rip out the phone and throw it at the bastard's meddlesome head.

After he was done lecturing her, she had to call Betty and let the dog lick her for a long time. Tongue wet and warm, brown

eyes forlorn. "Betty," she said, "this doesn't look good. Help."
Betty blinked up at her. Rubbed her head against Rin's knee.

Now Rin puts down the book, goes out to the barn to pick up
her medical kit, and heads back to the fence. For the first time
in years, she feels the way she felt so often in the army, dragging
herself through the days with a sense of foreboding so tangible
it feels like a cage tightening over her ribs.

At the wolf pen, she calls Silver, who limps over, coat matted,
legs trembling. Her normally bright eyes are dim and so mourn-
ful they seem to be saying *I'm done for. Give up.*

Rin steps inside the pen, endures Gray's inspection, and
coaxes Silver to sit on her haunches and open her mouth—she
has trained her to do this much, at least. Gray hovers nearby,
keeping an eye on them both.

It is always something of a shock to look in a wolf's mouth.
Canines as long as a thumb. Incisors serrated like knives. Not to
mention breath strong enough to knock out your sinuses. Rin
lifts Silver's lips. Her gums are indeed inflamed: red where they
should be black, ragged where they should be smooth. Bleeding
where there shouldn't be blood.

"Hi, Mrs. Drummond." Tariq has popped out of nowhere in
his usual gopherish way. "Is Juney home?"

"Shh. Don't talk." Rin has her hand in a wolf's mouth. Not the
time to deal with a half-pint Hajji and all he might trigger in her.

He falls silent. And while he stands there, quiet as grass, Rin
feels his presence soothe Silver, just as Juney's does. Silver was
tense and shivering a moment ago, probably afraid Rin would
hurt her, but under his gaze she lets out a little whimpery-whine,
exactly the sound she used to make as a pup, and releases her
muscles. Gray ambles over to the fence to let Tariq scratch him.

Rin finishes the exam, rubs some ointment onto Silver's
gums, whispers, "Good girl," and wipes the saliva off on her

pants. Keeping an eye on Gray, she slides through the double door of the fence and locks it behind her.

"She's sick, isn't she?" Tariq says after Gray has trotted off to sniff Silver. "Do you think she's got worms? She looks so skinny."

"What do you know about worms?"

"I read about them in a book."

"My wolves don't get worms. It does look like she has gum disease, though. If she were human, she'd be fitted with dentures. I need to give her a softer diet."

"I've been reading a lot about wolves. I read that famous book *White Fang*."

Rin looks down at him. His earnest little face. "What did you think?"

"I think it's stupid! He makes it sound like wolves are all savage and cruel."

"They are. That why I like 'em."

"They are not! They are loyal and wise and beautiful!"

Rin raises an eyebrow at that. "Why are you reading so much about wolves?" She packs up the medical kit and moves toward the house, trying not to let Tariq see her anxiety. Betty moves up beside her leg. Gives her knee another lick.

Tariq hurries to catch up. "I'm doing a school project on them."

Rin looks at him sharply. "What kind of project?" Last thing she needs is Tariq blabbing to his flibbertigibbet teachers about her wolves—that would really bring the cops here in a hurry.

"It's for biology. We're doing animal behavior. Don't worry, Mrs. Drummond. I won't say anything about your wolves. Or you or Juney, either. I know you like to be left alone."

Rin reaches out and pats his back, although she is not normally given to touching any humans aside from Juney. "Someday I'll teach you how to doctor wolves. Would you like that?"

"Yes please!" He looks up her, his face suffused with pleasure.

"Are you feeling any better?" she asks then. "I see your stitches are out at last."

He drops his eyes. "Yeah."

"How did it happen?"

"Just some kid."

"Was it bad?"

"Doesn't matter. I'm fine now."

Rin figures Tariq must get pulled into quite a few fights. He has to be a target with his one leg and his name. He has Outsider stamped all over him, just like Juney. He is quieter than he used to be, though—has been ever since he showed up with that ugly gash across the front of his scalp, bruises like a black bandanna over his brow. There is a new solemnity about him, too, an aura of melancholy he didn't have before. Juney senses it, as well. On the occasions he sits in long hushes, drawn into himself, she tries to offer comfort, either with words or by running her hand over his face, as if searching for a smile. It touches Rin that her daughter so wants the people she loves to be happy.

Jay would have liked this friendship, perhaps more than she does. She can just see him in her living room, a benign ghost, maybe sprawled in an armchair, maybe lounging against a windowsill, smiling at the children while they sit chatting on the floor. She wonders if he would find their friendship as ironic as she does. Their daughter, the only kid in town born of two OIF parents, and her best buddy is Iraqi. God's joke? Or perhaps she should say Allah's.

"I bet you can stand up for yourself though, huh?" she says to Tariq now. She is trying to be kind, but he doesn't answer, so she leaves the subject alone. She does ask something else, though, something she has been wondering about for a while, even though most of her doesn't want to know.

"Juney tells me your dad was a soldier. That true?" She hopes he's not going to say his father was one of Saddam's goons.

"Yes," he replies easily. "He worked for the U.S. Army. He was an interpreter."

Rin stops and looks at him. The son of a terp! That changes everything. *If,* that is, his dad was one of the terps the army could trust and not a two-timing slimebag of a spy.

"And your mom? What's she do?"

"She's a pediatrician. She used to work at the VA clinic till the storm wrecked it." And then he runs off because the dogs have started up the welcoming barks that mean Juney is home.

Rin stares after him, her veins filling with sand.

❈

Once Tariq has helped Juney take off her backpack in the kitchen and the two of them have finished the snack of apples and milk Rin gives them without a word, they snuggle beside each other on the woolly brown rug in the living room to start their homework. The walls of the room are paneled in dark, rough-hewn wood, as is the ceiling, so it always reminds Tariq of the forts he and Flanner used to build out of branches and bark in the woods; cozy triangular spaces filled with green light and the musky scents of earth and birch. He loved those forts, just as he loves this room, so different from the minimal decor of his mother's house. The jury-rigged lamps beaming from unexpected corners. The blankets and sweaters dangling fuzzily from hooks. The snoring dogs, buzzing cats, hair-matted armchairs, and mutt-brown couch. The books lining the shelves on either side of the fieldstone fireplace, promising long evenings of stories and dreams. The room feels like the safest, most settled place he has ever been; a place of history and family, of everything he and his mother have lost.

"What've you got for homework?" Juney asks, opening a book and running her fingers across it. "Mine's braille practice."

"Math." He watches her hands a moment, the nimble way her fingertips spider over the page. "Can I try reading that?"

"You mean my book?"

"Yes. Show me how." He leans forward and puts his right hand in hers.

"Okay. But make your hand floppy." She shakes his wrist. "It won't work if you're stiff like that. Good. Now here." Taking his forefinger, she feels the page with her other hand, then guides his finger to a spot. "Feel that?"

He concentrates. "That's one dot, right?"

"Yes. That's an *a*." She moves his finger over. "How many is this one?"

He closes his eyes. "Three?"

"Right. And what shape are they making?"

"Uh." His finger seems big and unwieldy now, as clumsy as the elbow he tried to see out of. "A triangle?"

"Don't press so hard. Try again."

He circles his finger slightly. "Oh, I get it. They're the shape of an *l*."

"Good! You just read the letter *h*."

"H? Why isn't it *l*?"

"Just isn't." She lifts her head, listening. "It's raining."

Tariq listens, too, but he can't hear it yet. "I hope it stops or I'm going to get soaked walking home."

Juney is still listening, although not to the rain anymore. "You sound sad again," she says after a time. "Are you?"

Withdrawing his hand, he looks down at the book on his lap, picking at its binding. He is sad, but he doesn't want to talk about it, even to Juney. He doesn't want to give shape to his fear that Flanner will tell people about the wolves, to the violent way

Flanner smashed him with that stick and yanked off his prosthetic leg, or to how that leg hasn't felt the same since. It has never
bothered him before and he's had it for four years, but it drags on
him now; a hard, unfleshed thing clinging to his body. Instead of
feeling like a mere extension of himself the way it used to, like a
glove on a hand or a sock on a foot, it feels like a parasite, a weight
that persists in reminding him that he is neither whole nor like
other people . . . that, like Juney, he is damaged.

There is more he cannot speak aloud, too. The way, when
Flanner pulled off his leg and left him helpless on the ground,
it spun him back to the years he had spent on crutches, always
precarious, vulnerable to being kicked over, knocked down; to
being made to look like a scrabbling, mutilated bug. The day
his leg was fitted when he was six years old and new to America, he stood up and simply ran. The very first time. He ran up
and down the clinic, ran and ran, laughing and laughing. It
was as if he had sprouted wings—as if he were flying just like
the wolves when they jumped for the apples. It was the most
wonderful day of his life.

Flanner took that wonderful day away. And now, at school,
he is trying to make everything even worse by turning the other
boys against Tariq, calling him an enemy and a traitor, only in
much uglier words. And Tariq can't even hate him for it because
Flanner's dad just died.

"I don't like fifth grade," is all Tariq says to Juney. "Everybody's turned mean."

She rocks back and forth. "Yes, Mommy told me that happens. That's why she wants to put me in a special school for the
blind next year. But I don't want to be in a special school. It'll
make people think I'm different."

Tariq unfastens his newly onerous prosthesis and puts it

aside, almost angry now. "But you are different. Me, too. And it sucks."

She stops rocking. "I don't think so." Her voice is grave.

But Tariq does. How many times, even before Flanner attacked him, has he wished he were like the other boys at school: American, whole-bodied, tough? How many times has he wanted to tell his mother to stop talking about war and death and staying strong, about being a refugee and being Iraqi and being Muslim and being and being and being ... How many times has he squeezed his eyes tight and hoped that when he opened them, he would find himself like everyone else?

Rin strides into the room just then, looking upset. She walks about, straightening a pile of dusty books here, tucking away a bunch of cat toys there, not really paying attention to what she is doing. She is just fiddling, Tariq can tell, and she keeps giving him the strangest looks.

She comes and stands over them.

"Mommy," Juney says, her voice a warning, "we're doing our homework."

"You two warm enough? Want me to light a fire?" Rin's voice sounds strained. "There's a chill in the air tonight."

"Ooh, yes! Our first fire of fall!" Juney loves fires, their caramel scent, their pops and fizzes, the warm pulses of heat they send along her limbs. But Tariq feels otherwise. Fires make him uneasy, stir something sinister at the periphery of his memory. He and his mother never light one at home.

Rin bustles about, snapping twigs and crumpling newspaper into balls. "Noisy!" Juney cries, clapping her hands over her ears. Certain sounds are unbearable to her—crackling paper like this, the squeak of a sponge in a glass—whereas other, more obviously disturbing sounds, such as the shrieking of brakes or wailing of sirens, hardly bother her at all.

"Sorry, bean, I'll be done in a minute." Rin lays the kindling, then the logs: two fat ones across, two slim ones upright, a little breathing space in between. She strikes a match and Tariq flinches. But when the logs catch, flaring neon orange, turquoise, and tangerine, he gazes into the fire, so mesmerized by the pictures forming in the flames he forgets his fears. A tiny soldier runs up a hill, bursts into sparks and flies away. A tree grows and spreads, then splits into an explosion of yellow and red. A woman holds up a baby, twists, convulses, and collapses into a glowing eye. . . .

"Tell me what it looks like." Juney edges over to him. "Tell me what you see."

He leans closer to her. "It looks like a little world in a sun." He stares intently into the fire, searching for images that aren't as bleak as the ones he saw just now. "There are trees and houses and soldiers and families. People are born and they dance and they disappear. I see a deer. And a lion and . . . a tiny elephant." He glances at Juney. "I see a wolf dancing with a girl just like you." She smiles. "Now they're twirling and turning and spinning and flying into tiny sparkly dots, floating up and up and up. . . . Gone."

She raises her face, the flames reflecting on her pale throat and the pink tip of her chin. "The fire feels white." She is swaying again now, and Tariq sways with her. "The fire feels white like the sun feels green." And then she adds, "It feels a little scary, too."

They sway gently together, the heat of the flames and smoke pulling them each into a heady, vertiginous dream.

❁

Rin watches the children for a long time, her tongue lying like a stone in her mouth. The pair of them are rocking in front of the fire as if they've been bewitched, Tariq with his prosthesis cast aside and the leg of his pants rolled up, Juney with a dreamy smile on her lips. Neither with the faintest idea of how dangerous Rin is.

"Tariq?" she finally makes herself say. "It's getting late and it's raining." She swallows, her mouth as sticky as paste. "Your mother, is she . . ." She swallows again. "She must be worried about you."

He gazes up at her with no comprehension whatsoever, still swaying along with Juney. The kids are downright stoned.

"Won't your mom be worried that you're out this late?" Rin repeats.

"My mom?" he says as if he's never heard the word. "Oh. What time is it?"

"Nearly seven."

That wakes him up. "*Seven*? Whoa. Yeah, I better go." He reaches for his leg, which is lying beside him in its sock and sneaker, and pulls it on, rolling his pants over it. He has taken to leaving that leg lying around a lot these days, along with the silicone lining he wears under it, which looks like a stocking made of discarded skin. Rin can't get used to it. It gives her a shock every time, stumbling across a dismembered limb and a puddle of skin in the middle of her living room floor.

She walks to the window, raises the shade and peers out, trying to collect herself. Interesting phrase that, *collect herself*. Little pieces of her lying about like dropped thumbtacks.

It's not raining; it's pouring.

"Listen, sweetheart . . ." (Did she just call him sweetheart? How mealy-mouthed is the voice of guilt.) "You can't walk home in this." She turns back to him and her spaced-out daughter, who is still rocking and smiling at the fire. "Can someone come pick you up? Your uncle, perhaps?"

"Oh no, Mrs. Drummond, I can't bother Louis now. His friend just got killed in a war."

Rin is knocked silent by that.

"I'll call my mom to come get me." And before she knows what's happening, he pulls a cell phone out of his pocket.

"Wait, don't." She can't have that woman here. Seeing her, recognizing her. "I'll drive you."

Juney returns to earth at that. "You'll drive?" Her mother never drives into town after dark. Never.

Rin clears the paste from her throat. "Yes."

Juney stands up. "Then I'm coming, too."

"Fine." Rin will need her, as Juney knows. Driving at night is bad enough, as that's when the hallucinations hit thick and fast, but driving to this particular house on top of it . . .

"Come on," Rin says, trying not to sound as stun-gunned as she feels. "Pack up your homework. Let's go."

Venturing out of her compound this late calls for her invisible wolves again, along with Betty in the backseat. "Just don't pet her," Rin reminds Tariq as he gets in beside the dog. "She isn't made for petting."

Juney wants to sit back there with them, of course, but knowing her mother needs her, she stays up front, her hand on Rin's knee. Still, by the time Rin has bounced her chunky old Buick over all the potholes to the end of her driveway, her heart is already lurching. Sure enough, hard as she strives against it, up it begins again. That little girl sitting on top of her PRIVATE KEEP OUT I MEAN IT sign, blood running from her eyes. Rin starts and looks away, sweat springing out of her every pore, drenching her lower back. . . . *Jay, where are you?*

Betty whimpers. The invisible wolves prick their ears. Juney strokes her knee, the acrid smell of her mother's alarm filling the car. "It's okay, Mommy, it's okay."

Rin turns right to head down the hill to Huntsville. A donkey carcass is lying beside the road, its body bloated. She scans for trip wires, shakes herself, drives on. Something white looms up out of the rain and she swerves, swearing.

Betty barks. A short, sharp bark. *Wake up, Drummond! Get back to reality.*

"Mommy?"

"Sorry, sorry. Hey, talk, will you? Just talk."

"Do you know where I live, Mrs. Drummond?" Tariq asks, leaning forward to poke his head between the front seats.

"Put your seat belt on. No, I don't."

"We're at Two Ninety-Five Softpatch Road. It's the green house on the corner of Babcock, the one with a wrecked-up roof."

"Storm damage?" Rin's voice sounds as though somebody's strangling her.

"Yes. Louis fixed most of it, but it still looks pretty crumpled."

Then she has to ask. "And your mom? Didn't you say she worked in the VA clinic? The one the hurricane destroyed? Is she . . . is she all right?" Wincing, wincing, her innards tangling like fighting snakes. Knuckles white on the steering wheel.

"Yes, she's fine. She wasn't for a long time, though."

Why, of all the doctors in the area, did his mother have to be this one? "So what—" *Jay, are you here yet? Can you help me out?* "What happened to her, exactly?"

"She nearly drowned. She was in the hospital for ages and ages." He turns quiet a moment. "She was the only one that happened to."

Rin's skull is shrinking. "Sorry to hear that."

"Mommy? You don't sound so good. You want to pull over a moment? The car feels kind of swingy."

It's true. Rin is weaving all over the place like a drunk. All she needs is one of the town's busybody cops—who knows, it might even be Flaherty—to pull her over and give her a blow test. She'd like to see him try. Foot in the fucking air, heel to toe—she'd walk a straighter line than any state trooper around here could. She would blow zeros all the way home, too, embarrass the hell out of him. She doesn't drink anymore, she'd tell him. Hasn't touched a drop since pregnancy wrung the need for booze out of her, along with her craving for tobacco. *I'm cleaner than you will ever be,* she'd say.

On the other hand, she does have some mighty precious cargo in here and the road is dangerously wet.

"No, it's okay," she says, slowing down. She leans forward to see better through the rain-splatted windshield, trying to keep the car straight and on the right side of the road, telling herself to ignore all visions of bloated dogs and donkeys, girls, ghosts, and snipers; of cops shooting her wolves. The roads in these parts hardly deserve the dignity of being called roads, she might add. They are more like tracks that happen to have a few patches of asphalt spilled on them here and there, flanked by dark channels of gravel and mud and bordered on either side by woods. Black trees rearing up without so much as a single streetlamp in sight. Thank the Lord, Allah, Krishna, Buddha, and Santa Claus, too, that the Iraq War wasn't fought in woods like these.

Betty is purring now, if dogs can be said to purr. She has a way of making a low hum in her throat when she senses Rin needs grounding. It's not a growl because there is nothing aggressive about it. If she were that librarian Rin imagined her to be, in glasses and a gray bun, she would be telling Rin to pull her skittering mind together and get this over with.

Juney is humming now, harmonizing with the dog. Rin wonders what Tariq thinks of her singing companions, a pudding brown mutt and a girl. The noise is pretty awful, but it is sweet, too, because they are doing it to anchor her. Juney starts up on her lyrics next, not self-conscious at all about the nonfamily member in the car. Rin has given Juney so little exposure to guests she has no idea that certain behaviors are not for outsiders, which makes Rin wonder if Juney sings like this at school and what the kids do about it.

"Mommy is driving Tariq home, Betty is singing, singing," she chants in that off-key way of hers.

"Mommy is driving,
Betty is singing,
Tariq is happy,
Mommy is fine.
La di la di la."

Rin is being nursemaided by two kids and a dog and she's still a basketcase. *Don't let that doctor see me and remember. Don't.*

"Turn right here, Mrs. Drummond," Tariq says above the singing, and Rin doesn't hear any laughter in his voice. She can only guess what he's thinking inside that old-before-his-time head of his, though.

"I'll just drop you off, so we can get back home for dinner," she tells him.

Juney stops singing. "Mommy, that's rude! Anyhow, I want to meet Tariq's mom. She's a hero, like you and Daddy."

Oh god of war, let me weep.

"Yeah, I want my mom to meet you, too," Tariq chimes in.

The girl with the bloodied eyes rises in Rin's mind again, the one she shot like a rat in Sadr City. The girl opens her mouth, teeth knocked out, tongue torn and bleeding. The girl is laughing.

22

THRESHOLD

Naema pulls up the blinds covering her front window and peers into the black wall of rain beyond, wondering why Tariq is so late. She assumes he is visiting Juney, but cannot think of him walking home alone at this hour and in this weather without a curl of fear wrapping her heart, so hurries across the room to fetch her phone. She no longer needs to draw in long, crackling breaths as she moves, but she can still feel a bronchial resistance holding her back like a leash.

The rain is driving harder now, battering urgently at her windows, the sound awakening the memories that are always hovering like an invading army in the corners of her mind. With a shiver, she pulls the phone from her purse just as a beam of light sweeps over the room. Peering out again, she sees Tariq running toward the house, head ducked against the downpour. She opens the door, clutching her hand to her chest in relief.

"Make some tea, please, Mama. We've got guests." He steps inside, shaking the water from his hair like a dog, and kicks the shoe off his good leg, leaving the other on.

"Why are you so late?" she asks in Arabic. "Take off your other shoe, please."

"Sorry. It's because of the rain." Then he says in English, "This is my friend Juney. And this is her mom, Mrs. Drummond." A woman appears out of the dark, holding a small girl by the hand, both of them bareheaded under the deluge and illuminated only by the yellow porch light over the door. They look familiar, although Naema cannot think why.

"Oh, good evening," she says, speaking English herself now, and opens the door wider to let them through. "I am so happy to meet you at last. Please, come out of the rain."

No response. The woman only stands there, a bulky shape in the doorway, the child beside her flickering like a candle.

"Hurry, Mommy. I'm getting wet." The child tugs at her hand.

"Yes, please. Do come in where it is dry," Naema says.

Juney yanks again at her mother's hand, but Rin's feet are locked to the ground. The rain hurtles down on their heads.

Realizing his friends need help, Tariq takes Juney's other arm and pulls. "Come on."

"Ow!" she yelps with a laugh. "I'm snapping in two!"

Rin tells herself to unfreeze and take a step. *Just one. Now another.* And so, shuffle by shuffle, she allows her daughter to wrench her over the threshold of an Iraqi home, the first such home she has entered since the war and the first time ever without a weapon, her Kevlar, and a team of fully armed U.S. soldiers at her back.

Tariq tells Juney to remove her shoes and pries his own sneaker off his prosthetic leg at last, revealing the molded silicone foot of which he used to be so proud but is now only ashamed. Taking her by the hand, he leads her off to fetch some towels while Naema smiles encouragingly at Rin.

"I am so glad to meet you!" she says again. "And thank you for bringing Tariq home on this terrible night. My son, he has been very happy to make a friend of your daughter and you have been so generous to have him to your house so often. I must now repay you with some Iraqi hospitality."

Her voice is welcoming, but to Rin she could hardly have

said anything worse. In her platoon, "Iraqi hospitality" meant being captured and tortured. She does, however, manage to get herself far enough inside the door for Naema to close it, quieting the racket of the storm and the grumble of Rin's still-running engine. Rin reminds herself that the car is there and ready, as is Betty, should she need to escape. Her invisible wolves, however, have unaccountably disappeared.

"Now, may I make you some hot tea?" Naema asks.

Rin understands she is obliged to accept, so manages a nod. Recognizing this is not enough, she adds, "Thanks," which comes out sounding like a cough.

Naema looks at her a moment, able to see her more clearly now that she is lit by the living room lamps. A round face, red-cheeked and gray-eyed, younger than on first impression but roughened by sun and wind. Stubbled hair, inky with rain. Body a square of muscle. Boots, jeans, and a man's white undershirt. Arms pocked with scars and a tattoo on her forearm so badly lasered-out that Naema can see exactly what it was: a bayonet encircled by a wreath. Naema has not worked at a VA clinic all these years without learning to recognize an army Combat Action Badge when she sees one. Perhaps she should not have mentioned Iraq.

Tariq reappears then, holding Juney's hand and carrying a towel for Rin. Juney has her own towel draped over her head like a scarf and is smiling happily, her bare feet pink and tender under the wet hem of her jeans. Naema examines her with curiosity. Her face the shape of a dewdrop, her chin a pleasing point. But her irises are reflective and blank, the color of bluish water; the color of near-nothing.

"Welcome to our home, Juney," she says. "Tariq, he has told me much about you."

"Thank you, Mrs. Jassim." Juney swings her head about like

a lily. Naema pats her shoulder, having long since given up explaining that Iraqi wives do not take their husbands' names. Jassim was the family name of her grandfather.

"Please, sit," she tells Rin then. Rin hasn't budged since she stepped over the threshold. "Tariq, go see if we have any cookies."

"We don't eat cookies," Rin blurts, jerking back to life. "And we're about to have dinner so we can't stay long." She swallows, wishing she had brought Betty inside with her. Even Juney is not enough here.

Naema blinks at this rudeness. She was raised to consider hospitality a sign of Allah's great goodness, not something to refuse on a whim. "Very well," she replies, determined to serve the cookies anyway. "But your dinner, it can wait a few minutes, no? Please, make yourself at home. Your boots you can put there." She points to a low rack along the wall by the door, heaped with shoes and slippers. "And do sit down and warm yourself. This is not a friendly night."

Rin nods stiffly. She doesn't want to take off her damn boots—it'll make it harder to run. But she rubs her head with the towel and crouches to untie them anyway, placing them where she can grab them, if need be. Then she crosses the room and sits on the bloodred couch. *Not a friendly night.*

In the kitchen, Naema finds the children raiding the cookie jar with the concentration of diamond thieves. Tariq looks at her guiltily, but she only puts a finger to her lips and winks. Juney is blissfully stuffing her mouth with as much cookie as she can get into it at a time. "Her mom won't let her eat sugar," Tariq whispers.

"Well, try not to gobble them all, Juney. Save some for your mother." Naema sets the kettle to boil and spoons tea leaves and cardamom into a small saucepan. Once the water is ready, she will pour it over the tea and then place the smaller pan inside a larger one to create a double boiler so the leaves can brew in the steam, thus creating the strong black chai of her homeland. She decides to use the enameled tea glasses she found in Damascus, the ones that normally sit so neglected on her sideboard. It is such a pleasure to formally serve a guest.

❁

Out in the living room, Rin is hunched on the edge of the Iraqi's gore-colored couch, feet wet and miserable in their socks, hands squeezed so hard between her knees they feel like rubber gloves, wishing she hadn't left Betty in the car. Does this woman really not recognize her, or is she only biding her time until she can take revenge?

Glancing about the room, she tries to reconnoiter her surroundings and reel in some sense of control. She needs to find a balance between the thoughts that might be reasonable and the fears that might not. Because right now she can't tell the difference.

On the surface, the room looks like any living/dining combo, if somewhat bare. The table on one side. A couple of armchairs in the same bloodred as the couch under her butt. A wooden coffee table as polished as a liar's smile, and a stretch of red carpet woven with the image of a tree, its branches writhing. The walls are naked but for a few Islamic tiles, no family photos anywhere. Rin knows this. She's seen it. Nothing to be scared of.

What if the Iraqi walks out of the kitchen not with tea but a gun . . . what if she kidnaps Juney . . . what if . . .

Rin studies the carpet, its branches squirming beneath her feet like worms, wishing she could squirm out of here with them. *I should never have come. I can't handle this, I can't . . .*

She jumps to her feet just as Tariq walks in balancing a platter of cookies, Juney close behind him, a hand on his shoulder for guidance. He lays the platter down on the coffee table and looks up at Rin. "There are five kinds of cookies here," he announces like a car salesman. "There must be one you'll eat."

She inhales and forces herself to focus on him. Then she takes in Juney. "Have you been helping yourself to these, young lady?" She is working to steady the shake in her voice and sound like a normal mom.

"Oh, no, I know they're not allowed." Juney slides her little hand down to hold Tariq by the wrist. Her mouth is smeared with chocolate and her chin is sparkling with sugar. Rin is about to scold her. Then she doesn't.

"Mommy, I can feel you standing and being weird. Sit."

Rin obeys. Her legs jiggle up and down. Her hands clench and unclench, badly missing a rifle. Her back is to the kitchen door and she is sweating so hard she feels her underwear getting wet.

She stands, moves to an armchair, and sits with her back to the wall. Better. Still, where are her invisible wolves?

A clattering in the kitchen. What is the woman doing? It doesn't take this much time or noise to boil a kettle. Then she abruptly appears, nods at Rin with a smile, crosses the room, and disappears again. Must be a second door to the kitchen, which means she could come in from two angles. Rin begins to shake.

Tariq and Juney are sitting on the floor beside the coffee table now, both cramming cookies in their mouths as if they haven't eaten for a week. Juney looks tremendously pleased with herself, but Rin knows she won't eat her dinner now, probably won't sleep, either, with all that sugar spinning inside her. She might even throw up, assaulting her pure little stomach as she is. They are in for a rough night—if they get out of here alive.

Jay, get us out of here alive.

Rin stands up again. "Betty. I shouldn't leave her in the car with the ignition on. She could get gassed. I'll just go fetch her."

Tariq glances at Rin, startled. "Um, Mrs. Drummond? I'm sorry, but we can't. I mean, my mom doesn't allow dogs in here."

She looks at him. Little nut face under his tangle of curls. Oh, right. Iraqis don't like dogs in their homes. She sits back down.

"Betty won't care," Juney says. "She's probably chasing raindrops on the windows."

But Rin needs Betty now. She also needs—and she is aware of this—to calm the hell down.

"Juney?" she says. Just one word, but Juney understands. She scoots along the floor to Rin, feels for her legs, and leans against them. The warmth of her little back, the shine of her hair. Rin puts her hand on Juney's head and feels her heart slow. For the moment.

A tinkling of glass against glass and the Iraqi enters, instantly triggering Rin's fearsweat again. She is carrying an oval brass tray laden with fancy glasses rimmed in gold, each one only a little bigger than a shot glass. Amid them stands a tall and narrow silver teapot, its spout curving up it like the stem of a tulip. She moves slowly, her breath strangely heavy, and Rin can hear a wheezing sound from her throat. What could that be?

Oh.

Fuck.

The Iraqi sets the tray on the coffee table and then herself on the couch Rin just left, folding her thin hands on her lap. She is wearing loose black pants and a pink button-down shirt, a long black braid draped over her shoulder—no hijab, abaya, burqa, or anything like that. Thank god. But her cheek is stamped with that shrapnel scar Rin remembers only too well, a star of fire and metal right there on her cheekbone.

She studies Rin's face.

Please don't recognize me. Please.

"Mrs. Drummond, I am thinking maybe we met before, no? Your daughter, was she ever a patient of mine? Are you one of my veteran parents?"

Rin can't say a word.

"Oh no," Juney chimes in. "I'd remember your voice if you were my doctor. I didn't like my doctor. But I like you." She takes another bite of cookie.

Rin's eyes refuse to blink. She has no idea if Juney is lying to protect her or if this is indeed what her memory has done with that unforgiving day.

"You were not in the clinic the morning of the hurricane?" the woman asks then. "Do excuse me, for my memory of that day, it is very hazy. I remember only rain and all that wind and water and noise. And then I was so sick afterwards, it is all like a bad dream now."

Good. Don't ever wake up.

"Yes, we did go to the clinic that day—it was so scary!" Juney says. Rin stares at her. Her daughter the Judas. "But my doctor was this lady who treated me like a baby. Not you."

The Iraqi frowns while Rin sits stiff as a shot deer. Then, after an interminable pause, the woman shakes her head. "Ah, perhaps you saw my colleague, Dr. Jordan. No matter. Come, the tea, it is ready. It is too strong for the children, Mrs. Drummond, but may I serve you? I think you will probably want sugar."

For the first time in her life Rin is glad that trauma plays havoc with memory. She accepts the tea and capitulates about the sugar, too, only on one condition. With each sip, she will swear in the secret blood of her every vein and artery that she will never, ever go near Tariq's mother again.

Later, as she drives home, having managed to escape the house with no more damage done than a daughter full of cookies and nerves cinched tight enough to snap, Juney sits beside her singing again, rocking even more than usual in her sugar high, her voice bouncing off Rin's ears like bubbles. Betty is asleep in the back, snoring her doggy snore, probably half poisoned by carbon monoxide. And Rin is in such a snarl of relief, confusion, and what might possibly be regret that she scarcely pays any notice to her usual nighttime visitations. Even the shot-up girl leaves her alone.

The driving demands attention, though, the rain sheeting down. It is solid black out here—so black she can barely see the road. She won't be able to see a cop car, either, at least not till it's right up behind her, and she expects to find Flaherty or the DEC on her tail at any moment. Oh god, how is she ever going to tell Juney? Juney has never known life without their wolves— she and Silver and Gray were born in the same year; her lupine sister and brother. How is Rin going to tell her that their family might be ripped apart? That Rin herself might even be arrested?

"Mommy? Isn't Tariq's mom nice?"

Deep breath. "We don't know her yet, bean. We can't tell if she's nice."

"But she gave us cookies and tea and she didn't ask any dumb questions about my eyes. I like the smell of her house, too. Spicy and minty and peppery, like a pie."

"Garlicky, you mean. The whole place stank of garlic and onions."

"It did not!"

She's right. It didn't.

Juney falls silent a moment, her singing gone. "Can you and Tariq's mom be friends now? I want you to have a friend like I do."

"No, I can't be friends with her. No."

"Why not? Why did you say that?"

"I didn't mean it. Wasn't thinking." Rin pauses, knowing she owes her more. "It's just hard when you've been trained to see Iraqi people as your enemy, when you've seen them kill . . ." She swallows. "People you love."

"You mean Daddy, don't you?"

"Yes, little bean. I mean Daddy."

Juney is sitting still now, so still it isn't like her at all. Betty wakes, no doubt sensing the tension. She sits up in the back and glares at Rin in the rearview mirror with her droopy black eyes, snout quivering.

"Juney, is something the matter?"

Juney waits a second before answering. "Mommy, I want you to listen." Although Rin can't look at her, having to keep her eyes on the nearly invisible and increasingly slippery road, she can feel Juney's mind focused on her like a searchlight. "Tariq and his mom didn't kill Daddy. Did they?"

"Not exactly. I mean no, of course not."

"And Americans kill people, too, right?"

"Yes, I am afraid we do."

"And we kill not just enemy people but other Americans. I heard about it at school. Kids even shoot other kids right in their own schools. Don't they?"

"Yes," Rin replies reluctantly. "But it's rare."

"Still, they've done it. Right?"

She sighs. "Right."

"So does that mean you can't ever be friends with a kid?"

Rin has no answer to that.

"Well, does it, Mommy?"

"No, little bean," she whispers. "No, it doesn't."

❊

Tariq, too, is pressing his mother for her opinion of his friends. "What do you think?" he says in their kitchen, wiping off the cookie platter, now empty of everything but crumbs. "Isn't Juney cool?"

Naema rinses out the teapot in the sink while she considers her answer. "She is a sweet child, yes. And I see you two know how to be naughty together." She shakes out the tea leaves stuck inside the spout. "But her mother seems troubled."

"No she isn't! Louis said that, too, but it's not true. She just isn't used to people." Tariq hands his mother a tea glass to wash. "You'll like her better when you get to know her, you'll see."

"I'm sure I will." Naema is touched by her son's generosity, but privately she hopes she will never have to know Mrs. Drummond at all. The woman disturbs her, not only because she is an obviously traumatized veteran, as well as ill-mannered and rough, but because she seems to touch in some way on Naema's buried and disquieting dreams. Perhaps she has not been wise to allow Tariq to spend so much time at Rin Drummond's house.

"I'll tell you why I like her," Tariq is saying. "She knows a whole lot about animals and she's superchill with her wolves."

"Wolves?" Naema turns a frown on him.

"I don't mean wolves, I mean dogs. She's got four dogs and three cats, but one died, so now she's got only two and—"

"Tariq, you're lying. You know I can always tell when you're lying. Remember what your grandmother used to say? 'The rope of lies is short'? Out with the truth now. What did you mean about wolves?"

Tariq examines the gilt enamel rimming one of the tea glasses. It is not as easy to keep up a secret life as he thought. Secrets just don't seem to want to stay in their hiding places, no matter how hard you work to keep them there. But he tries once more. "Please don't make me tell you, Mama. I promised I wouldn't."

"Whom did you promise?"

"Juney. Well, really Mrs. Drummond."

Naema dries her hands. "Come." She walks out of the kitchen in her newly careful way and sits on the sofa, patting the cushion beside her. Tariq trails in and sinks down, staring at his knees.

"*Habibi*, it is never a good sign when an adult asks a child to keep a secret. Adults should not demand such things of children. Please, don't make me waste my breath. Just tell me the truth." Her voice wheezes to a halt.

Tariq pulls in an extra-deep breath for her, torn between his two consciences: the one that belongs to his newly fragile mother and the one that belongs to Juney and the wolves. He sighs, kicks his legs, and rubs both hands in his curls. And then he gives in.

"All right. But it's not a bad secret, Mama; it's a wonderful one. A happy one!" His face is alight now. "Mrs. Drummond keeps wolves. She's got three of them and they're the most awesome animals in the world. They like me. I speak to them and they understand, they really do!"

"Are you making this up?"

"No, but don't worry, she keeps them behind a great big fence, just like in a zoo, much too tall for them to jump over. Me and Juney don't go in there with them, honest. Only Mrs. Drummond does that."

"I do not like the sound of this. I don't want you spending time near such dangerous animals or with a woman as disturbed as Mrs. Drummond."

"Oh no, it's not like that at all, Mama. She's very nice to me and she always makes sure we're safe." He reaches for his mother's braid and winds the end of it around his hand. "People don't understand wolves. They think they're evil. They might try to take them away or shoot them if they know about them. That's why Juney and her mom said it's got to be a secret. Juney needs those wolves. They both do. The wolves are like their family. They really love them, and I do, too, so please don't stop me from going there."

Naema knows Tariq has been unhappy in school lately, just as she knows how important Juney is to him, so she holds up her hands in defeat. "Very well, I will let you go. But first you must promise to keep well away from those wolves. And no more lying."

"I promise. But you won't tell anybody about the wolves, will you? Please?"

"Not even Louis? He would like to hear about this, I think."

"Not even Louis."

She hesitates. "All right, I will tell no one. Now, give me back my hair and go warm up the supper—it's in the blue casserole. And make one of your delicious salads, would you? I need to lie down."

Once he is gone, Naema stretches out on the sofa, drained by the events of the evening. That dense burl of a woman with her darting, frightened eyes. The tension thickening the air like exhaust. The discomfiting tug at the back of her memory.

She nestles deeper into the cushions, wishing Louis were here. Even if she can't mention the wolves, she would like to talk the evening over with him, find out what he thinks of Rin and whether Tariq should spend so much time with her, for she trusts Louis to be honest with her and always has. Once, early in their acquaintance, he asked her why she trusted him like this when she hadn't Jimmy Donnell, and she replied that were she to see every American as her enemy, she would never be able to call this country home. "You know our saying in Iraq?" she asked him. "'*Lo khuliyet, qulibet.*' If the world were empty of good people, it would end." But in truth, her anger about the war and the murders of her brother and father and Khalil did still smolder within her like scorched earth, as did her blame of Donnell.

Naema has never forgiven herself for failing to convince Khalil not to rely on Donnell, even that last evening of her husband's life. He had come home without warning, missing her and Tariq too acutely to stay away, and as soon as he called her, she rushed out of the kitchen and flung herself on him. "It's a torture living like this, never knowing if you're dead or alive," she cried. "Tell Sergeant Donnell you refuse do this insane work any longer. It's not worth it."

Khalil stepped out of her arms. "There's no need to worry, *ayuni*. Jimmy will keep me safe."

"A drowning man will cling even to a snake."

"And what is that supposed to mean?"

"It means I don't understand why you put your life in this soldier's hands! Besides, whatever he says, you're still doing a job that makes everybody hate you."

Khalil frowned at her. "I didn't come home to argue. We've gone over this a thousand times. And you know I do this work not only for our survival, but for my honor."

"What honor? Have you forgotten what the Americans have done to us?"

He rubbed the crease between his eyebrows. He looked so worn, her husband; eyes sunken, trousers drooping at the waist, face as grizzled as a bandit's. "I've told you. This is the only way I know to help prevent the misunderstandings that cause so many needless deaths—to make clear when people are innocent."

"Aren't we all innocent? Aren't we only trying to defend ourselves?"

"You know it's not as simple as that. But enough. I must leave early tomorrow. I need rest and I need peace."

"I will give you peace," she replied, folding her arms in an angry barrier. "But understand this, Khalil. If you die because of working for this soldier of yours, if you add your death to those of my brother and father, you will also kill me."

That night, they went to bed too angry to talk. For months, she had been longing for her husband, yet all she could do was lie beside him in stubborn silence. But the following morning, she awoke ashamed. "I should have remained calmer. Forgive me?" Khalil held her, apologizing too. Yet they both knew they had resolved nothing.

After a quick breakfast, Naema stood in the doorway, watching in sorrow as Khalil crossed the courtyard to unlock the gate and greet his old father, who was waiting by the car.

"Baba, wait!" Tariq cried, and before she could stop him, he dodged past her into the street, his little legs surprisingly fast. "Baba!"

"Tariq!" she called, running to catch him. "Come back!"

Khalil turned to blow him a kiss. Then he pulled open the door.

A terrible noise. A shower of blood, more blood than she ever could have imagined. Tariq flying into her, knocking her over. Her heart liquid with terror.

23

COLLATERAL

Beth shivers in her tight black dress and heels, her matching jacket flapping in a cold wind, trying to make herself feel something—anything at all—as she squints against the October sky, washed to a brazen blue by the previous night's rain. Whichever way she looks, she is surrounded by a pegboard of death. Row after row of upright slabs marching to the horizon, some fourteen thousand military men and women reduced to rectangles as white as their bones.

Smoothing back her hair, which she has fastened into a tidy ballerina knot on top of her head, she reaches for Flanner beside her, his shoulders two small knobs under his miniature jacket, his mouth seamed tight. The last time they stood stiff and dolled up like this, they were waiting for Todd, too.

Louis hovers behind them, adorned in his military best, having driven them from Huntsville to the Saratoga National Cemetery, KISS FM turned up high to drown out the fact that not one of them could find a worthwhile word to say. Beth's parents are here as well, delivered by airplane from Miami, sitting behind her in folding metal chairs, her father baggy in a royal blue suit, her mother in something chiffony and purple, both of them leathered by the Florida sun. And on their left, flanked by family and friends, sits Todd's tall and rangy mother, hidden under a huge plate of a black straw hat. Beth wonders where the new husband is, the one who pulled Todd's indifferent mother into even deeper indifference.

Far in front of them, in a tight-knit row amid the graves, seven marines stand at attention in their navy blue uniforms, rifles barrel up and ready, the brims of their white caps low over their eyes, chin straps seizing their jaws. Tiny toy figures, stiff as molded tin.

No sounds but the flap of Beth's jacket and the sudden sobs of Todd's mother; not, it seems, so indifferent after all. Behind them, a hearse waits on the road; a great, gleaming beetle, its back door lifted like a wing.

Beth tries to pull herself free of her anesthesia, regretting now that she took all those pills her doctor prescribed to help her "deal with her loss," as he put it. (*Loss? What kind of a word is that for death? You lose a wallet or a glove, not a husband.*) She feels trapped in a grim circus. The marines with their rifles and shiny white caps and belts, their rows of gold buttons, their Mickey Mouse gloves. She has an overpowering urge to laugh.

Six more marines materialize from somewhere behind her in those same caps and belts and march in brisk formation over to the beetle. Lining up three to a side, they slide out the casket, draped in an American flag, and heave it onto their shoulders. The wind picks up, but otherwise all remains silent as they carry the casket toward the open grave in front of her. Their pace is slow and halting, as if they have forgotten where they are going. The flag ripples.

Beth glances at the coffin, a momentary fear drilling through her—Todd is lying in there, close enough to leap out and grab her. Those marines must be enormously strong, she thinks a second later, to carry her big brutal mess of a husband like that, as if he weighs no more than a stick.

She sways, suddenly light-headed, until a hand grips her

elbow: Louis, his three fingers steadying her. His other hand, his whole one, is on Flanner's shoulder. A stand-in dad. Why didn't Billy come to play this role? Too busy tending his weed in California, no doubt. Billy never liked Todd. Never liked his sister, either, to tell the truth. Never liked being little brother to the high school hottie. Moved as far away as he could . . . Billy the pothead doing just fine without Huntsville or anyone in it.

Louis lowers her to a foldout chair, seating Flanner beside her and pulling his own chair up behind them. Beth's jacket, short, linen and annoyingly buttonless, continues to flap.

The six marines are holding the coffin over the grave now, staring ahead as if hypnotized, their faces nothing but noses and chins. She finds herself counting.

Nose.

Chin.

Coffin.

Nose.

Chin.

Coffin.

Abruptly, the marines hoist the casket aloft and suspend it above their heads, as though waiting for applause. Then they slowly lower it to the bars spanning the hole beneath.

What was that, another circus trick?

Stooping, they lift the flag, straighten it, and drape it back over the coffin. For a second, Beth expects them to sit down, legs dangling into the grave, and break open fried chicken and beer. But they only spring upright again, salute, and back away. She drops her eyes to the grave, the sparkly Astroturf around it making her think of miniature golf and martinis.

The chaplain steps forward then and starts intoning about Todd's Purple Heart, his honor and bravery, God and death, dust and ashes. Beth closes her eyes, Todd's fingers pressing into her throat.

Shut up! I don't give a shit about hearts and ashes.

At long last, the chaplain falls quiet. Another silence. Beth fidgets, looks at her nails, painted navy blue in honor of . . . in honor of something. A movement catches her eye. The other marines, the toy ones lined up in the distance, are raising their rifles to their shoulders in perfect synchrony. They turn. Aim.

Crack!

She starts violently.

They pull the rifles back. Align them vertically to their noses. Pause. Turn. Raise them once more.

Crack!

She starts again. *Stop!* she wants to shout at them. *Stop that right now!*

But they won't. Again, they pull the rifles to their faces. Pause. Turn. Lift.

Crack!

She starts for a third time. *Stopstopstopforchrissake . . .*

She glares at the row of chins behind the rifles. What does all this useless noise have to do with her and Todd? Not the recent Todd, but the one who would curl up with her on the bedroom floor and play her his latest favorite song. "How cool this is?" he'd say, and put on something about a woman shivering in the pines or a heart-shaped box—something strange and intriguing while he eased off her jeans, spread open her legs . . .

But when the shooting ceases and a lone bugle plays "Taps" with its iconic call to sorrow, her tears come after all. Great fat ones rolling obligingly down her face as she watches the pallbearers lift the flag off the coffin and begin to fold it. Yet she still cannot shake the sense that she is acting in a macabre circus, imitating all those war widows she has watched on television, faces distorting, eyes streaming, bodies crumpling in front of coffins and graves.

The marines fold the flag, smaller and smaller, slowly, ceremoniously, meticulously, until it has shrunk to a perfect triangle. They hand it to the chaplain, who, in turn, approaches Beth and bows, laying it as gently in her arms as if it were a newborn.

She clasps it to her stomach, weeping, feeling honored in spite of herself, even as she hates the flag, the marines, the chaplain, and, at that moment, the entire United States of America and everyone in it.

❦

Louis is holding himself as still as he can, within and without, until this ordeal is over. Military stiff in his dress uniform, unearthed from his attic for the occasion, he sits with one hand still on Flanner's shoulder, the other hovering by Beth's elbow, thinking of Todd and his compliant march through the Adirondacks. Louis is certain Todd didn't die because of the enemy sniper Beth was told had killed him. He died because he wanted to.

Louis stares out at the rows of glowing white headstones. All those thousands of dead, and all the thousands of shadowed dead unburied behind them: the bodies never recovered, the AWOLs and dishonorable discharges—the collateral damage, like Melody. And here he is, with no more to pay for his sins than the loss of two fingers, a woman he loves but will never get, and a remorse about his wife like a shard in the heart.

He feels Beth slump again, so slips his arm around her to hold her up. Flanner is slouched in his chair now, a little peg of a boy who barely understands what is happening to him. Louis glances over at Todd's mother, a tall, lean woman yellowed by years of smoking, half-obscured by her hat, her face sliding like melted wax.

Beth's parents are sitting beside him, staring into space. They didn't like Todd much—nobody did, to be honest, but Beth. Todd in his coffin being lowered right now into the grave with a series of unseemly clanks and jerks. Who was Todd anyway? Todd in the Adirondacks, so indifferent to the flaring trees, the silken lakes, the shell-pink skies.

And then, at last, and not a minute too soon, it's over. The bugle has fallen silent. The marines have shouldered their rifles, swiveled about in their boots, and marched into the distance. The black cars have opened their mouths and swallowed the other mourners, whoever they were—Louis has no idea. Todd's mother has been whisked off by a friend. And suddenly he, Flanner, Beth, and her parents are alone, standing by his car on this wildly beautiful day, the October sun and dancing foliage seeming to have no other purpose than to mock them.

"Performance over," Beth says. "I need a drink."

24

PATIENCE

Tariq and Juney are lying on their backs in the grass, talking about colors. October has edged into its third week by now and Tariq is trying to convey to her the wonder of watching the leaves change by the day. "You know how fire feels?" he says. "It's like that for your eyes."

"Warm and flickery and a little scary?"

"Warm and flickery, yes. Scary, no."

She wriggles deeper into the leaves, listening to them crackling beneath her, the sound somewhere between the snap of flames Tariq was just talking about and the crunch in her head when she chews a celery stalk. She picks up a leaf and sniffs it: maple. "This one is . . ." She runs her fingers along its veins, the brittle edges and sharp points, the moist and flappy middle. "This one's turquoise. Here." She feels for Tariq's face and balances it on top of his nose.

He leaves it there and they stop talking a moment, both of them splayed faceup, as gangly as foals. At school, Tariq has noticed that some of the older girls aren't so gangly anymore, having returned from summer with new soft curves on their hips and round bumps under their shirts. Juney, though, is still all child, and this makes him feel warm and safe and protective all at once.

"What does fall smell like to you?" he asks her.

She rolls over and pokes her nose into the ground. "Grass and worms and a little like burned sugar." She rolls back again. "Summer smells like steam and sun lotion and rot. Winter's burning wood and wet wolves. Spring smells like my mom."

He sits up. "Let's go see Gray. I want to see how thick his coat is now."

They stand, take each other's hands, and walk over to the fence, Juney calling her wolf cry again. Gray runs up right away, looking bigger than ever now that his two layers of thermal coat are growing: the downy, insulating layer underneath and the waterproof guard hair on top. Ebony shows up, too, his black coat also thicker now and tipped with even more of those shimmery threads of white. But Silver is nowhere to be seen.

"Is Silver here?" Juney asks. "I can't smell her." She has explained to Tariq that every wolf has its own scent, depending not only on what it eats but what it rolls in, like Gray with his fish scales. But then, Tariq supposes, every human must have its own scent, too.

He peers through the woods: the thick trunks black and mossy; the dense crochet of leaves between. "I don't see her." He watches Gray and Ebony a moment. They seem uneasy. Gray is particularly agitated, pacing back and forth, glancing now and then into the woods behind him. "I think something's wrong."

"Let's go tell Mommy."

They make their way to the barn, where Rin is bent under the hood of her car, cleaning spark plugs and scraping corrosion powder off her battery. She has decided to get the old Buick into the best condition possible so that if and when Flaherty or the DEC show up, she can send them into the woods to take their chances with the wolves, bundle Juney in the car, and escape. Better to run than to have her witness the wolves being kidnapped, or worse.

"Mommy?"

Rin pulls her head out, her arms smeared with grease. The children are standing in front of her, their faces serious.

"Hey, you two, what's up? You hungry?" She glances at her watch.

"Silver's disappeared," Juney says.

Rin puts down her tools. "What do you mean?"

Tariq answers this time. "We called the wolves but only Gray and Ebony came. You think something's the matter, Mrs. Drummond?"

She frowns, wiping the grease from her hands on an old towel. Striding over to a shelf, she takes down her medical kit. "Come."

The children hurry after her, holding hands again so Juney won't trip. Gray and Ebony are still there, sitting on their haunches. The minute Gray sees Rin, he stands and makes a noise deep in his throat, a kind of gruntgreeting, walks a few paces toward the trees, and turns to look at her.

"I think he wants you to follow him," Tariq says.

"I think so, too." Rin puts her hands on the children's shoulders. "Now listen. I need you both to be very grown-up here and calm. You understand?"

Tariq nods. Juney says, "Yep."

"Good. I'm going in there to see if Silver needs help, so I want you to stay quiet and watch them. Tariq, if Gray or Ebony circles behind me, or if Silver appears from anywhere I can't see, I want you to tell me right away. Don't shout. Just say it calmly and clearly. Okay? And Juney, if you smell any change in them, you let me know, too."

"Don't worry, Mommy, it'll be fine." Juney sniffs. "Right now I smell they need you."

Rin pats her shoulder. "Allright, here I go." Unlocking the catch pen and then the inner gate, she walks through.

This is only the second time Tariq has seen her inside the fence with the wolves, and he watches her closely, half in fear, half in envy. He would love to go in there one day if she would let him, in spite of his assurances to his mother. He would love to pet Gray, bury his face in that magnificent coat and hug him.

For a long moment, Rin stands without moving, her hands by her sides, fingers tucked inside her palms, her breathing deliberately steady. Everything about her is trying to convey patience rather than threat.

Gray approaches her first, as always, ears pricked, snout thrust forward. Rin doesn't flinch. He is clearly determined to give her a thorough inspection today, for he sniffs one curled hand, then the other, and then each of her boots and legs, taking his time while she stands still and quiet. Tariq draws in his breath and holds it, sending a message to Gray in their private language. *She isn't going to hurt you, Father Wolf, so please don't hurt her. She is only trying to help.*

Gray finishes sniffing, lifts his great head, and trots off into the woods, Ebony beside him. Gray stops, looks back at Rin just as he did before. Trots on.

She follows, step by slow step, Gray and Ebony leading the way. Neither of them circles behind her; neither of them turns to look at her again. They only lead her deeper and deeper into the shadows.

❖

The trick is to keep calm and move steadily. Wolves are highstrung critters, as is Rin, so they all need to be careful of one another. She doubts Gray or Ebony would ever turn on her, not intentionally. But if they grow overexcited or afraid, or just in the mood to tussle, she could be in trouble. She has a long scar on her thigh to prove it.

Keeping calm is easier for her with wolves than it is with humans, but even so she doesn't like venturing this far into the woods with them alone. When she pets Silver, she always makes sure to stay by the catch pen in case things turn rough, so right now she would be happier to remain near the kids. Tariq's eyes on her back are her eyes at the moment and Juney's sense of smell is not to be underestimated. But Gray has taken her far out of their range by now, whether she likes it or not.

She doesn't catch sight of Silver until she and Gray have walked for nearly five minutes, and even then she is not sure what she's seeing. Silver looks like a rolled-up shag rug lying there on her side, half-hidden behind a rock, her white fur tangled with dirt and burrs. She is panting unhealthily fast, her ribs heaving up and down—she has deteriorated badly since Rin last saw her. Rin knows not to go up to her right away, though. She knows to stop first and wait for Gray to tell her what to do.

He walks over to Silver and smells her. He smells her all over, but mostly her snout and eyes. Wolves mate for life, and Rin can sense the sorrow in him as he hovers over her, whimpering. If Flaherty does succeed in taking the wolves away, she hopes whoever is put in charge will at least allow Gray and Silver to stay together.

Finally, after licking Silver's nose, Gray leaves her be and walks a few paces away, followed by Ebony. Then they sit once more and wait for Rin to do what she must.

Slowly, keeping her eye on Gray, she approaches Silver from the front and crouches by her head, murmuring reassurances and holding out her curled fist. Silver sniffs it. Licks it. Whines.

Rin looks at Silver's eyes, her extraordinary honey-gold eyes, glazed now with a milky film. Her nose is paler than it should be and clogged with mucus, her coat balding around her legs and snout. Her hip bones rise from her torso like sails.

Having made sure Silver doesn't object, Rin feels her ears, examines the inside of her mouth, runs her hand over the soft hair on her flanks. Silver lies without moving, struggling to breathe.

By the time Rin returns to the fence, she is too saddened to hide it, even from Juney. Padlocking the gate behind her, she squats down to hold her. Tariq as well, now that the two of them are attached at the hip.

"Kids, it doesn't look good. She's just too sick."

Juney grows still. "Too sick for what, Mommy? You mean she has to die?"

"Yes, little bean."

"Isn't there anything we can do?" Tariq says. "She can't leave Gray all alone! He'll be so lonely. She can't leave him! She's too beautiful to die!"

Rin pulls him closer. God, why did she do that to his mother?

"I know she's beautiful, sweetheart." She folds him into her for another hug. "But death happens to us all; you know that." Of course he knows, more than most children his age—as does Juney. These fatherless kids in her arms. "Come on, let's go inside. It's time I called the vet."

25

STAKE

Beth tucks herself into the corner of her cream-colored couch, her feet folded under her. "So why did you enlist?" she asks, leaning forward to pick up her vodka tonic from the glass-covered coffee table. She takes a long swallow. "I know why Todd did. But you? The money or what?"

Louis, who is pressed up against the far corner of the same couch, gazes into his own vodka, watching the ice cubes hollow out in the middle, tiny prisms of melting light. He learned long ago, when he moved to this mostly white town, to keep his private life to himself. But he has to say something.

"Money was part of it, yeah. And it wasn't like there was a lot else going where I grew up." He takes a nip.

"Where was that? Someplace Hispanic?" She uncurls and stretches out until her bare feet touch his thigh.

"Binghamton."

"Oh." She folds over her legs with her dancer's ease and refills her drink. "Your family still there?"

"No."

"Why not?"

He pauses. "My parents split and . . . well, we all went our separate ways."

"That stinks." She rattles her ice around in her glass. "My family wasn't too good at sticking together, either, specially

249

not after I married Todd. They wanted me to dump him, you know. We had big fights over that." She takes another swallow. "Maybe they were right."

Leaning forward again, she strokes Louis's hand—the good hand, not the mutilated one. "That have anything to do with you enlisting?"

"What?" Louis spends so much of his time with a woman he longs to embrace but can't that the sensation of Beth's fingers on his skin, her toes against his leg, is disabling his powers of concentration.

"Did your parents' split have anything to do with you joining the army?" she repeats.

This being none of her business, he says nothing.

Withdrawing her fingers, she drains her glass and drops back against the cushions, an ache pressing against her eyes. Ever since those two ghouls drove up to her door with their scripted concern and rehearsed condolences ("First Sergeant McAllister died bravely, ma'am. And we can assure you that he died instantly and felt no pain whatsoever"), she has felt split in half, one minute hurting more than she imagined a person could, the next utterly numb. It is as if she married two Todds, one prewar, the other post, and now she has to be two widows: the widow who is going to awake every morning to an unbearable weight bearing down on her, and the widow who is so glad to be rid of him she can't even face herself in the mirror.

"Louis?" she says, her voice quavering. "You think if Todd had been able to come home and stay awhile, he would have turned back into who he was before?"

Louis moves his eyes over the room. The never-used fireplace, the mirror above it a shimmering blank. The yellow walls. The thick white carpet as shampooed as a freshly groomed poodle. He has come to see Beth three times since

Todd's funeral, feeling duty-bound to offer comfort, and each time she has asked this same unanswerable question.

"I guess he would have mellowed out some, sure. Maybe he wouldn't have been exactly the same. But parts of his old self would have come back. Probably." He doesn't believe a word he is saying.

"But what made him like that? Is it because he killed people? You think he did? Kill people, I mean?"

"Beth . . ."

"Innocent people?"

Louis shifts around to face her. "Stop torturing yourself like this. You must have thought of all this before, right? When he joined up? And while he was away for all those deployments? There's no point now."

She stares into her glass. "It's just hard to know that he died before he got a chance to turn good again."

"He *was* good. He was a brave marine. Just be proud of him and let it rest at that. Just try . . ." But Louis falters here because he doesn't know what to advise her to try. If he tells her that Todd despised himself for who he'd become, that he was glad to be taken away so he couldn't hurt her anymore, surely that would only make her feel worse. Anyway, Louis has mourned enough people to know words don't help. Nothing helps. Nothing but a long, cruel burn of time.

"I know he was brave," Beth is murmuring. "It's only . . . well, I never wished him dead or anything. But it feels like I did."

"Beth, don't do this to yourself, it isn't . . ." He trails off because she is gazing into his face now with a new, curious expression.

"What color do you call your eyes?" she says in an entirely

different tone. "I've been trying to figure it out forever. I've never seen anyone with eyes your color before."

Louis looks back into his drink. "Green, I guess."

"No. They're not just green. Look at me."

He glances at her, then away again.

"I said *look*." He does. She leans forward and peers right into his irises, and for the first time he notices a light dusting of freckles over her nose: Flanner's freckles. "They're so clear, like beer-bottle glass. I see a little yellow in there, too.... Moss! That bright star-shaped kind—that's the color they are. You have star moss eyes! Where did they come from? Which parent?"

"Uh, my mother. A lot of my Dominican side has eyes this color."

"So, you *are* Hispanic! Was your mom white?"

"Not exactly. A mix, you know."

"What about your dad? Was he Dominican, too?"

"No. Haitian—well, his grandparents were."

"Ah, so you're a mutt!" She leans back into the pillows with a lopsided smile, and he realizes she is drunk. "Mixed-race people are supposed to be the best-looking and the smartest, too. Did you know that?" She angles her head and examines him. "The looks part certainly applies. Don't know about the rest." Chuckling, she stands up and peers around the room. "Where's the vodka?"

It's still on the coffee table, but he picks it up while her back is turned and puts it out of sight on the floor. "Beth, I think you should go to bed. You've had a hell of a week."

She hesitates, then nods. "Maybe you're right. I should check on Flan first, though."

"It's almost midnight. He went to bed hours ago. Come

on." Louis rises. "You want some help getting upstairs? You need to sleep."

"Huh, yeah. Probably do." Beth is not as drunk as he thinks, but she leans into him for the comfort, curling her arm around his waist.

He walks her over to the staircase, her pelvis moving under his hand, her left breast brushing his arm. He draws her closer and, hip-to-hip, they gingerly mount the stairs.

❀

At the top of those stairs, in his narrow bedroom, Flanner is staring in terror at his doorway. His father is standing there, a stake through his chest like a sword.

"Why did you do this to me, Flan?" his father moans.

Flanner struggles to open his mouth. *I didn't mean it,* he tries to say. *I didn't, I promise!* But his voice won't speak and his mouth won't move. He is as paralyzed as if encased in cement.

❀

Louis maneuvers Beth into her room and helps her onto the bed. "I'll get you some water," he says, trying with no success whatsoever to stop his eyes from roaming over her supine body: the slender hips, the divide of her vulva clear under her jeans; her breasts reaching to him from beneath her white sweater, which has risen to reveal an enticing wedge of belly. He has a powerful urge to bury his face right there in that strip of velvety skin, and then down and down till he makes her moan.

Out in the hallway, he stops to listen at Flanner's door to make sure he is asleep and, seeing a new fall of rain outside, shuts the landing window. In the bathroom, he washes out the toothbrush glass and fills it with water, scowling at himself in the mirror. *Louis Martin, she's drunk. You're not. She's a mess of a new widow. You're not. Don't you goddamn dare.*

When he steps back into her room, closing the door behind him for reasons he would rather not examine, he is startled to find her in nothing but a pair of pink satin underpants as narrow as a ribbon and a matching bra, its shiny cups barely covering her nipples. He remembers something Todd said to him once when they were out drinking. "Beth is a dancer, you know that, right? Flexible as hell. You ever fucked a dancer, Martin?"

"Um, here." Louis puts the water on her bedside table, untangles the sheet at the foot of her bed, and pulls it up to her chin, careful not to touch her. "Go to sleep now."

"Too hot." She kicks it back off. "Sit."

He does, but only on the edge of the bed. She fixes her gaze on him. "You've listened to me all night about Todd," she says then. "It's your turn now. Tell me . . . tell me about Melody."

Louis recoils. "Another time." He moves to stand up.

"Not fair!" She grabs his arm and pulls him back down. "You can't do all the knowing about me and not let me know about you." She gives him a long stare. "Were you happy together?"

He looks over at the window.

"Well?"

"Beth, I can't . . ."

"You have to. Start with how you met." She nudges his thigh with her foot, giving him a flash of her scantily clad crotch. "Where did you find her?"

He forces his eyes away. "College. In Albany. We married young."

"And?"

He lets out a long breath. "And then OIF started, so I had to drop my classes and go. I deployed right after our wedding."

"Just like me and Todd." Her voice trembles. "Go on. Please."

Louis looks down at his missing fingers. "Well, she got her degree in psychology. Joined a practice. And . . . and I came back . . . different. . . . You know."

"How different? Like Todd different?"

He inhales. "No. Well, yes. Kind of. It got bad pretty quick."

"What do you mean, 'bad'?" Beth's voice is a whimper now. "You never hurt her, did you?"

"No. But I . . . I didn't help. And after . . . I felt it was my fault, just like you do about Todd."

"You did? Why?"

Louis rubs his eyes. "She was asking me to save her and I . . ." He rubs his eyes harder, pressing the eyeballs in and in.

He was only just home from Iraq when it happened. He had been in Mosul with the First Armored Division, scouting out weapon caches, unearthing insurgent strongholds, interrogating suspects with a violence he cannot face even now. It was his toughest tour yet. Three of his buddies killed in his first week, his fingers blown off, more bodies in his head than in all his previous deployments combined. He had come home as jacked up as a junkie, ghost digits throbbing. Not listening to her. Taking too many painkillers. Then he had gone out to talk war talk with his soldier buddies, the only talk that made him feel grounded, leaving her alone even though she begged him not to.

She found his M4 in the attic—the rifle he had bought to keep her safe.

Took it into the shower. Sat on the floor in all her clothes, muzzle in her mouth.

Turned on the water to minimize the mess.

And then the police.

His wife.

His rifle.

His failure.

His night on the shower floor, arms around his belly, rocking and rocking in the blood. . .

"Hey!" Beth kicks him. "Aren't you listening?"

"Sorry, what did you say?"

"I said I can't feel that Todd's dead!"

"Beth, shush. It's too soon. It's because you're in shock. Let's stop talking about all this now. I don't see how it's going to help."

She looks at him a long moment. "Come," she says in a near sob, grasping his shoulders and pulling him down. "Kiss."

"Oh Beth, I don't know."

"Now."

"I don't think this is a good idea."

She arches her back. Draws him nearer.

"You sure? You really sure?" he just manages to say.

"Shh," she replies, raising her lips to his.

❁

Flanner is startled out of his nightmare by a cry. He sits up, sweat-limned and terrified, trying to work out whether what he is hearing is real or something from his dream. He hears another cry, a drawn-out moan. Is there a raccoon outside the window? They make creepy noises in the night, even snort like pigs. Or is it a fox? Foxes sometimes sound as if they're suffering horrible wounds in the woods. Or maybe it's Louis, who has been hanging around the house lately like a flea-bitten stray. Holding his breath, Flanner listens again. Hears a giggle and then another long moan.

Oh.

Sliding under his sheets, he presses both hands to his ears so he won't have to hear any more. His mother is disgusting. Louis, too. But his mom is worse. A disgusting drunken slut, just like his dad called her. And Flanner suddenly wants his father back so badly that for the first time since Beth told him Todd died, the rage in him gives way and he weeps.

The sobs come hard and fast, shaking his spindly shoulders, the thread of his narrow spine. And then the dream comes back to him. His sharpened stake. His father's voice. The tears in his father's eyes.

26

TONGUE

Juney is leaning against the wolf fence, trying to smell what is wrong with Silver. Tariq isn't here today, so she is by herself. She lifts her head and listens. For once her mother is nowhere nearby, and the knowledge makes her feel light and bold.

Juney resents her mother for never allowing her to touch the wolves. Her mother says this is because Juney won't be able to see if they grow agitated, but it prevents her from sensing the shape of them. It helped when Tariq told her they were like the dogs, only with bigger heads, taller ears, and longer legs, because she has cuddled the dogs enough to know their every inch. Still, she is jealous that he can pet the wolves when she can't.

She tries again to smell Silver, but the sugary scents of dying leaves and resin emanating from the woods are too strong. So she raises her face and calls out her wolf cry. Not loudly enough to attract her mother, but loudly enough for wolves.

She holds herself still and waits. And then she hears it: a rhythmic panting, a snapping of leaves. And finally a new scent—the pungent, wild scent of earth and heated hair and meat-breath that makes her feel so cozy inside, along with a touch of something akin to hot chicken soup.

"Come here, Ebony," she coos, her fingers clasping the

chain link, the side of her face pressed up to it in just the way her mother forbids. She feels the wires crisscrossing her cheek, cold and hard and right on the edge of sharp.

The panting comes closer. The chicken scent, too. And suddenly here he is, breathing right onto her hands while a slimy thing brushes her fingers. The slimy thing is round and cool. It must be his nose. Then a hot dripping slab of something else curls over her fingers.

"Your tongue!" she whispers. "Tickles!"

She presses her body against the fence, hoping Ebony will press back the way Tariq says Gray does for him. But Ebony only keeps licking. First one finger, then another. She wonders if he tastes the salt on them. She hopes he doesn't think she's food.

The fence rattles a little, and then he does lean into it after all. She can feel him right up against her belly. He is surprisingly dense, his body hard and his coat neither soft nor rough, but thick and springy. When she holds Betty, it is like holding a warm and throbbing pillow. Ebony's body feels more like the head of a wild-haired giant.

Moving one hand down the fence, she pokes her fingers through and tries to stroke him. It is difficult to reach much through the holes, so she gets at only one tiny patch. She can't tell if it's his back or his side. She rubs it a little, but the hairs catch in her fingernails and she accidentally tugs them. She feels his body stiffen, so pulls her hand back quickly. An instant later, he growls.

See, Mommy? I'm fine. I can tell what Ebony will let me do and what he won't just as well you can.

Ebony runs off then and Juney returns to the task of trying to smell Silver. Her nostrils are full of Ebony's odor now, yet she can detect something else nearby. She grows still to make herself concentrate. The scent is something like her mother's breath when she is sick and won't eat, and something like the dead possum Juney once found in the barn: a vomity, decaying odor that made her wrinkle her nose. Could that be Silver?

"Please don't be," she whispers. "Mommy needs you. She needs you not to die."

27

RABBIT

Mike Flaherty is eating his coffee and bagel breakfast at his desk before starting on the first shift of what he suspects will be a very long day. His head feels considerably foggier than usual because he had to stay up till all hours dealing with a DUI over in Clarksville: some bozo of a teenager showing off to his girlfriend, first by driving into a ditch, then by turning belligerent. Flaherty had to cuff the kid and take him in, charging him not only with blowing a point one zero but resisting arrest, too, all of which led to late-night paperwork, more arguing than any cop needs, the calling of distraught parents, and coping with the weeping girlfriend to boot, who had to be found a ride home from the middle of nowhere in the middle of the night. He was tempted to leave the girl hanging out to dry to teach her to develop a better taste in boys.

He sighs and bites into his bagel, the cream cheese squeezing out with an irksome plop onto his newspaper. For the past five years, he was a street cop in Albany, but he grew sick of all the gunshot victims and abused children, so switched to state trooper. Now he spends his time patrolling the back roads and little towns between Slingerlands and Cairo, dealing with wife batterers, methheads, juicers, and junkies, half of whom he's known since kindergarten. He tugs at his duty belt, which is gripping tighter than usual, making his guts ache. This job is turning him fat, forcing him to sit in his patrol car all day, eating crap.

Speaking of crap, his bagel is the consistency of drywall and his coffee has gone cold. He pushes them aside just as his desk phone rings. Megan Hutchins, whose job is to answer the phones, hasn't come in yet—she is always late with one excuse or another—so he answers for her. Nobody else is around anyhow.

"New York State Police, Huntsville."

"Mike? It's Beth. I've got a question."

Flaherty flushes, his old high school butterflies starting up again. "Hey, Beth. What's up?" And then he recalls the obit that ran in the *Huntsville Bugle* only last week: the usual picture of a scrubbed young face under a white cap and beneath it an article describing the deceased as a football star (a vast exaggeration of Todd McAllister's meager abilities, as Flaherty remembers it) and a war hero (when, he'd like to know, is a dead marine not called a war hero?). "I'm so sorry. I just remembered. My condolences."

Beth swallows. "Can we stick to the point?"

"Yeah. Of course." Was there a point?

"I want to know what you've done about Rin Drummond's wolves."

Flaherty was expecting this. "I called like you wanted and she said she doesn't have any. Just huskies."

"She's lying. One of those wolves to tried to attack my son, and I can promise you it was no husky."

"You sure?"

"Of course I'm sure!"

"Sorry to hear that. Was he hurt?"

"No, but he was damned scared, Mike. That woman's a menace. I want to file charges."

"All right. Why don't you come in and we'll take care of it. Then maybe we could talk, um, over a coffee or something?"

Beth tries to recall if Mike Flaherty is married. She believes he is. With a couple of kids—unless that's somebody else. "Okay, I'll be there today after work."

That afternoon, when she pulls up to the state police head-quarters, nothing but a cube of dirty brown bricks with no windows and a chipped gray door, she sits in the car for some time, trying to master the press of misery in her chest. Finally, she climbs out, buttons up her stonewashed denim jacket, pulls her tight matching jeans down over her white high heels, and walks in.

There, she is met by a sheet of bulletproof glass, behind which a female police officer is typing intently on a laptop. "Hello?" Beth ventures.

The cop glances up, takes one look at Beth and puckers her mouth into an expression Beth can only interpret as disdain, which makes her wonder if her choice of powder-blue denim was wise. Perhaps she should have worn something more somber; something that would attest to her new status as a widow.

"I've come to see Officer Flaherty? He's expecting me?"

"Sit." The cop returns to her typing.

Beth lingers a moment, about to suggest the cop might consider taking her name, but the woman's implacable face drains her of courage, so she turns into the room behind her, which is blank, windowless, and grim. A vending machine full of bottled water is leaning against one end, as if recovering from a beating, and two rows of black plastic chairs are lined up against the walls, the space between them so narrow that no occupant could sit and cross her legs without kicking someone else in the knee.

Beth sits and, being alone, crosses her legs. Opening her purse, a small white leather box with a gold chain for a handle, she takes out her cell phone and checks the messages. Nothing, just as there has been nothing all day. Nothing from Louis. Nothing from anybody. Clicking off the phone, she stuffs it with a surge of despair back into her purse, extracts a piece of paper, and unfolds it.

"I WAS WALKING IN THE WOODS MINDING MY OWN BIZNESS WHEN I HERD A NOYZ." (Beth thought it would be more affecting if she let Flanner write his report himself, misspellings and all.) "I SAW A HUGE FEERCE ANIMAL. IT WAS A WOLF! A GINORMUS DANGRUS WOLF WITH FANGS AND TEETH AND SLOBBER. AND WHEN IT SAW ME IT GROWLED AND JUMPED AND TRIED TO KILL ME! I THAWT I WOULD DIE!"

Poor boy! She should have followed up on this long ago— she would have if Todd hadn't turned her life inside out. But now she wants to make it up to Flanner, show him how much she cares about him and how determined she is to protect him, too. Folding the paper carefully, she returns it to her purse and drops her head in her hands, massaging her temples, which have been throbbing all day. She must have had more to drink with that bastard Louis last night than she thought.

When Flaherty comes through the door, she stands and they each take a moment to absorb how the other has changed in the seventeen years since they last met. Flaherty sees the same Beth he always used to see; older, of course, but still with that mane of glorious auburn hair and delectable figure, somehow sexier than ever. She, on the other hand, sees a middle-sized pink man with a little-boy face, a balding head, and a potbelly. The sexiest thing about him is his uniform.

"Hey, Beth, good to see you." His voice has changed since high school—she noticed this on the phone, too. It is deeper now, crustier; the voice of a cop. "My condolences again."

"Thanks, I . . ." She can't finish the sentence, silenced by a new wrench of remembering Todd—both when she loved him and when she didn't.

"Follow me." Flaherty leads her down a long gray hallway into a small gray office and closes the door. Pointing her to a chair facing a cluttered desk, he plants himself behind it, folds his blond-fuzzed hands on the desktop, and leans forward. Beth notices his nails are buffed to a shine and immaculately clean. "Now, what exactly happened again?"

"It was just like I said. Flanner was in the woods minding his own business and that wolf tried to kill him! He wrote it all down here." She hands him Flanner's report.

Flaherty runs his eyes over it and slips it into a file. "Case opened." He leans back, which makes his potbelly pot out even more. Beth can't remember Mike Flaherty being this confident. He was always something of a rabbit in high school, his crush on her embarrassingly obvious to everyone. But then becoming a cop, anointed with a badge and a gun, presumably would give a man confidence. As the folks in Huntsville like to say, "When a cop's right, he's right. And when a cop's wrong, he's right."

"I've done a little more investigation on Rin Drummond since you called this morning," he says then. "Seems like she's quite a piece of work."

"I told you. She's a thug." Beth rubs her temples again.

"Yeah. We've had to go to her house at least three times, according to our files. Once when she set her dogs after a prowler. He had a record of breaking and entering and he was trespassing, though, so no charges there. Plus, she's an Iraq vet—don't know if you knew that."

"Everybody knows that. I know about the prowler, too. It was in the *Bugle*. She shot him, didn't she?"

"No, it was just the dogs. The second time she did the same, only that guy was a Jehovah's Witness. He wasn't hurt that bad, but he filed a complaint anyhow. Third time was when she threatened her neighbors 'cause they wanted to cut down a bunch of trees on their mutual property line. They claimed she said that if they so much as 'murdered one tree'"—Flaherty wiggles his finger in the air to make quotation marks—"she'd shoot them. The lady's definitely got some screws loose, know what I mean?"

"But what about the wolf license? Does she have one?"

"I was just getting to that. She doesn't, no. She hasn't proved she has huskies, either. She hasn't done anything I told her to do."

Beth barely refrains from rolling her eyes. Obviously, Mike dropped the ball. Typical of a lazy local cop. A marine would never have been so irresponsible. She rubs her head once more, a new wave of pain tightening her skull.

"You okay?" Flaherty asks. "You look kind of miserable."

"It's only a headache. I wouldn't mind some water, if you have any."

"Sure, no problem. There's a cooler in the hallway." He gets up, lumbers out of the room and reappears with a flimsy plastic cup of water. He hands it over, spilling a fair amount on her leg. "Shit . . . sorry."

"Doesn't matter." She brushes it off and drinks what's left while he returns to his seat. "So what do you do now?"

"Pay her a visit with the DEC." Flaherty leans forward. "I get a break in five minutes. How about that coffee?"

"But . . . wait. What happens then?"

"We read her the riot act, take away the wolves, and ticket her."

"*Ticket* her? That's all? She's putting my kid in danger, Mike! Flanner told me she pointed a gun at him! Doesn't law enforcement care about the safety of children at all?"

Flaherty fiddles with a pen here, a stapler there, the blond hairs on his hands glittering under his desk lamp. His desk, Beth notices, is laden not only with papers, telephone messages, pens, paper clips, a computer, and file folders but with a lump of clay that vaguely resembles an owl and a fuzzy blue pig made out of a washcloth.

"Well, the problem is," he finally says, "your son was on her property. And how can we be sure that a wolf actually tried to attack him?"

"Because he said so right here in his report!" Beth remembers now why she was never much interested in Mike Flaherty. He has the mind of a banana.

"He's a kid, Beth. Kids are prone to . . . well, exaggerate when they're upset. As he must be right now, if you don't mind my saying. And then a lot of time has passed. I mean, when did this happen—almost two months ago, according to the date on your son's report, right?"

"My son does not exaggerate. Or lie, either, if that's what you're implying."

Flaherty raises his clean pink hands. "No, no, I'm sure he doesn't." He leans forward again. "Listen, I know this must be a pain for you, specially at this, uh, difficult time, and I'm sorry. I'll go pay this lady a visit for sure, get her to explain herself."

He stands and adjusts his utility belt. "Now, coffee or no coffee?"

Beth stands, too, glancing at the wall clock. "I can't, I have to pick up Flanner from football practice."

"Another time, then?"

"Maybe." It is beyond her to even think about this proposition right at the moment.

Flaherty runs his eyes over her once more. "Okeydoke, I'll give you a call. Oh, and Beth? The DEC are police officers, too. Which means that they're armed. In case Ms. Drummond decides to go a little hog wild with her guns."

28

ATONEMENT

Naema is alone in her kitchen, preparing kebab *iroog* for dinner and thinking about the death of Todd McAllister. She wonders whether it is true that misfortune arrives in clusters, as Hibah used to insist. "Luck is like a magnet," she would say. "The bad collects the bad, the good the good. Allah wills it so." This has certainly been true for Naema, losing so many family members in quick succession, and then escaping a war only to almost drown in a flood. And now it has happened to Beth and Flanner, too. Yet perhaps the adage reflects nothing about Allah's will, or luck, either, but only the fact that life is so full of misfortunes there is no room for them to arrive in any other way.

She hears a knock at the door just as she is chopping vegetables, so wipes her hands on a towel and goes to open it, assuming it is Tariq, having forgotten his keys again. But no, there is Louis, standing on her doorstep for the first time in a week, looking oddly bashful.

"Come in and join me for supper—I am just making it now," she tells him with a lift of spirits. He has never stayed away so long before, let alone neither called nor sent her a text, and this has disturbed her more than she cares to admit. She notices he is more formally dressed than usual: a green button-down shirt strained tight over his shoulders, black trousers instead of his usual jeans, dress shoes rather than his typical scuffed-up desert boots.

"You sure you have enough food?" he says. "I didn't show up to make you feed me."

"Of course I have enough." She looks at him in surprise—she always has enough food.

He steps into the house. "Tariq here?"

"Not yet. He has gone to see Juney again. I thought her mother unpleasant when I met her, but she has clearly made him feel at home. He is always at their place these days. I can hardly get him to stay at home for more than five minutes."

"But he should be helping you. Your strength isn't all the way back yet."

She waves a hand. "I am perfectly all right, and he is helping me enough by being happy. Come, you can fix the vegetables. I am making aubergine."

He removes his shoes and follows her into the kitchen, listening to her breathing. Nearly seven weeks have passed since she came home from the hospital, yet he can still hear the strain in her chest.

"Now," she says as she returns to chopping the peppers, onions, garlic, and tomatoes she has gathered into a pungent heap on the counter, "tell me what you have been doing all week and why you look so nice."

"Oh, working. It's the usual fall craziness. I'm dressed like this 'cause I came from a meeting." He washes his hands, avoiding her eyes, and steps around her in the narrow kitchen to take two eggplants out of the refrigerator. In fact, he dressed up for her, as if to clothe himself in atonement.

"I suppose you must have been looking after poor Beth, too. How is she managing?"

He takes some time slicing the eggplant before he can answer.

"She's fine." He realizes how absurd this sounds. "Not so good, to tell the truth."

Naema scoops her chopped vegetables into a bowl of ground beef and kneads them together. "I feel sorry for her, I do, for what she went through with her husband, and now his death."

Louis can add nothing to that.

"And Flanner? How is he? When Khalil, he was killed, Tariq was so small he has been able to forget him. Well, almost. But Flanner, he is old enough to remember forever."

Louis has no idea how Flanner is. Several times, he has been on the verge of calling Beth to ask, only to lose courage at the thought she might interpret his concern as courtship and reentangle him. And again he sees himself in her bed, spinning down from intoxication to the cold fact of what he had done: Todd's widow. Todd's house. Todd in the woods. Todd in his coffin. Careful not to wake her, he'd slipped out from under the sheets, written a quick note of apology, and fled to spend the rest of the week hiding in self-disgust.

"I'm not sure how Flanner's doing," he replies. "But he looked pretty shut down at the funeral."

"I worry about that child. Beth has no control over him. Look at what he did to my poor Tariq."

Louis snatches a glance at Naema while she shapes the beef into oval patties and lays them on a platter. She shows no sign of having heard anything about him and Beth, even though gossip can race through this town of theirs with the speed of a flu virus, but he would rather not press his luck by discussing Flanner any further. "But how are you?" he says quickly. "I'm sorry I've been out of touch. Between work and—"

"Yes, you have been neglecting me terribly." Flashing him a teasing smile, she squeezes beside him at the sink, rinses her hands, and moves back to the stove. She is about to light the burner when she drops her arms and turns away. Crossing the room, she sinks into the chair in the corner. "I am all right, my friend. But . . ." She trails off.

"But what?"

"Oh . . ." She looks up at him. "I had not a good day today."

"Why, what happened?"

She pulls at her long fingers, an old habit she resorts to when distressed. She is achingly beautiful to him right now, her hair loose, her slender figure bending like an iris under her soft blue tunic. He remembers when she went through a phase of try-ing to look more American, dressing in tight clothes and cover-ing her scar with makeup. It was during the year after she had fled Jimmy Donnell's house to live in that run-down apartment in Albany, when she was sewing mattresses at a Soft-Tex fac-tory during the day and attending medical school at night. "The other students, they look at me so strangely," she said to Louis one day. "I will never make friends looking like this." But after she saw a photograph Tariq had taken of her—the foundation over her scar like a slab of putty, the stiffness with which she was holding herself in her tight skirt—she never made such attempts again. Now she wears the modest garments in which she is comfortable, eschews all makeup but kohl, and, to Louis, is lovelier than ever.

"Nothing happened," she replies. "It is just that I do not like this new job."

He pulls a chair out from under the table and sits facing her. "What's wrong with it? Are the other doctors treating you badly again?"

"Sometimes. But that is not what I mean. I feel lost, Louis. Ever since the VA clinic, it was destroyed, I have lost my way." She pauses, pulling again at her hands. "I do not belong in this city emergency room. It is all teenage gang members with gunshot wounds, or who have hurt themselves with drugs. Children who have been beaten by other children or adults. Girls who cut or starve themselves. Addicts. Boys who try to commit suicide . . ."

She looks at him again. "I know these children, they need a doctor as much as anyone else, but I am not the right person to help them. It is hard to avoid growing angry at a girl who is starving herself when one has lived through the deprivations we did in Basra. And it is hard not to resent a child who tries to throw away his life when my brother's own life was taken at thirteen and he so loved to live. Does this sound very heartless?"

"Of course not. You—"

"I want to undo the war. If I can heal an innocent child who has been hurt by the war in my country, even the child of an American, then I have undone one small piece of the harm caused by this terrible inhumanity. But this city hospital, it is too removed from that. Too distant. You understand?"

"I do. I understand." And he does. He, too, would give any-thing to be able to undo the war one human being at a time. But as a veteran with the blood of so many humans on his hands, he cannot imagine how.

"So it is like this," she is saying. "I spend my days with these troubled teenagers, or with children run over by drunks or sick with asthma or bad food, or who have swallowed paper clips or toys, and meanwhile in Iraq, thousands of children, they are born without legs or arms or eyes because of the toxins left by our wars and yours, while others are losing their limbs to mines or bombs, like my Tariq. And now, with the rise of all these new extremists, it is happening again, more and more killings, more and more brutality!" She stands in distress. "Oh, Louis, why am I not there to help?"

He stands, too, and takes her hands in his. "Shh," he murmurs.

"You are a wonderful doctor, doing wonderful things. It's too dangerous for you to go back. You know that. But you'll find a way to do what you want here, I'm sure. We'll figure out something." And without thinking, he enfolds her in his arms.

She rests her head against his chest. It does not occur to her to step back out of propriety, the way she always has in the past. She only lays her cheek against him, basking in the comfort of being encircled by her dearest friend in the world. Why, she wonders now, has she never let him hold her like this before? It is as if Khalil's death and the decimation of her family have sunk her to the bottom of a river, where she has lain for seven entire years, as cold and senseless as if sealed under ice.

As for Louis, he is in delicious agony, scarcely able to believe it is Naema pressed up against him, Naema so soft and alive in his arms. He yearns to run his hands over the curve of her back with its play of tiny muscles, the dip of her waist, the swell of her hips. Cautiously, afraid of ruining the moment with one wrong move, he rests his lips on her head; her smooth hair scented with jasmine and a touch of cardamom from her cooking.

"Naema," he whispers, unable to hold back the words. "I don't want you to go anywhere. I want you to stay here with me."

He draws her closer, still afraid she will push back in outrage. But she only holds him tighter. "Is this all right?" he whispers. "Is this really all right?"

"Yes, yes. Don't let go."

Clasping her as fervently as he dares, he breathes her into him. And when she raises her face, her lips parted, he knows, the way a man in love does know, exactly what she wants.

29

ARROW

Now that Silver's growing sicker by the day, the kids spend almost all their time together at the wolf fence, calling out to her and pushing little treats through the hatch in the hope of tempting her to eat. She has crawled out of the woods to be nearer the food, but all she can manage is to lie panting on her side, eyes glazed, ribs more visible than ever. Rin can hardly stand to watch. Painful as it will be for her if Silver dies or Flaherty takes her and the other wolves away, she can't even think of what it will do to Juney and Tariq.

"You want to stay for dinner?" she asks Tariq today. She figures the kids need each other with all this sadness in the air. "Call your mom and tell her I'll run you home later." Rin can do that now. It is not, she realizes, so very impossible.

"Thanks, Mrs. Drummond. I'd like that." He pulls out that phone of his and taps on it with his thumbs so fast they turn into blurs. A second later the phone emits a small *bing*, like a tiny doorbell. Rin has never really understood cell phones. "She says it's fine."

In the kitchen, Rin puts on some potatoes to boil and sets Tariq to chopping carrots and Juney to washing tomatoes— Rin doesn't like her handling knives. Then she goes into her back nook to call the veterinarian again, leaving the children to themselves.

"I wonder if wolves move anywhere else after they die," Tariq says once she's gone.

Juney rubs a sticky spot off a tomato. "No, they just crumble into earth like Hiccup."

Tariq thinks of his father's remains soaking into the soil, the ear-shattering blast that haunts his dreams, and then of Juney's own father, photographs of whom are all over the house: a tall, blond man with a high-boned face and lanky limbs, either lounging in jeans or standing upright and serious in an army uniform and cap.

"I don't know. I bet they turn into somebody else. Somebody with a soul." He scoops up the carrots he has chopped so far, a heap of bright orange coins, and drops them one by one into a saucepan.

"Like a ghost, you mean?" Juney turns off the water and listens to the dropping carrots, which make little ringing sounds, like the tapping of a miniature tin drum.

"No, not a ghost." Tariq searches for words to describe the sense he has when he looks into Gray's eyes. "I just don't think Silver will really go away if she dies. I think she'll still be here looking after you and your mom, even if nobody can see her."

Juney feels for the tomatoes she has piled into a pyramid beside the sink and balances the one she just washed on top. "Like a fairy godmother? Silver would be good at that, yeah. Just kind of stinky." She giggles but then grows serious again. "I don't know. I wish that was true, 'cause Mommy's going to miss her so much. But I've held a lot of dead animals, and when they're dead, they're just dead."

❖

Rin closes her study door to make sure the children can't hear and picks up her phone, the good old-fashioned kind that doesn't sound like a doorbell or allow the feds to spy on her from right inside her own pocket. She likes this veterinarian, who is down-to-earth and sensible. Rin calls her "Doctor Doolittle" because, like her, she is better with animals than people.

When Doctor D. answers, Rin describes Silver's symptoms. "My guess is it's cancer. She won't eat, and I can tell she's in pain."

"I could sedate her and bring her in for X-rays, if you'd like. It's expensive, though."

"No one's shooting sedatives into my wolves, thank you. I'm going to let nature take its course. I just want to ease her suffering."

And this is another reason Rin likes Doctor D. She doesn't try to guilt-trip Rin into spending money she doesn't have for fancy treatments she doesn't want. She only says in her atonal way, "All right. I'll send you a prescription for painkillers. You can mix them with her food. Give her soft food for now; see if she'll take it. She probably can't handle much else."

Rin thanks her and hangs up, a weight sinking through her. Poor Silver. She was such a good mother to Ebony, licking him, feeding him, teaching him how to hunt and play and howl. Such a good mate to Gray, too. If she and Gray were in the wild, he would chew and regurgitate food to feed her now that she's sick—wolves do that for their ailing mates, just as the mothers do for their pups. He might do it yet, although Rin will feed mush to Silver in case he doesn't. But now she has to make a decision: whether to let Silver suffer out her last days in the woods, as she would in the wild, or put an end to her misery herself. Rin does, after all, own more than one gun.

Standing at the window, she thinks this over while a late

autumn fly thuds mechanically against the glass, its movements clumsy now that it's winding down to winter catatonia. The trees outside look stripped and cold, their naked branches tangling against the soot-smeared sky, and the leaf-smothered lawn is already matted. Rin is not a fan of winter.

The dogs startle her just then by breaking into a cacophony of barking. The wolves begin howling as well, the howl of GET-OFFANDGOAWAY—a howl they only make when they know the dogs are seriously alarmed. Rin runs to the kitchen and grabs her M16 from its rack. "Stay inside!" she yells at the children, and crashes through the front door.

First one vehicle comes up her driveway, then another. The front one is a patrol car, the usual dark blue shark with a yellow stripe down its middle and a bar of lights across its roof. The back one is a big blue van, POLICE stamped in huge yellow letters on its side, along with the words NEW YORK STATE ENVIRON-MENTAL CONSERVATION.

So. They've come.

Both vehicles pull up to her gate and stop, flashing their panic flashes. The doors open and a phalanx of armed men in uniform tumbles out and stands there.

Too late now to sneak Juney into the car and flee. Too late to lure the cops to the woods or hide her wolves, either; she can only hope they'll hide themselves. But not too late to offer her usual welcome.

"Get off my property now!"

The dogs are charging already, barking and growling, hackles raised like collars of thorns. They hurl themselves against the gate, nothing between them and the uniformed stiffs but Rin's jury-rigged barrier. They clearly want to tear the heads off those cocky-faced bastards. Rin wouldn't mind if they did.

But the cops don't budge. Not one of them. And then she

sees something she never wants to see again. A fat, round-faced cop in front yanks out his pistol and aims it right at Betty.

That does it. Rin is not letting any chickenshit civilian cop shoot her animals.

"Leave my dogs alone!" she screams and raises her rifle, sighting it above his head. Then she sees something else. The three other cops drop down by their cars. And the one in front lifts his pistol, training it dead on her.

"MA'AM PUT DOWN YOUR WEAPON," a voice bellows through a megaphone. "PUT DOWN YOUR WEAPON AND CALL OFF THE DOGS."

Convoy to Tikrit, moondust storm in our eyes, scarves over our mouths . . . gust of wind, sudden clearing . . . heads poking above a berm, black scarves over their own faces . . . RPG . . . incoming . . . Jay . . . your blood and your blood and your blood . . .

❈

"Mommy wait!" Juney screams, stumbling into chairs, tables, stools, cats as she flies to the door. "*MommyMommy!*" But Mommy doesn't hear because Mommy is shouting and yelling in her other world. Tariq catapults out after Juney, trying to reach her, to hold her back, to call *wait and wait and don't and don't!* The two of them hurtle through the door, across the porch and up to Rin. "*MommyMommy . . .*"

Rin aims her warning shot over the cop's head.

The cop points the muzzle of his gun directly at her.

Two bullets, one an arc, one an arrow, slice through the air.

30

PEACE

When the sun has slipped far enough down that evening to send beams through Naema's narrow windows, lighting up her attic bedroom like a lantern, she untangles herself from her bedspread and slides her leg over Louis's. Outside, a cardinal whistles in the distant woods, its song seesawing through the trees. Inside, the only sounds are Louis's breathing and the whispering rustle of sheets. "Naema?" He parts her hair so he can see her eyes. "If only you knew . . ."

"Shh. It does not need words."

She rests her head on his chest, nestling against his long body, his skin warm and silken. "Well, perhaps there is one thing I will say," she murmurs, smiling at herself. "I have always known I had to wait for a truly good-hearted man. And this is you, my friend . . . of course it is you."

Louis is about to reply in kind when familiar hot fingers of shame grip his neck. He shifts in the bed, still holding her, although uneasily now. "But I don't understand. Why me? I thought you wanted to be with Mustapha."

"Mustapha?" She lifts herself to her elbow to look at him. "Oh, no. He is much too broken for love."

"More broken than I am?" Louis says wryly.

"Of course." She frowns, reminding him that she has no patience for the self-pity of American soldiers. "I never told you this because it is his private business, but his wife and both his children, two little girls, they were all killed when a bomb fell on their house in Mosul. If I were to love him—and I do not—he would cling to me like a man drowning. And I would drown with him."

Louis takes a moment to absorb this. "But that's what I mean. How can you be with me after what we did to your country? Why am I any better than Jimmy Donnell?"

She caresses his cheek. "Louis." Her voice is softer now. She knows he is only expressing the remorse of every American who has retained a conscience about the war, and she has made her peace with that. She has had to, raising her son as an American, working with the children of American veterans. She has had to teach herself that not all Americans—not even soldiers like Donnell and Louis—are the same as their leaders, any more than she was the same as Saddam. "You are my best friend and that is what counts. And you and I have already overcome much of this, have we not? So we shall keep trying, agreed?"

"Of course." He pulls her to him again. *But,* he adds silently, *I've still done what I've done and I don't see how we'll ever overcome that.*

When her cell phone rings moments later, they are deep in a kiss. "I am sorry, but a doctor must always answer," she says with regret, so Louis eases himself off her. She turns and picks up the phone.

"Dr. Jassim?" a gruff male voice barks. It sounds more like a command than a question.

"Yes, who is speaking?" She shifts back a little, pressing her buttocks teasingly against Louis.

"Are you the mother of Tariq Jassim?"

She springs up. "Who are you?"

Louis sits up, too.

"This is the police, ma'am. We need you to come to Saint Peter's Hospital. We're heading there with your son."

"Allah save me! Is he hurt? Oh please, please no."

But there is no answer.

She jumps out of bed, pulling on her clothes. "We must go. The hospital, it has Tariq." She neither cries nor screams, only switches into physician mode: cool and efficient. But she can feel the ground tipping on its side, ready to plunge her yet again into tragedy.

A few minutes later, Louis is hurtling with soldier speed through the evening rush hour toward Albany.

The drive is short but feels unbearably long. Every traffic light creeps by as if sleepwalking; every yawning commuter inches along as if intentionally blocking their way. Naema is praying fervently to Allah in her head; Louis to his own panoply of nongods.

"I can't believe that fucker didn't tell you if he's hurt," he says through his teeth as he swerves past a Volvo. "But if it was really bad, they would've said, I'm sure."

She grips her knees with both hands, trying to believe this. "But what could have happened to him?" Then she gasps, "The wolves!"

"What? You mean they're real?"

"Yes! Oh, Louis, he promised to stay away from them!"

❁

Mike Flaherty is pacing the waiting room just inside the hospital's emergency entrance, casting uneasy looks at the child sobbing in the corner. He was only doing his duty, right? A police officer is trained to shoot back when shot at, and surely what happens next is up to fate. But what will the investigative board say, let alone his superiors? And the press? *Oh Jesus, Mary, and Joseph, the press.* He wishes with every bone in his body he could be at home with his wife, who always helps him figure out what to do. *Damn that Beth Wycombe. She's never brought me anything but misery.*

At last, the two people he's been waiting for come running in wearing the wild expressions he sees all the time in his job—he can tell from the face on the woman, who is panting heavily, that she's the lady he called. She runs right past him, but the man with her, big and dark and, judging from his haircut and posture, a veteran, gives Flaherty a look that roots him to the spot.

Naema flies over to the sobbing child curled tight as a snail on a corner bench. "Tariq, are you all right?" She runs her hands over him quickly and gathers him into a hug. "*Alhamdulillah,* you are not hurt! But what happened? Tell me, *habibi*, quick."

He grips her tightly, sobbing so hard he can barely speak. But finally, he pulls out of her arms and points at Flaherty, who backs toward the door. "Make that man go away, Mama. He's scaring me! He's the one who shot her! He shot her right down!"

Part Four

NOVEMBER

31

FLAG

"Flanner?" Beth calls up the stairs. "Come here."

No answer.

"Honey, come! I need to talk with you."

Still no answer.

With a sigh, she mounts the steps, watching her feet sink into the white carpet one after the other, her toes inside their stockings looking like netted shrimp.

She knocks on his door. No doubt he is playing another of his violent video games or looking at war porn. That's how he spends most of his free time these days. She knocks again.

"What?"

She pushes the door open. He is indeed sitting on his bed, rattling away on his laptop.

"Flan?" She walks over. "Close that thing a moment, would you? I've got something important to tell you."

He scowls but does as she says.

She sits beside him, running her eyes around his room, which has become forbidden territory to her these past weeks. The rumpled red-and-black NASCAR bedspread. The posters of football stars grinning out at her, teeth polished, necks like sides of beef. The meager collection of sports trophies gathering dust on a near-empty bookshelf.

She looks up to see a new Marine Corps recruitment

advertisement tacked to the ceiling over the bed, a soot-smeared grunt grimacing down at her, his enormous assault rifle pointed right at her nose. She wonders where on earth Flanner found that.

"Flan, look at me."

He glances at her with the wary expression of someone expecting punishment. Nearly three weeks have passed since Todd's death, yet she has never succeeded in getting Flanner to talk about it. Sometimes she senses him watching her, but as soon as she catches his eye, hoping he's ready, he hurries away. Still, she tries again now.

"Are you all right, honey? Because you don't seem all right."

His narrow jaw tightens. But he says nothing.

"Listen, I've been thinking. How would you like to move?"

He drops his eyes back to his laptop. "Move?"

"Yes. Move away from this house. Away from this town. Go to New York City."

"When?"

"Now. As soon as we can pack. I'll put the house up for sale and we can just go."

"You mean in the middle of school and everything?"

"Yes. In the middle of school and everything."

Flanner opens his laptop. "Sure. Whatever."

For the next three days, Beth allows Flanner to stay home so the two of them can empty the house room by room, selecting what to pack, what to toss, and what to store. Beth bundles up every last shred of Todd's Marine Corps belongings: photographs, boots, uniforms, medals, belts, and socks, along with all her honeybee soaps and towels, throws what she most abhors away and takes the rest to Dump King O'Malley, a former marine himself with the purpled nose and ballooned belly of a drinker.

"You sure you want to leave this stuff here?" he says as he paws through it. "This is nice shit, Beth."

"Shit, yes. Nice, I don't think so. Give it away. Keep it. Burn it—I never want to see it again."

Flanner tosses out everything that reminds him of Tariq, camp, childhood, or school. All he keeps are a few clothes, his father's knife and the baseball mitt, and, most important of all, Todd's Purple Heart and Combat Action Badge, which he fishes out of the garbage while Beth isn't looking and hides in one of his socks.

The expensive furniture she puts in storage: the white couch and chairs, the velvet cushions and beds and smug yellow curtains, all of which now nauseate her. And then she packs some more, until she has reduced an entire household full of objects to whatever she can stuff into the little red Fiesta she bought with the Camaro insurance money. After all, she thinks as she walks through the denuded house for a last check, what does she have to keep her here? She never cared for her job at DanciHi or anyone in it. Louis has let her down. She can no longer face Naema. She certainly wants nothing to do with Mike Flaherty, not after that terrible thing he did. And the idea of staying in this town of her childhood and marriage makes her feel as if someone is holding a pillow over her face. But what she does have is Todd's life insurance, the death benefits due to her as a military widow, and the proceeds to come from the sale of the house, which the real estate agent told her should happen in no time. "Nice location," he said, dollar signs flashing in his eyes. "And you've kept it in such good shape, too."

Another thing she accomplished with no help from a husband.

By the fourth morning, the house is empty, the car packed, and she and Flanner are standing in the daffodil hallway with their jackets on. "Ready?" she says, the car keys swinging from her hand.

"Yep." He heads out the front door without so much as a glance behind him. "Bye, house," he adds, and ducks into the car while Beth climbs in beside him. She allows him to sit in front only because the back is crammed with suitcases, the television, both their laptops, and a jumbo sack of her shoes, as well as— and this she doesn't know—the folded flag from Todd's coffin, which Flanner also rescued from the garbage and secreted at the bottom of his suitcase.

"Ready to leave for New York City and a brand-new life?" she asks him.

He looks over at her, his eyes and hair and freckles all a matching ginger under the metallic November sky. "What're we gonna do first?"

"Find a hotel, then an apartment, and then a school for you and a job for me. I thought we'd try Brooklyn, see if we can afford it. It's supposed to be cool. Sound good?"

"I guess. Better than this dumbass town anyhow." He hits the dashboard exactly the way Todd used to. "Let's blow this place forever."

And so they do.

32

UNDERGROUND

The road to Rin Drummond's house is damp and shadowed under the gray light of November, the woods on either side so dense they shut out all but a glimmer of sky. Tariq rolls down the back window of Louis's car and sniffs. He wonders if Juney can smell the dying leaves wherever she is. If, that is, she can smell anything at all.

At the sign PRIVATE KEEP OUT I MEAN IT, Louis turns into Rin's pitted driveway and bumps along it for some time, careful not to lose his tailpipe to one of its potholes. Planted at regular intervals on both sides are the hand-painted NO ENTRY, GO AWAY signs he remembers, along with as much concertina wire as he used to see around a forward operating base. He reaches the heavily fortified gate and stops.

"Mrs. Drummond, she must have been very afraid to have put up all these barriers," Naema remarks.

Louis nods and squeezes her knee.

"If the dogs are here they might not let us in," Tariq says, the first words he has spoken the entire drive.

"But they know you well enough by now to be friendly, don't they?" Louis asks.

"Maybe. I don't know what they'll be like without Juney or her mom here." Tariq opens the door and climbs out, his throat pulpy.

Not a single bark or growl. Nobody runs to meet him. Nothing moves.

The gate turns out to be ajar, its padlocks cut, electricity off, so he pushes it open to let Louis through. Louis parks on the grass and he and Naema get out to stand beside Tariq, huddling against the cold in their winter jackets as they look around. The old red barn, its roof caved in at the back. The tumbledown animal huts. The lawn hidden under a quilt of orange and brown leaves. The shattered willow lying with its head in a stream. The remains of the oak, roughly sawn into logs and stacked in a pile by the barn.

Without speaking, they turn toward the main house, which to Naema, who has never seen it before, appears on the verge of collapse. The roof is sagging, the walls patched, the rooms attached to its corners barely holding on. Four wicker chairs clutter the porch, along with a row of potted geraniums, several knocked over, stems broken, flowers crushed. The floor is stained with a long streak of rust-colored blood.

"Wait here. I'm going inside," Tariq says, his voice low. He climbs the stairs, leaving Naema and Louis out on the grass. "Betty? Rufus?" he calls. "Ricky? Pop? Purr? Patch?"

Nothing.

He steps over the blood, careful not to look at it, and tries the handle of the front door. It opens. Slipping inside, he stands a moment to listen. The foyer is dark, the house suspended in silence.

He tiptoes into the living room, which is equally lifeless, equally silent. How different it is from that cozy evening when he was sitting here by the fire, telling Juney the stories in the flames. He thought this room the friendliest place in the world then. But now the fireplace is dead, and even though sweaters are still dangling from hooks, the rugs still rumpled, and the couch and chairs as dog-haired as ever, the air has lost all its embracing scents of sizzling wood and sleeping animals.

Unable to bear the desolation, he hurries into the kitchen. But here it is even worse. The glass of milk Juney was drinking while Rin called the veterinarian is still on the table. The saucepan on the stove is still full of the water and potatoes Rin was about to boil for dinner. The tomatoes Juney was washing, the carrots he was chopping—all are untouched. On the floor in the corner, the cat food bowls are empty and licked clean. "Purr?" His voice is scarcely a whisper. "Patch?"

And then, at last, a tentative meow. And the motley nose of a tabby pokes out from behind the refrigerator.

"Purr." He crouches to see if he can spot Patch, the tortoiseshell, too. "Here." He fills a water bowl from the faucet and another with the ground meat he knows to find in the pantry alongside the wolf food. Then he puts them by the refrigerator to entice the cats out, pretending Juney will appear as well, slip into the kitchen from wherever she is hiding and say, "Tariq, you've come!" But the last he saw of her, she was being pushed into a police car, screaming for her mother, who lay in a mass of blood.

Purr is the only one to emerge. She laps the water thirstily and gulps down the food while he waits. Then she looks at him, meowing until he picks her up. Tucking her in the crook of his arm, he strokes her head and carries her outside.

"Let's go around the back," he says to his mother and Louis.

They follow him in silence, Louis reaching out to clasp Naema's chilled fingers. He knows she has been trying to persuade the Child Protection authorities to reveal where they placed Juney so she can take her away from there and bring her home, as Tariq has been begging her to do. "I may not be able to save the children of Iraq, but I can help to undo the war for two

children right here," she said to Louis. But so far her efforts have
been stymied by the slow-moving cogs of bureaucracy and the
apparent unwillingness of every human being within it to help.
"Blind children need special care," they keep telling her. "We
have to consider your qualifications."

Tariq leads his mother and Louis over to the goat pen beside
the barn: empty. Then to the chicken hutch, its door blown
open, the eggs cracked and eaten, not a hen to be seen. Next,
he takes them to the vegetable garden out back—Juney's garden—uprooted and decimated, deer, rabbits, moles, foxes, and
groundhogs having broken through Rin's netting and gobbled
everything in sight now that there are no dogs to stop them.
Juney's bird feeder is empty, as well. Everything is as still as if
holding its breath.

Tariq walks around all this without a word, clutching Purr.
Finally, he turns to his mother and Louis. "I'm going to call the
wolves. You can come, but don't speak when we get near, okay?
Just be quiet and don't move." Purr is struggling now, so he puts
her down. She seems content to slink along beside him.

Approaching the fence, he scans the woods beyond for any
sign of movement. The wind has dropped now and the sun is
low enough to have drained the trees of their remaining color,
leaving them hunched and dull in the waning light, like a crowd
in the rain at a bus stop. He presses himself against the wire,
hoping Gray will catch his scent and come, as he has so often
before. He waits.

Naema and Louis wait, too. Now that Naema sees the eight-
foot fence topped by a coil of razor wire, the hefty lean-ins holding it steady, the heavily chained and padlocked double door at
its entrance, she realizes there never has been anything to fear
from Rin Drummond's wolves, just as Tariq said.

Tariq stands still and alert for a long while, sending all his will and longing out to Gray. *Come,* he tries to telepathize, *come, father wolf, your boy is here. Ta'al, el-theeb el-'ab, ebnek hna.* But the trees only look back at him indifferently and not a shadow moves. So he lifts his head and in the same imitation of Juney he tried before, he calls, "Gra-aay, Silverrrr, Eboneeey."

Naema shudders, for the call sounds alien and haunting and utterly unlike her son. But Louis has the odd sense he has heard this sound before. Then he remembers: the loons of the Adirondack lakes. Their unearthly wails of warning.

Tariq waits with the patience he has learned from his months of watching the wolves. Then he calls again.

Far back in the woods, hidden in a den deep beneath a large granite rock, Silver pricks her ears. A shiver of hope runs through her and she tries to stand, struggling to heave herself up on her front legs. But she is too weak and can only collapse. She is nothing but ribs and fur now; blind, her mouth crusted and dry, her white coat thin and filthy. Her mate has stopped coming to feed her, as has the other creature. Her son is never here to groom her. She has no water, aside from the rivulets that trickle in with the rain.

With a great effort, she lifts her head off the ground and returns the call with the loudest and most desperate howl she can muster.

Had Juney been here, she might have heard, deep underground though Silver is. But a breeze has stirred up again and a sibilant rustle of dry leaves is sweeping through the woods, so Tariq hears nothing.

He scoops up Purr again and buries his face in her neck, trying not to cry. "They're not here," he says to his mother and Louis, his voice trembling. "Oh, Mama, where has everyone gone?"

33

CANE

It is so dark in here. Everything in this place is sharp and hard. The bed frames and doors and tables and chairs. They bump into Juney. Gash her shins. Bang her toes.

Ms. Jackson has given her a cane because Juney lost hers when the police arrested her. She says Juney should use it all the time so things don't bump her so much.

But at home, Juney didn't need her cane all the time. She could see with her nose and her fingers and ears and her dogs and Tariq. She could see with her mother.

Ms. Jackson won't let her visit her mother. They didn't kill her, Ms. Jackson told her, so Juney is not an orphan like some of the other children here. But what else is she if they won't let her visit?

She heard them whispering in another room, Ms. Jackson and some man. They don't know how well she can hear. She heard them talking about a prison and a place for the blind. She doesn't want to go to a prison for the blind. She wants to go home to her mother.

She wants her mother. She wants Tariq. She wants Ebony and Silver and Gray, and RufusBettyRickyPop and Purrand-Patch. She wants her bird feeder and her flowers and Hiccup's grave and her tomatoes. She wants the weeds in the garden and the eggs under the chickens and the rugs under her feet.

She wants the fire. She wants the sun. It is so dark in here.

34

PACK

The doctors are giving Rin enough painkillers to numb a buffalo. Morphine, Percocet, Vicodin, OxyContin—she has long since lost track. But even though she has been locked up in this hospital for eleven days now, they won't tell her anything about Juney. Where she is. How she is being treated. Whether she can find her way around. If there is anyone to console her.

Rin heard her screaming. Even through the pain and shock, even through the sky spinning into her head, she heard her. Juney must be so scared, so very scared. *Will your sea urchin fingers help you now, little bean? Your radar senses? Your songs and your happy rocking?*

"I need to see my daughter!" Rin yells and yells all day long. "I need to see my child!" Nobody listens.

They chained one of her arms to the bed. The door to her room is guarded day and night by a cop. "Why?" she asks him. "I can't even walk, my leg is shot up so bad. I have to piss in a goddamn bedpan. What did you expect me to do, come tearing out and attack you with my IV bag?"

But she doesn't care what they do to her here. She only cares about Juney.

Flaherty did do quite a number on Rin, though. The doctors tell her she's lucky to have the leg at all, given that he shot her with a Glock 37—she still might end up like Tariq. All she did was fire a warning shot. Way over his head, no less. If he had been army-trained and less damned trigger-happy, he would have known better than to open fire on a woman standing on her own goddamn porch with two kids beside her. It's a miracle he didn't hit Juney. Or Tariq.

Is there no one in this godforsaken town full of godforsaken people who is willing to help me get my daughter back?

Meanwhile, visitors keep bothering her all the time. Doctors and nurses, of course, interns and first years. But also cops, lawyers, DEC officers, Child Protection snoops. Even reporters.

The cops come to tell her she's in about the deepest shit a person can be, having shot at one of their sacred clan. Fact that she didn't shoot *at* him but *over* him interests them not at all.

The lawyers come to promise they'll fight the charges. Pull up her PTSD records, her service, her honorable discharge. Shock the court by pointing out that those so-called officers of the peace came tearing onto her property with no warning, pointing guns at her service dog and her blind daughter over nothing but a stupid license. Rin listens, nods, rolls her eyes. Who are they kidding? Nobody's going to give a hoot about any of that, not when she threatened a police officer. "Dream on, boys," she tells them. "Dream on."

The reporters come to ask her why she did it and was it the war and does she feel she's being treated right. She rattles her chain and says, "You tell me."

The Child Protection snoops come to say they are "looking into" a permanent home for Juney, meanwhile still refusing to say where she is or when Rin can see her, until she screams them out of the room.

The DEC officers come to discuss her wolves. She finds it hard to believe these are the same folks who run those nerdy little forest rangers giving leaf-peeping tours in the Catskills.

"You were keeping your wolves well," they say—they being two bottle-tan men with thick-thatched yellow hair. "We were going to advise you to go for the exhibition license, given that you raised your wolves in captivity, if you'd listened to us instead of shooting."

So why did you arrive at my house armed to the teeth like a SWAT team? Cowards.

Oh well, too late now. She's fucked everything up in style. What comes around goes around, as they say. She steps on a doctor and almost drowns her to save her own. Cops shoot her to save theirs.

As for her dogs, they pumped them full of tranquilizers and took them to the pound. That will be the death of them, as she trained them to be so unfriendly to strangers. Rufus was such a good Seeing Eye for Juney, taking her to and from the school bus every day; Betty so loyal, with her soft, black eyes and pudding-brown coat.

Rin has no idea what happened to her cats and goats and chickens. Running wild, no doubt, prey for foxes and the packs of coyotes who show up regularly in her woods like a gang of muggers. But her wolves—Gray and Ebony, poor sick Silver—nobody will tell her what has been done with them. And when she asks, those DEC bastards only get all skitter-eyed and back out of the room.

I need to see Juney. Tomorrow, maybe, they say. A new word, tomorrowmaybe. I wait and I wait, I plead and I plead, but tomorrowmaybe never turns into today.

Still, the visitors keep on pouring in. A physical therapist who tortures her by forcing her to lift her shattered leg and wiggle the ankle. A creep calling himself her "pain manager" who pumps up her morphine as if hell-bent on turning her addicted. A second team of lawyers who orders her not to talk to any more cops or reporters and gives her bad news disguised as good. "Public sympathy is on your side," they say at one point. "Your case has become so notorious we may have to move your trial," they say the next.

Even a clump of hippies turns up, claiming to be veterans.

"Hi, comrade," says one, which immediately puts her off. "We're from VVFTWOOV."

She eyes them from the bed. A motley crew of aging geezers in gray ponytails, their addled brains topped by baseball caps festooned with peace signs and patches from the Vietnam War. "What the hell is Vee Vee F-T WooVee?"

"Vietnam Veterans for the Welfare of Other Veterans."

She looks at them in disbelief. "What do you want?"

The lead geezer grins at her, white hair straggling out from under his cap, ten teeth missing. Former methhead if she ever saw one, just like her brother. Either that or a junkie. She met a lot of junkies in the army—three in her own platoon, all dead within a year of getting out. "We want you to know we've got your back."

"Listen," she tells him, heaving herself up in the bed as best she can, which isn't far, given her leg and the chain. "First, I don't consider a bunch of decrepit old Deadheads my comrades, so you can quit saying that right now. Second, did you notice that I happen to be a female? So why didn't you come with a woman if you're so keen on my frigging welfare? Third, if you're going to call yourselves veterans, clean the fuck up. You look like something dredged out of the bottom of Woodstock."

They leave in a collective huff.

But amid all these parasites, torturers, liars, and loonies, a couple of visitors arrive who give her a true surprise. The first is Tariq's mom, wearing her white doctor coat and her shrapnel scar, who seems destined to haunt Rin's life whether she likes it or not. The second, coming in right behind her, is that hooah army guy Tariq calls his uncle.

"Are they treating you well, Mrs. Drummond?" Naema asks.

Rin stares at her as if she's one of her phantoms. The woman's back sinking under her foot.

Naema walks up to the bed and brushes the sweaty hair off Rin's forehead like a mother. This is the first gesture of kindness Rin has received in this place. From her, of all people. A rocklike weight shifts inside Rin and she nearly breaks down and weeps.

"If you call chaining me to my bed and not letting me see my daughter 'treating me well,' sure," she says, yanking herself together. "But I guess they're doing the medical stuff right."

"Yes, you do not have to worry about that. I checked their procedures and they are correct. But you must be in pain. Are they giving you enough painkillers?"

"Yeah, but I don't want them. I'm not interested in turning into a morphinehead. You got any news of Juney?"

A flicker passes over the woman's face, a flicker Rin doesn't like the look of at all. "We do. She is in a foster home in Albany, a private house with some eight or ten other children. But this is only temporary—"

"A foster home?" All the stories Rin has ever heard about child molesters and beatings and kids locked in basements come clamoring into her head. She was hoping Juney was in some place responsible, at least, like a boarding school for the blind run by people who know what they're doing. "Why is she in a foster home?"

Naema's brow pinches up and she pulls at her skinny brown fingers. She glances at the hooah guy with the look a woman gives the man she trusts. He steps over to stand beside her, a towering hunk of a war vet next to a fragile stick of an Iraqi. Takes all kinds, Rin supposes.

Naema speaks again. "The authorities, they said it is because they could not find any relatives to take her."

Rin examines her. She is so like Tariq. That same acorn skin; same narrow face and delicate body. And for once, Rin knows exactly what she must do. "Get her out of there. Get my daughter out of there and take her home with you. Please?"

Naema glances at Hooah. "Mrs. Drummond, this is exactly what we came here to ask you today. We, too, wish to take her out of that place. We want her to stay with us for as long as she needs to—to stay with Tariq, who loves her."

Rin's eyes sting. She closes them quickly, the relief coursing through her stronger than any morphine. She pictures Juney living with Tariq, having him as a brother. She pictures them doing their homework together on the floor, swaying in front of the fire.

"Thanks." For the moment, she can say no more. Did she just thank an Iraqi for taking her daughter? She hasn't felt this flippy-floppy since she was driven out of the army for being pregnant and raped. She feels like a weeping fish.

Opening her eyes, she wipes them dry and tries to master her voice. "Have you seen her?"

"Not yet." Naema is still pulling her fingers. "The bureaucracy, it is very slow. But we will persist."

"Are you sure they'll let you take her?"

"I think so, yes. These agencies, they are happy to find private homes for the children. It is less expensive for them that way."

Hooah speaks up then. "It might speed things up if you write a letter vouching for us."

"Sure, but I doubt it'll help. Not now they've decided I'm such an unfit mother they won't even let me talk to my kid." Rin stops speaking. Breathes. Digs around for her voice. "Does she know I'm all right?"

"Yes," Naema replies. "She knows you are recovering in a hospital." And once more, she leans over to smooth Rin's head. She smells of the starch in her coat but also of a flower Rin knows, a scent she remembers . . . jasmine, that's it. A favorite perfume in Iraq, which, for some reason, is not triggering her right now.

"Tariq, he spoke to Juney on the phone yesterday," Naema continues. "We are able to do that, at least, thanks to my former nurse. She knows the woman who runs the foster home. Sarah Jackson is her name. She told us we can visit Juney next week."

Listen, god-I-don't-believe-in, make this Jackson person kind. Make her understand Juney. Make her gentle.

"Mrs. Drummond . . ." Naema is still stroking Rin's brow, her hand dry and cool, and Rin is surprised by how soothing it is. "As a mother, I understand something of how painful this must be for you. We will telephone Juney every day until they let us see her. Tariq, he will give her your messages and her messages we will bring to you."

Rin lets her head fall back against the pillow and stares at the ceiling, trying to hold on to this one tiny shred of light for as long as she can: Juney and Tariq talking.

"When Tariq spoke to her, what did she say?" Her voice comes out more of a croak than a voice.

Silence.

"She's unhappy, isn't she?" Rin whispers.

"Yes, I am afraid she is. She wants only to leave that place and be with you. But she is safe; we are sure of that."

This time, Rin can't even feel ashamed of weeping, soldier though she is. Wiping her face hastily with her sheet, she glances around the room. "Where is Tariq anyway?"

"They would not let us bring him, I am afraid."

"Oh, right." She rattles her chain again. "I'm a dangerous maniac now. So how come they let you see me?"

304   *Wolf Season*

"The press." Hooah is speaking this time. "Your story's all over the place, embarrassing the hell out of the cops. It doesn't look good when a state trooper shoots at little kids. Or female veterans. They're trying to rustle up better PR by allowing you visitors."

"They give Flaherty a medal yet?" Rin doesn't even try to hide her disgust.

Hooah shakes his head. A mighty handsome head, she just noticed. He's got a couple fingers missing, and she can guess where from. This warms her to him somehow. "He's under investigation." He raises a telling eyebrow.

Rin tries again to push herself higher on the pillows, about to give Naema a message for Juney, when a scrawny nurse marches through the door, face like a dried apricot.

"Visiting hours are over. You have to leave now."

"We will leave when we are ready, thank you, Nurse," Naema replies, her tone as crisp as her coat. That shuts the nurse up. Rin likes that.

"Mrs. Drummond," Naema says then. "One more thing before we go. Tariq, he wants us to ask you—what happened to the wolves?"

After Tariq's mom and Hooah leave, Rin lies back and closes her eyes, their faces dancing like shadow puppets behind her lids. She has made such a mess of things; she needs to face that now. She has let Jay down, and even worse, she has let Juney down. She won't make any excuses. But their daughter is going to live with Iraqis now, or so she hopes. *I know this isn't how you would want it, Jay, but they are good people, I promise. These ones are, at any rate. As for the irony in all this, make of it what you will.*

When the members of a wolf pack turn against one another, the pack destroys itself. She remembers Jay telling her that. Her pack turned on her, the very men in her platoon she thought she could trust. Why, she can only guess. Because they couldn't have her while she was his? Because she refused to play their power games? Or maybe because she was widowed, pregnant, and devastated, and so, like wolves, they smelled her as weak and pegged her as prey?

She won't be a person who betrays her pack like that. She might have lost Gray and Silver and Ebony, but her pack is still Juney and the memory of Jay. So even though she is bound for prison (and what is prison after war?), she will devote her life to doing what's best for Juney. And if it turns out that the best for Juney is to be free of her, so be it. For it does occur to Rin, as she lies here having made such an almighty screwup of everything, that Juney might be better off without a mother as crazed as she is. Yes, even though it will crush Rin's heart, Juney might be better off without her at all.

35
===

HOWL

Far away in the upper reaches of western New York, two wolves pace their pens, their heads sagging. Once in a while, they approach the hurricane fence that separates them and lick each other's muzzles through the holes. But otherwise, each is left alone to prowl, wait, and to mourn.

The young wolf, black from nose to tail but for tips of white on his winter coat, searches for his family. He searches for his mother, his den, his woods, for the places he used to run and climb and hunt. He searches for his favorite beds. He searches and he whimpers. But this is not his territory. These are not his woods. Nothing here is his.

The great timber wolf, with his thick silver mane, arching eyebrows and simmering golden eyes, is searching, too. Many times a day he approaches the fence of this new, unpleasant place and sits looking out at the world. Different animals come to stare at him. Some are tall, some short, some dark, some light. Some smell friendly; most smell afraid. Many smell hostile.

He examines each one of them with keen attention, opening his nostrils to take in their scents, hoping to find what he needs. But the scents are wrong. The bodies are wrong, the faces are wrong, the voices are wrong.

He turns, and with a weary tread, drags himself to the

highest ground he can find. And there he sits until the night closes in and the moon sails into the sky, when he raises his head to howl.

He howls as he will howl night after night, week afer week, determined to wait as long as he must for an answer.

ACKNOWLEDGMENTS

When I embarked on this novel some seven years ago, I had no idea how essential the Iraqis and soldiers I met would be to its realization. Former interpreter Yasir Mohammed Abbas offered me invaluable help with Arabic and indulged me in long conversations about war and the conscience. Nour al-Khal, who was also an interpreter and was shot and nearly killed for her efforts, taught me much about Naema and the life of a refugee. Hala Alazzawi and her daughter, Hiba Alsaffar, welcomed me into their home, responding to my numerous questions with enthusiasm and patience. And Mohanad Alobaide kindly told me much about working with the military as an interpreter and his adjustment to a new life in the United States. My deep gratitude to you all for understanding why literature matters and for showing me how to react to oppression not with hatred but with wisdom.

I was also partly inspired to write this novel by Maj. Jason Faler, a former U.S. Army National Guardsman who saved his Iraqi interpreter and his family from death by bringing them to his home in Oregon. Faler went on to create the Checkpoint One Foundation, which rescued more than a hundred interpreters from 2007 to 2012 by helping them obtain visas to emigrate here. Their work is being carried on by the organizations listed on page 312. I thank Major Faler for helping me check my facts and for being so ready to answer questions.

Captain John Ryan was also gracious enough to lend his time to reading parts of my work, as were the many other veterans I have met and interviewed over the years. Thank you all. Any mistakes are, of course, mine.

I also thank Dunia Kamal for her knowledge and help about her native Damascus: she would have been my guide had civil war not torn her country apart. And once again, my gratitude to Zainab Chaudhry and Susan Davies, who have worked tirelessly to help the Iraqi refugees settled in and around Albany, New York.

I am grateful to many others, too. The staff at Wolf Mountain Nature Center for letting me spend many hours with wolves. Jennifer Lyons, for keeping faith and working so hard for this book. Erika Goldman, inspired and inspiring editor. The Virginia Center for the Creative Arts, the Blue Mountain Center, the American Academy in Rome, the Ucross Foundation, the Ragdale Foundation, and the Tyrone Guthrie Centre in Ireland for granting me residencies filled with peace, nourishment, and beauty while I was writing this book.

And last but never least, the friends and family who encouraged, read, reread, critiqued, tolerated, and listened: the brilliant writers Rebecca Stowe, Robert Marshall, Cara Hoffman, and David Groff; Simon and Emma Benedict O'Connor, who fill me with joy and let me pick their brains about language and music and elbows; Andrea Cashman for giving us her delightful self and Iggy; and, most of all, Stephen O'Connor, for his many reads, exacting eye, and for still believing in me while I write for year after year about war.

—Helen Benedict, 2017

AUTHOR'S NOTE

Since the United States invaded Iraq in 2003, some one million Iraqis have died, two million women have been widowed, and one million children have been orphaned, according to Physicians for Social Responsibility and others. More than four million Iraqis have been displaced, either within the country or without, meaning that one in five people have been forced from their homes.

Among the majority of Iraq civilians who are not and never were enemies of the United States arc the more than seventy thousand women and men who worked as interpreters for the military, the government, or journalists. These interpreters, all of whom were meticulously vetted before being hired, saved countless lives, both Iraqi and American, but, like Khalil, were targeted from all sides, seen as collaborators and traitors by some, spies by others. Hundreds, if not thousands, have been tortured or killed by militias (the Taliban also murders interpreters and their families in Afghanistan), while others have been driven to live under assumed names, never daring to see their families or stay in one place for more than a few days at a time. As I write, the violence is growing ever worse in Iraq, endangering all citizens, interpreters or not, more than ever.

The United States has been unconscionably slow to help interpreters. The State Department did eventually create the Special Immigrant Visa to allow those in danger to move to the U.S., yet only a fraction of these visas have been granted, and, as I write, the future of this visa program is in question. As of October 2016, some thirty-six thousand persecuted Iraqi refugees with U.S. ties were stranded in Iraq, according to the Urban Justice League. Since then, the Trump administration has been playing fast and loose with these refugees' lives, regardless of their sacrifices or the fact that they have undergone every security check possible. Naema represents one of the lucky few who escaped.

Several organizations have been created to help Iraqi and Afghan interpreters, as well as other refugees, escape persecution:

The International Refugee Assistance Project (IRAP) at the Urban Justice League: refugeerights.org.

The Iraqi and American Reconciliation Project: reconciliationproject.org.

The List Project to Resettle Iraqi Allies: thelistproject.org.

No One Left Behind, nooneleft.org.

For more information about the plight of Iraqis, see this report by Physicians for Social Responsibility*: psr.org/news-events/press-releases/doctors-group-releases-startling-analysis.html.*

BOOK CLUB EXTRAS

A Conversation with Helen Benedict

You interviewed dozens of veterans as well as Iraqi refugees before writing about them in your nonfiction book *The Lonely Soldier*, your novel *Sand Queen*, and now, in *Wolf Season*. What is it about their stories that continues to inspire your writing?

All the Iraqis I met, and most of the veterans, had been through truly terrible traumas—war, after all, offers little else. What inspired me was their resilience and their honesty. Parents who had lost children, soldiers who had lost friends, adults who had lost brothers and sisters and spouses, and women who had been sexually attacked or tortured—all revealed a determination and generosity of spirit I found deeply moving. They told me their stories because they wanted to help others who had lived through similar circumstances. The impulse of many who have been through trauma is to help others. This speaks to the best side of the human spirit, just as war often reveals the worst.

Your novel prominently features three mothers. Rin is an Iraq war veteran and Naema is an Iraqi refugee. Beth, on the other hand, is neither a soldier nor a refugee but the wife of a deployed marine. What inspired the creation of her character? What were you hoping she would add to the narrative?

As this novel is about the aftereffects of war—about war brought home—I thought a military spouse like Beth belonged in the story. More American women experience war through their husbands or sons, boyfriends or fathers than they do by serving themselves. Beth is one of these. Also, I liked the idea of the three women in the novel representing different views of war: Rin as a veteran, Naema as an Iraqi, Beth as a military spouse.

Rin reacts to the world around her in deeply honest yet troubling ways. Were you concerned that readers might find her unsympathetic?

I like characters who make me, as a reader, keep changing my mind. People are puzzling and self-contradictory and vulnerable and imperfect, and even the most flawed character can be sympathetic and heartbreaking. I hope readers will feel this way about Rin.

Programs that pair veterans with rescue animals have shown great success in helping to alleviate some of the symptoms of post-traumatic stress disorder. Were those programs on your mind when you made Rin's wolves such an integral part of this novel?

I was not thinking of therapy animals when I brought the wolves into *Wolf Season* but of a real veteran I once interviewed who lived in the woods with wolves. Rin is not like her at all, but the idea intrigued me. Later, long after I'd written a draft of *Wolf Season*, I found out that quite a few veterans do like to keep wolves, and that some therapy programs do indeed pair wolves and vets. However, I suspect many vets are drawn to wolves not so much as therapeutic animals but because wolves represent something pure and wild and untamable and strong, as well as dangerous and protective. This is certainly why they appeal to Rin.

Readers were first introduced to the character of Naema in *Sand Queen*, when she was a medical student in Iraq. In *Wolf Season*, we meet her again, now working as a doctor in a VA medical clinic. When did you know you hadn't finished telling her story? Will we meet her or Tariq again?

I decided to continue Naema's story in 2010, as I came to know more Iraqi refugees and saw the terrible fallout from the Iraq War all over the globe. Having been so moved by the Iraqis I met and interviewed, I felt saddened by the negative stereotypes of Muslims gaining popularity around the world, and I wanted to push against that with Naema and Tariq. Now it seems more important than ever for us to pay attention to people like Naema and Tariq in all their humanity. So yes, Naema and Tariq are not going away yet.

Louis, an Army veteran, and Todd, an active-duty marine, reveal other aspects of war's toll on the human psyche. Do you believe that men and women experience war and its aftermath in essentially different ways?

I don't like to generalize about men and women because no one truth belongs to everybody, but I will say that many women do experience war and its aftermath differently than men. Civilian women and children die in greater numbers in today's wars than men, for one. And as I found while researching my nonfiction book, *The Lonely Soldier: The Private War of Women Serving in Iraq*, women soldiers are still often treated as outcasts by their comrades, along with being sexually assaulted at a rate of nearly one in three, which means many women veterans suffer the double trauma of combat and sexual assault. Furthermore, some 90 percent of women are sexually harassed in the military. (Men are harassed and assaulted within the military, too, but not in nearly the same proportions.) Having to fight without the compensation of camaraderie is a cruelty experienced by far too many military women, and this alters their view of both the military and war.

The three children in *Wolf Season* handle the challenges they face in very different ways. Why are their perspectives so vital to the story? Was it a challenge to capture their voices in such an authentic way?

The juxtaposition of children and war is particularly poignant, for their very frankness and innocence strips away the glamorizing lies that so often cloak our discussions of war. Valor and strength, weaponry and heroism—what do these matter to a boy who has lost his father and his leg, or to a girl who has lost her sight, or to a child whose family has been torn apart by the trauma of war? Worldwide, children suffer and die from war more than anyone else, yet they are rarely given a voice.

Also, I have written from the point of view of children before, particularly in my earlier novel, *The Edge of Eden*. Taking on the voice of a child enables me to cut through to the heart of things. And then, I am a mother and have learned to listen to and relish the way children talk.

Novelists sometimes talk about being surprised by their characters. Did any of the characters in *Wolf Season* surprise you?

All my characters surprised me. Rin, with her complications—her distrust of people and her love of her daughter and wolves—was a constant surprise. The children with their quirks and stubbornness. Naema, with her hard-earned patience. If a writer isn't surprised by her characters, something is wrong. Creating a character is like getting to know a friend: if she never surprises, she is not going to be interesting.

Wolf Season takes place in upstate New York, and its towns and woods almost become characters themselves. Why was it important to set the story in a small American community?

Many enlisted soldiers come from economically depressed small towns all over the United States, especially towns that offer few jobs or opportunities. My fictional Huntsville and Potterstown are placed near the real Slingerlands in Albany County, where a large proportion of families have sons and daughters in the military. Furthermore, as I found out after I began writing, hundreds of Iraqi refugees have been settled in that area, so I was able to make Naema's story historically accurate, too.

What were you trying to explore in Wolf Season that separates it from your earlier work?

Everyone who has been through the horror of war brings it home in one way or another, and this, in turn, affects families and communities. Put another way, when a soldier is wounded, physically or psychologically, so is everyone who loves her. Likewise with a victim of war. Sand Queen took place mostly in Iraq, during the war itself. With Wolf Season, I wanted to follow Naema and her family after they fled the war, and to explore how the Iraq War has affected all of us at home in America.

Book Club Extras

Conversation Starters for Your Book Club

1. This book explores the long-reaching effects of war, not only on those directly engaged in it but on those close to them. How are the three mothers in the novel—Rin, Naema, and Beth—affected by war, and how does it affect their children, Juney, Tariq, and Flanner?

2. *Wolf Season* opens with an approaching hurricane. What is the fallout from the storm on each character? What is the effect of opening the novel with such an event?

3. Wolves have long been symbols in folktales and literature all over the world, from ancient myths, such as those of Native peoples in America, to the European story of "Little Red Riding Hood." Sometimes wolves stand for nobility and courage, sometimes evil, sometimes threat. What do you think the wolves represent for Rin and Juney or Naema and Beth, and how do those symbols evolve throughout the novel? What did the wolves represent to you?

4. After we meet Naema, the Iraqi doctor, we do not see her again for a few chapters. What effect does this have on the way Naema's history and character are revealed? How does the author use her absence to develop the other characters?

5. Louis, one of the veterans in the novel, is something of an enigma. What makes him so guarded and private? Why does Beth make him so uncomfortable?

6. What pulls Louis and Naema to befriend each other despite the differences in their backgrounds?

7. What did *Wolf Season* make you think about war and how it affects people's hearts and morals?

8. What does the novel reveal about how men and women experience war and military service? Are the experiences of women soldiers different than those of men? What could the small community in this novel have done to better support the families struggling with the aftermath of war and the deployment of their loved ones?

9. How does this novel portray the refugee experience and the process of immigrating to America? Would any of the issues Naema's family faced have been different had she immigrated to a larger city?

10. How do Tariq and Juney cope with their disabilities? How do those conditions affect the relationships between them and the other characters, particularly Rin and Naema?

11. How would you describe Tariq, Juney, and Flanner? In what ways have their parents influenced them? In thinking over what happens to them in the novel, why do they react differently to the circumstances they face?

12. What do you imagine will happen to Rin and Juney after the end of the novel? What choices are available to Rin? What do you think she should choose?

13. What do you think the author is trying to convey in the novel's final scene with the wolves?

To invite Helen Benedict to your book club, please visit www.helenbenedict.com

To download reading group guides and enjoy more BLP Conversations, please visit www.blpress.org

Book Club Extras

Bellevue Literary Press is devoted to publishing
literary fiction and nonfiction at the intersection of
the arts and sciences because we believe that science and the
humanities are natural companions for understanding the human
experience. With each book we publish, our goal is to foster a rich,
interdisciplinary dialogue that will forge new tools for thinking and
engaging with the world.

To support our press and its mission, and for our full catalogue of
published titles, please visit us at blpress.org.

Bellevue Literary Press
New York